REVEALING THE VISCOUNT

Marrying a Mabry, Book 3

Lexi Post

ARE YOU SIGNED UP FOR DRAGONBLADE'S BLOG?

You'll get the latest news and information on exclusive giveaways, exclusive excerpts, coming releases, sales, free books, cover reveals and more.

Check out our complete list of authors, too!

No spam, no junk. That's a promise!

Sign Up Here

www.dragonbladepublishing.com

Dearest Reader;

Thank you for your support of a small press. At Dragonblade Publishing, we strive to bring you the highest quality Historical Romance from some of the best authors in the business. Without your support, there is no 'us', so we sincerely hope you adore these stories and find some new favorite authors along the way.

Happy Reading!

CEO, Dragonblade Publishing

Acknowledgments

For my wonderful husband, Bob Fabich, Sr., who has seen so much yet remains such a kind and gentle soul. I am very lucky.

For my awesome sister, Paige Wood, who found the weak points in my story and had the best ideas for strengthening them.

I'm so grateful to my critique partner, Marie Patrick, who enjoys talking about our stories throughout the process, making it so much more fun.

I also want to thank Mariah Fair-Wall, a Dragonblade reader, who not only came up with the names Legend and Lore, but also gave me a great idea for the rest of the horse names for the Viscount of Blackmore.

Lastly, I want to say a huge thank you to you, my reader, for allowing the Mabry sisters the honor of entertaining you. Without you, there would be no reason to tell their love stories.

Author's Note

The Marrying a Mabry series was inspired by one of my favorite books of all time, Louisa May Alcott's novel, *Little Women*, published in two volumes in 1868 and 1869. This was an American coming of age story about four young ladies in New England. They were Margaret, Josephine, Elizabeth, and Amy March, or Meg, Jo, Beth, and Amy respectively. Each tries to live up to their mother's expectations of them, which were to become good people and respectable women.

Revealing the Viscount is specifically inspired by Meg March and her journey to happiness. For Mariel Mabry, it is a journey from heartbreak to having all she longed for. Basically, what if Meg March lived in Regency England and was the young widow of an old marquess? How would a woman determined to be the perfect lady and sacrifice her own wants for everyone else, be selfish enough to fulfill her destiny with the man she's always loved but thought dead? What can she do when faced with the fact he's alive and has been hiding from her? Can she stop loving him for what he's done, or is her heart stronger than her head?

There is, however, a minor content warning for this story: it has an incident of rape witnessed by the hero that is explained briefly as part of his past. This takes place off the page and is not depicted in detail, but please be aware of its presence.

On a weather note, it should be explained that 1816 was denoted as the Year Without a Summer. This was due to exceedingly cold temperatures and torrents of rainfall, freezing rain, and snow in the northern hemisphere causing catastrophic loss of life. Our current science is quite confident this event was caused by one of the largest volcanic eruptions on Earth. The volcano was Mount Tambora in the Dutch East Indies, or present-day Indonesia, which erupted in April 1815. Its ash cloud was so extensive that it changed the weather, causing crops to fail in all countries affected, including England. The fall out, no pun intended, would cause famine, riots, looting, soaring prices, and believe it or not, due to the cost of feeding horses, most likely the invention of the bicycle.

⁂

CHAPTER ONE

Northampton
March 1817

Lady Mariel Mabry Beaumont pulled on the reins until Zephyrus came to a halt. "Now what do we have here?" Patting the horse on his neck, she studied the long row of carriages lining the entrance into Ravenridge Manor. "It appears the viscount is having a lawn party." The idea that Marcus could be hosting guests when her heart was in tatters had her gripping the reins as if a storm was about to sweep through.

Discovering a sennight ago that the man she loved, the man she'd planned to marry, the man who had died in the war against Napoleon, was alive and well and had been living in England for the last two years but never once thought to contact her, had buckled her knees. The layers of pain were so jumbled in her heart that she vacillated from hurt to rage and everything in between.

Two years! Though her brain told her he obviously didn't feel anything for her to have hidden away for so long, her heart refused to believe that he no longer loved her. Something or someone had kept him from her. It was the only possible explanation that she could accept. He'd pledged his undying love for her not only in words, but also with letters, and gifts. She touched the octagonal garnet outlined in tiny diamonds that still hung around her neck. Even while she'd been married to Lord Beaumont, she'd never taken it off. Marcus' words the day he gave it to her, the day he left for the continent, were forever etched in her mind. *This is my heart. It is forever with you. Keep it safe.* And she had.

Since learning of his subterfuge, she'd reached up to rip the necklace from her body at least a dozen times, but something held her back. She could not in good conscience relegate him to a mistake of her past without hearing his reasons for what he'd done to her...to them.

But confronting him as an uninvited guest would be far beyond the pale. Their conversation was not for society's ears. As much as she wished to know why, she was too well bred to make a scene, especially among so many. About to turn Zephyrus around, she halted as a carriage came through the stone columns, expecting it to pass.

Instead, it stopped before her. The door opened and a young blonde woman poked her head out. "If you're hoping to see Lord Blackmore, you'd best return on the morrow." The woman wrinkled her nose. "Though he may not be at home then either."

Unable to ignore her own curiosity, she nudged Zephyrus forward.

The young woman pulled back inside a bit as the large horse came closer.

Mariel wasn't surprised. Most people had that reaction to her midnight black thoroughbred stallion. "What do you mean?"

The woman splayed both her hands as if in warning. "The lord hasn't been home the entire month, yet he is nowhere else. I'm beginning to believe he's a ghost." She brushed a curl away from her cheek. "But if you're like me and the rest of us," she waved her hand back toward Ravenridge, "you'll be back tomorrow. It's not every day North Hampton has a new bachelor, especially when the season has already begun."

Mariel looked down the line of carriages, another one starting up the drive toward them. "Are you saying all these carriages are people calling on the viscount?"

The young woman rolled her eyes. "Of course. Why else would we be here? Unless you wish to spend time with his mother, I suggest you turn about. I did." She looked over her shoulder at something someone inside said, before continuing. "You may want to go to London though if you're in search of a husband. I'm quite sure one of us here will catch him." With that, the blonde closed the door and the carriage continued on its way, just as the next one came abreast of her. A pretty brunette stared at her from the window, but the conveyance didn't stop.

She may not have her sister Joanna's intelligence, but she did have a better grasp of society, and it was quite clear what was happening here.

Marcus was hiding.

An unreasonable feeling of glee passed through her at how uncomfortable he must be. He had a bevy of young debutantes calling on him as the new viscount, and he wanted nothing to do with them. Her heart skipped a beat. Was it because he still loved her? She shook her head. No, if that were the case, he would have contacted her as soon as his feet touched English soil, if not sooner.

Again she touched the necklace's red stone. Maybe he loved someone else. Frustrated with her lack of information, she dropped her hand and picked up the reins as another carriage rolled through the stone columns. She'd waited long enough. Turning her mount around, she walked him back into the forest that bordered Ravenridge on its northern side. It had been in this very wood when she'd first met Marcus with only a footman accompanying her. She hadn't known at the time that she had wandered off Silver Meadows' grounds where her family visited her Aunt Mabry and found herself on the Viscount of Black-more's estate. She'd never forget Marcus' gray, rebellious gaze or how tousled his thick, black hair looked from his ride.

She mentally shook herself. That was not what she needed to

think about. She'd planned to ride up to the front door, demand entrance and confront the man she'd loved, not moon over a past memory. The new Viscount of Blackmore owed her an explanation, and she planned to have it.

Coming to a fork in the path, she guided Zephyrus to the right. It had been years since she'd ridden here, but she knew the way to Marcus' favorite place on his father's, now his, estate. Coming to the edge of the wood, she slowed. The stables were a brief gallop away and far from the prying eyes of the carriages on the front drive. Giving her stallion his head, she raced across the short field, usually filled with lily of the valley flowers in the summer, but now nothing but dry grass and dirt. Pulling up before the large stone building, she dismounted and looped the reins through a ring nearby and moved toward the open doors.

"Ebba, you can eat more than that. No, not my ear, you flirt."

At the sound of his voice, she stilled, her breath lodged in her chest. Though she'd seen it in print, she hadn't truly comprehended that Marcus was indeed alive. A rush of longing swept through her, and she grabbed onto the doorframe to keep from falling. Tears stung the backs of her eyes so she stepped back, leaning against the cold stone of the building.

A memory flashed through her mind of Marcus holding her gently, cupping her face in the moonlight and kissing her. The love in his gaze so clear, she'd melted into him. She closed her eyes, fisting her hands and forcing herself to remember he'd never contacted her. She'd been a widow by the time he'd arrived in England and yet he hadn't let her know he lived. He couldn't even extend that simple courtesy to her. Pulling on her anger, she pushed away from the wall and stepped into the stable.

The darkness blinded her to everything at first, and she waited until she could see clearly. Noises coming from the fourth stall on the left let her know where he was. Quietly, she walked forward until she could clearly see him. His back was to her, giving her a chance to accept it really was him and to adjust to the changes in him. His torso was broader than it used to be and his waist more narrow. His black hair was far shorter than she remembered. She latched onto those changes to keep her memories at bay. Steeling herself, she buried her hands in her skirts. "You're alive."

He spun at her voice. "Mariel." The love and longing deep inside her were reflected in his gaze, and clear in his voice, as he spoke her name on almost a whisper. Everything she remembered about him and how he made her feel flooded her.

And then he changed before her eyes. The love she'd missed disappeared, the lines about his face grew deeper as it hardened, and his shoulders stiffened. "What are you doing here?"

It was as if Marcus never existed and before her was a stranger. His abrupt question lit the match to her simmering anger. "I came to see if it's true."

"It's true. You can leave now." He turned away from her, moving deeper into the stall, dismissing her as he turned the Irish Hunter around.

Not bloody likely. She stepped into the stall. "I want an explanation."

"The rumors of my death were obviously exaggerated." He kept his attention on the horse as if it were of far more importance than she.

"Obviously." She let the full force of her sarcasm intone her response.

His head jerked up at that. "You've grown cold."

She was anything but cold. Her pain burst deep beneath the growing heat of her fury. "Only with people who have betrayed me."

His eyes narrowed. "I have done nothing to warrant such an accusation."

"You haven't?" She held her left palm up and tapped it with her index finger. "You were alive, but didn't send word to your betrothed." She tapped her palm again, harder this time. "You returned to England and still didn't send her word." She tapped her palm a third time. "When she arrives, you tell her to leave."

She dropped her hands. "That sounds like a betrayal to me. A betrayal of our oath to each other. A betrayal of the love you promised." She swallowed hard, refusing to cry. "A betrayal of our families."

He dropped the bucket in his hand and took a step toward her then stopped, his hands fisting at his sides. "I did not betray anyone. There were circumstances beyond my power to control."

"Such as?"

He stood there glaring at her, his jaw clenched, but didn't say anything.

She lost her patience. "Very well, I'll simply ask your mother."

"No!"

His immediate response was what she'd hoped for. "Whyever not?"

"She's been through enough." The words were uttered between gritted teeth.

The double implication that his mother seeing her was too much, and that she herself had not been through enough snapped her ever-present control. She slammed her hands on her hips. "Then you'd best tell me. Now!"

At her shout, he finally moved, stopping within arm's reach. The scent of tonka wafted over her, the nutty aroma mixing with the scents of horse and hay, the combination threatening to fill her with heartbreaking memories. She swallowed hard. "Well?"

"You are a widow. Why does it matter to you, when after they reported my death, you so quickly married another? It's clear to me that whatever feelings you had, whatever loyalty to me, had been far less than I realized. There was no reason to contact you."

She widened her eyes in shock, his assumptions too wrong to allow. "When we received the letter from your brother that you had been killed, my heart died." She stepped forward and poked him in the chest with her finger. "I didn't see any reason to mourn because I didn't see any reason to continue living. You had my heart and took it to the grave with you."

He stepped back from her. "You're a widow."

"Because I found a purpose."

He scowled. "To be someone else's wife."

She gave him a hard stare. "No. To save my family from financial ruin. My heart was dead, so I married Lord Beaumont to insure my family would continue to thrive. His death set me free, but to what? To find out that you've been living here, hiding?"

Suddenly, the truth hit her in the gut. He *had* been hiding, from her. But inheriting the title had thrown him back into society whether he wanted it or not. She pointed behind her. "Well, you can't hide anymore, Viscount Blackmore. You have a duty to your family, to your mother, to marry some chit and have heirs. It is unfortunate that you hadn't searched me out. I could have saved you from all this."

Reaching up, she grasped the jewel on her chest and yanked. "To think I've worn this every day since you left. I had no idea you had left me so long ago. Here's your heart back." Throwing the stone into the hay at his feet, she turned on her heel and strode out.

She barely made it to Zephyrus before the tears started to fall. Climbing up onto him, she kicked him into a gallop, not caring where he took her. Not caring about anything.

MARCUS CROUCHED DOWN and picked up the garnet necklace. Memories filled his head, and his heart started to pound so loud he was sure Ebba could hear it.

She'd kept it. She'd worn it against her heart. He closed his fingers over the stone, even as his breathing remained erratic, the pain in his chest intensifying. His memory of Mariel was but a shade of the truth. Her height remained the same, but her chestnut hair seemed to shine with warmth, her green eyes were so brilliant as to make the leaves on the trees appear dull, and her skin, glowing with wrath appeared as soft as the orange blossoms she loved so much. Her dark brown riding habit accentuated the fact that her slender build had filled in, especially her bosom, which now encased her closed heart.

Bootsteps on the brick floor of the stable had him rising.

"So that was Lady Mariel Mabry?" Anthony came to a stop at the entrance to the stall.

He nodded, his throat too tight to speak.

"I thought you loved her."

Again he nodded before turning back to Ebba. With anyone else, even his mother, he'd simply ignore the question. But Anthony was the reason he made it back to English soil. He owed him his life, such as it was.

"I'm confused. If you love her, why didn't you tell her the truth?"

He forced himself to focus on Anthony's words and not on Mariel. "*Because* I love her."

His friend crossed his arms. "I'm not sure I understand. Or is that it? You don't think she'd understand your injury."

He slipped the jewel into the fob pocket of his pantaloons before giving the horse a pat on her rump and exiting the stall, brushing by Anthony, forcing him to move. He closed the stall gate before facing his friend "No. Mariel would understand. She's the most understanding person I've ever met. But I can't let her waste her life on me. She can still marry another and have the children she always wanted."

"How do you know she wants that?"

He shook his head and started toward the open doors to the outside. "I know her. I know what she's dreamed of. She told me. I can't take that from her."

Anthony fell into step beside him. "People change. It's been at least four years since you last saw her, hasn't it? You've changed."

He gave Anthony a stern look. "I went to war. I was shot. I saw...I witnessed atrocities committed on both sides. She was safe here. Safe to attend balls, choose her favorite dress, race Zephyrus over hill and dale at Thornwood." He shook his head. "How much could she have changed?"

"She was married and lost her husband. Maybe she had children."

He headed out of the stable. "She doesn't. I inquired about that before I came home. I wanted to know in the unlikely event that she found me. Which she did." He stepped into the warm sunlight, shading his eyes with his hand before choosing the pathway back to the house. His brother's death had wreaked havoc in his life. Not only had he lost his best friend, but he'd gained a title, something he'd never wanted, except once, when he'd first met Lady Mariel Mabry.

"She had no groom with her. She must feel comfortable riding between your properties."

At Anthony's observation, he looked at him. "She probably left him in the wood. She always has a groom with her. She is the epitome of a lady. She would make someone the perfect wife." At his own statement, his insides twisted around like a gnarled tree. Returning his attention to the path, he defended his actions once more. "She's wrong if she thinks we would suit each other now."

"She had one thing right though."

He stifled a snort. Mariel had everything right. She was perfect. A woman of kindness, love, and manners who loved horses as much as he. There would never be anyone else for him, even if that were a true possibility. "Which of her many comments do you refer to?"

Anthony walked past him and halted before the steps of the side door, blocking his path. "I'm referring to her comment that if you had sought her out when you first arrived back in England, you wouldn't have to contend with the score of women who keep flocking to your door."

"It isn't a score." He barely kept the growl from his voice as he reached around the man and pulled open the door that led into his study. "Maybe a dozen, but they are persistent. Besides, I'm perfectly happy avoiding them all."

Anthony followed him inside. "I'm sure you are, but what of your mother? Even my mother didn't have to be nice to so many upper crust ladies on a daily basis and she owned a shop."

"Bloody hell." He reached for the decanter of whisky, the need to feel it burn its way down his throat too strong to ignore.

His friend's hand covered the glass. "I thought you didn't want to slip into a stupor ever again." Anthony's face changed, sympathy showing in his gaze. "Are you in pain?"

He yanked the glass out from under Anthony's hand. "Yes. I just told the woman I love to stay the hell away from me and broke her heart for a second time. Why am I still here? Why didn't I just die like I was supposed to?" He hated that his voice rose.

Setting both the decanter and glass down on the side board, he strode to the fireplace and looked up at the portrait of his brother. "And why is it that everyone I loved is gone except for the woman I love, who I can't have, and my poor mother, who is caught in the middle of my pain?" He gripped the mantel, the solidness of it like a loaded canon in a battle.

Anthony clasped his shoulder from behind. "Nothing can take away the pain of your losses, but maybe it's time to stop hiding."

He closed his eyes and swallowed his denial. The man had been the voice of reason so many times in the last three years. His words were worth listening to. "What do you suggest?"

"I suggest that you call on Lady Mariel tomorrow and offer her an apology for your behavior."

He opened his eyes and stared at Anthony as if he too had become but a ghost. "I don't think I heard you correctly."

Anthony let go of his shoulder and moved toward the door. "Yes. You did." Then with no further explanation, the man slipped from the room.

There was no possibility that he would go to Silver Meadows and apologize to Mariel. Having her hate him was for the best. She'd always been too good for him, not simply in social status, but also in character. Now the gap between them was even wider.

But as he remembered her outrage, he shuddered. He hated seeing her so angry and hurt. He slipped his hand into the pocket of his pantaloons and pulled out the large garnet. Looking at it now, it reminded him of his own dried blood. Quickly, he dropped it back into his pocket. Whatever it meant to him now, it didn't lessen what it meant to her. Anthony made a valid suggestion. No matter how much he didn't want to see her again, he needed to apologize for propriety's sake. At his decision, a new plan formed.

When he left for the war, he'd been a young man filled with conviction and life. Now he was filled with cynicism and a wish to retire from the world. But that was not an option for a titled aristocrat, and if he'd learned anything from the military, it was that he must fulfill his duty, no matter how distasteful it might be, even if it meant dying.

He shook off the thought. Maybe it was time to stop hiding as Anthony also suggested. It hadn't helped anyway. Now that he was Viscount Blackmore, he no longer needed the small cottage in Scotland. Maybe he'd give it to Anthony. It was the least the man deserved after France.

First, he needed to relieve his mother of the strain of being his gatekeeper. Though she enjoyed having visitors, the steady stream had to be difficult for her, her eldest son having died barely six months ago. She was all he had left of his family, and it was his duty to take care of her.

Stepping out of the study, he strode toward the servants' stairs when Gibson stepped from the shadows.

"Do you need something, my lord?"

"Yes. Please tell the ladies calling upon my mother that she is no longer taking callers and have her come to my study."

"Of course." Though Gibson didn't ask, curiosity filled his gaze.

Heading back to his study, he strode to the far window which had a view of the end of the drive. He waited impatiently before a carriage drove toward the edge of the estate. When another followed, he felt the stiffness in his shoulders ease. It was on the fourth carriage's exit that the door to his study opened.

"Marcus, is something wrong?"

His mother's worried expression had him hurrying to reassure her. "No, not with me."

She placed her hand over her chest. "Thank the heavens. Gibson told me to send my callers away."

He walked toward her, still amazed that she looked so beautiful even at two score and ten. Only the silver starting to streak her black hair gave any hint of her age, a silver that was not in residence when he'd left for the war. He held his hand out toward one of the two chairs before the unlit fireplace. "Please, join me."

She strode forward as if walking on air and sat as befitted a queen. She'd never been petite, but she had always carried herself with grace. "Has something happened?"

"Yes. I've grown tired of the endless stream of ladies taking up your time. I wanted to steal you away during daylight hours for a change." He gave her a warm smile.

She relaxed into the dark green chair, her lavender dress covering it like a fragile flower upon a rigorous vine. "I very much appreciate the change of venue. Spending time with you is always my preference."

It was very typical of his mother to express her likes and dislikes in a positive fashion. She was the epitome of a lady. *That was one of the things she had loved about Mariel.* Ignoring his thought, he smiled. "And I enjoy your company over all others."

"Marcus, I know you. You are only charming when you have a boon to request."

He smirked, having forgotten how much she did know him, or rather who he used to be. "Actually, I want to offer my apology to you."

"Whatever for?" She sat straight up, clearly puzzled.

He laid his hand upon hers where it rested on the arm of the chair. "I have ignored my duty as the Viscount of Blackmore and allowed you to suffer under the onslaught of femininity that has descended upon us since I came home."

"Oh that." She patted his hand with her other one. "It really has been no bother." Her eyes lit up with delight. "Have you finally decided on a few ladies to call upon? Oh, you must tell me."

He barely held back a grimace. It hadn't occurred to him that she would think he'd taken her observations at dinner on all the ladies that had come to call to decide on a potential wife. But he should have. "I am still thinking on it. However, I feel that you have quite done your duty here and wish you to proceed to London for the rest of the season."

She pulled her hands back and set them in her lap. "You want me to go to London without you?"

The hurt in her voice was a shot to his gut. "I was only thinking of you. Do you not wish to see your friends and enjoy the festivities?"

Her brow furrowed, clearly not excited by the prospect. "I am more concerned that you find a proper wife and allow me the pleasure of seeing my grandchildren."

He stiffened. He could not tell his mother that her hopes for grandchildren had died with his brother. That the memories of what he'd witnessed made it impossible for him to have intercourse. Nor could he tell her he'd never marry. What the bloody hell was he supposed to do? As a child, he'd never been able to lie, an inordinate amount of blinking accompanying every one until all in his family had recognized the sign. However, he'd outgrown that problem for better or worse. "I understand, but I do not think the search should be limited to Northampton, do you?"

Her face brightened. "Of course! I can go to London and see who is available and best suited to you. Then you can follow, and I will tell you all that I have learned." She clapped her hands together and held them tight. "I think that's a wonderful idea. You send word to Blackmore House, and I'll have Mrs. Hammons begin packing straight away. I believe I could be settled in at Town by week's end."

She rose and he stood with her, a stiff smile on his face. "I will tell Gibson to let any future callers know that you are not receiving. That should give you more time."

"You think of everything." She paused then took his hand. "I'm so very glad you came home to me."

He swallowed hard. She'd been through so much in only three years. First, the notice that he had died, then his father's death at the hands of a criminal, and most recently his brother's and sister-in-law's deaths from typhoid fever. He was all she had left, and that wasn't much. "You always have my heart."

She grinned slyly and let go of his hand. "I'm happy to share it with your wife." Then with a soft twirl of skirts, she turned and floated as if on air to the door.

He watched her until she left, then slumped back into his chair. Her idea to look for his potential wife in London was the last thing he wanted. While it pleased him that she was so happy, he didn't see a happy resolution to his dilemma. He would either appear to be too picky and selfish or he would have to tell her and break her heart again.

Which begged the question, if he did so much damage to the women he loved, would they have been better off if he'd died on that battlefield like his men had expected him to?

CHAPTER TWO

MARIEL DESCENDED THE grand staircase at Silver Meadows, the place of her sister's new school, her emotions under tight control. It would not be appropriate to rant and rave before the duke. A full day of crying and a sleepless night was enough. The Viscount of Blackmore deserved no more of her time.

Reaching the entryway of the grand home, she moved through the parlor and into the drawing room where her hosts the Duke and Duchess of Northwick sat reading their respective news sheets. She could see the duke's face above his reading material. His dark brows knit and his blue eyes were steadily moving. His dark brown hair had begun to curl at the nape. He would no doubt have it cut soon as he preferred it shorter.

The duchess, her sister Joanna, looked up first and quickly set down her sheets. "Mariel." She rose and approached with her arms held wide, her hazel eyes brimming with sympathy.

She quickly held up a hand to stop Joanna. Any touch might cause her to lose her composure. "I am fine."

When her sister hesitated, but didn't move, she softened her voice. "Please."

Joanna's arms came down and she gave a curt nod. Flicking a black curl over her shoulder, she moved back to her chair, her pretty bright blue dress reminding Mariel of the sky outside.

Relieved that no sisterly hug was forthcoming, she moved to

the sideboard as a servant arrived with a new pot of tea. There were numerous tasty treats from seed cakes, to toast and jam, to honey cakes. Though she thought it quite a lot considering all the young ladies of Joanna's school, Belinda's School for Curious Ladies, were in London for the season, she refrained from commenting because she did so love a honey cake.

She made her selection then joined her sister and the duke at the table. The duke set aside his newsprint and smiled politely. "Good morning."

She gave him a polite nod. "Good morning. Is there anything of interest in the country news?"

He grimaced. "Hardly, unless, of course, you have a stake in the fate of Mr. Lowel's two pigs."

"Mr. Lowel?" She poured her tea and added sugar.

"Yes. He is a farmer not far from here, and it appears his pigs walked into Widow Barough's kitchen through an open door and enjoyed the dinner meant for the august widow."

She stared at him in disbelief. "You are jesting."

James Huntington raised dark brows and managed an extremely arrogant posture, but the laughter in his blue eyes belied his affectation. "I assure you, my lady, I do no such thing."

Her lips tugged upward at the silliness of the story. "And what, pray tell, is to be the fate of farmer Lowel's pigs for such a horrifying deed?"

"Well, the widow demanded they be put to death for their perfidy and be served to her in multiple dinners."

Trying hard to match the gravity of the duke's demeanor, she clasped her hands together. "Oh, do tell me they met not such a fate."

"I admit, the judge found a compromise, and as soon as the sow's piglets are weaned, they are to be turned over to the widow for raising and, dare I say, eating."

"Oh, James." Joanna rolled her eyes. "Don't pay him any attention, Mariel. I'm sure there was no such story in the paper."

She unclasped her hands and gave the duke a friendly smile.

"I don't think I care to know if it's true or not. Thank you, James."

"I'm pleased I was able to entertain you." He rose and moved toward the sideboard himself, though it was obvious he'd already eaten.

"How are you feeling this morning?" Joanna's question was anything but polite conversation.

"I am tired, and I fear my eyes are quite swollen despite the ice you sent up, but I shall continue on as I have."

Joanna reached across the table and took her hand. "You have always been so strong, and so helpful. Is there anything I can do?"

She shook her head. "No. I think I'll take Xeres out for a ride today and enjoy this beautifully crisp weather. It's such a relief to see the sun after this past year."

Joanna gave her hand a squeeze before releasing it. "After yesterday, I made the decision to stay on here at Silver Meadows until you are ready to travel to London."

Travel to London? She'd been so set on her plan to confront Marcus that she'd failed to think of anything else. That was not like her. She always had a plan.

"Unless you don't wish to go to Town this year. I would understand." Joanna's words gave her pause.

"I haven't thought about it. I suppose I want to go. It's what we always do."

"Not me." James spoke from the sideboard. "In fact, I'm perfectly happy to skip the season for the next ten years."

She and her sister looked at the duke. "We know." The burgeoning tension she felt in her stomach eased at their joint comment.

"Good. Then I will leave you two to decide my fate." The duke strode toward the parlor, but stopped in the pillared opening. "I will be in the library finishing my most recent acquisition." With that, he continued out of the room with a small plate in his hand, leaving them alone.

She had no doubt the newest acquisition was a book. When

she turned back to the table, she found Joanna staring at her. "There is no need to look so concerned. I will continue to live."

"I have no doubt of that. But if you could enlighten me a bit on what you must overcome, perhaps I can be of assistance."

If Joanna had offered such aid a year ago, she would have demurred, but now that her intelligent sister had fallen in love, at least she felt the emotion as well as understood it. "He wishes nothing to do with me. In his opinion, I married before his body turned cold, which it never did, but his heart has."

"Oh." Joanna remained silent for a moment. "You did disabuse him of his obvious notion that you married for love."

"I did. However, he is much changed." Though she'd seen a glimpse of the man she knew, he'd been replaced with a stranger. "He is not someone I wish to have any further contact with."

"And there's no reason why you should." Joanna smiled reassuringly, but her concern was clear in her gaze.

"Thank you. I just need to create a plan for this year, so that I have activities to look forward to." Planning made her feel comfortable and safe.

"I was just thinking you would make a wonderful teacher here at Belinda's School for Curious Ladies."

"Oh, my, no." She shook her head vigorously. "All that I know is what every other lady acquires in her journey to being a wife. That is hardly what you teach here."

Joanna leaned forward and lowered her voice. "Now that you have learned that our neighbor is not who you thought, would you consider becoming a wife again?"

At Joanna's carefully worded question, a cold chill ran through her. "Do I need to? I had thought you said I have enough to purchase a small manor."

"You do, but we would all miss having you with us. What would we do without you?"

She cocked her head and raised her brows.

Joanna chuckled relaxing back into her chair. "Now what did I say to deserve *the face.*"

"You know very well that none of you need me as a chaperone anymore. Both you and Amelia are happy with your marriages. You have your school and Amelia has her painting. I am not so intelligent or talented as you both."

Joanna frowned and opened her mouth to object.

She held up her hand. "No, do not flatter me with some hidden skill you think I have. I am not like you, or Amelia. I'm more like our dear Belinda." At the mention of their late younger sister, Joanna closed her mouth. "The painting Amelia did of Belinda in the parlor is truly a masterpiece."

Joanna, who could see the painting from where she sat, sighed. "It's a comfort to me. I know it's strange, but she seems so real that sometimes when I'm alone, I find myself talking to her."

She understood completely. Though she'd not admit it, she too spoke to Belinda. "I can see why. She was always calm and happy. Whenever I feel at my wit's end, I think of her and I immediately know I can make it through."

Joanna's keen gaze settled back on her. "You speak as if you've been in such a state many times."

Drat. She hadn't meant to reveal herself. She never wanted her family to know how much being married to George Walford of Beaumont had affected her. She shrugged, "Haven't we all? I mean, even Zephyrus can cause me to wish I were anywhere but with him."

Joanna's eyes widened and a wide smile lit her face. "That is it."

"That is what? He's not a bad horse. He just becomes stubborn at times and can get quite, well, mulish."

Joanna rose even as she waved away her comment. "No, not Zephyrus. I mean the horses. You have a way about horses that none of us has, not even old Mr. Haggett."

Oh, dear. When Joanna got excited, that usually meant trouble was forthcoming. "I doubt I know my horses any better than your stableman knows yours. I've just spent more time with mine than you have."

"Exactly." Joanna started to pace across the drawing room, her blue skirts swishing against her legs with her long strides. "You know your horses, but you also know horses in general, their temperament, the best training for them, even the best horse for the best task."

Once again, she felt her stomach tighten. When Joanna had an epiphany and wished to act upon it, there was usually nothing to be done but hope all would turn out well. That Joanna's focus had turned to her was of great concern. "I do not know why that would be of any import."

Her sister turned and stopped in midstride. "You could breed horses!"

"What?" Horror filled her at once. "I'm a lady. Ladies do not breed horses. How could you think of such an endeavor for me? It's just not done."

"Oh, come, Mariel. It's not done for a lady to open a school for ladies of the peerage and to educate them on anything men are educated on. But I've done just that."

"You are a duchess. Allowances are made."

Joanna opened her arms wide. "What about Amelia? She's becoming famous because of her paintings. That's certainly not done."

She shook her head, placing her napkin to the side of her plate. "Amelia exhibited with other female artists, so it is becoming accepted, and I don't believe that selling a few paintings makes her a famous artist."

"Sixteen."

"Sixteen?"

"Yes. Amelia has sold sixteen paintings in mere weeks to three different lords."

Why hadn't she known that? Probably because she'd been so focused on a particular viscount who had risen from the dead, or so it seemed. "Joanna, I'm not like you and Amelia. I don't wish for something beyond being a wife and a moth—lady. That is who I am."

Joanna's shoulders slumped.

Now she felt like she'd just told her sister there would never be another bowl of mascarpone ice cream made for eternity. "I would posit that Belinda and I were alike in this."

"Perhaps." Joanna returned to her seat. "I just want to see you happy."

"But I am happy." At Joanna's doubtful look, she explained further. "I have two wonderful sisters, both our parents, and even a bit of independence as a widow."

"Is that truly enough?"

Joanna's look of disbelief almost made her laugh out loud. "Poor Joanna. Your mind just never rests. It is impossible for you to understand. No, it's not enough." She had dearly wished for a house and children of her own. "I also need Zephyrus and my stable of horses."

Her sister's hazel eyes immediately lit up again.

"To ride. Not to breed."

"Very well, I will yield to your better knowledge of yourself...for now."

"Thank you." She smiled warmly. She was very happy for both her sisters and looked forward to being an aunt to their children. Maybe one of their daughters would need lessons in arranging dinner parties or embroidery. That would be enough for her.

Joanna lifted the tea pot and poured them more tea. "I suppose we should discuss when to go to London. Though James is happy to stay here or at Burhleigh Park, we do have students in Town who are being tended to by Lady Astor, so I will have to insist that we take over those duties."

"It would also be remiss of me to not be at Craymore Hall to help Mother with her dinner parties and ball." Even as she mentioned it, she found herself yearning to be of help once again.

"And we will need to attend to our wardrobe for the season, of course." Joanna winked.

That warned her they'd be having many fittings when they

arrived in Town, which she would quite enjoy. "Now that you are wed, will you change your preferred dress hues?"

"Whatever for?"

Part of her wished to wear the jewel-colored tones her sister wore, but they did not look as well on her. "You are a proper duchess now."

"But as you mentioned, not so proper as to be head of an experimental school. Actually, I believe my color choices will fit much better with my new matronly status. But what of you? You do not need to wear such somber shades anymore."

In other words, now that the man she'd loved since before she'd come out was no longer dead, she could wear brighter shades. Though Joanna didn't say it, it was clear in her face. "You do not think the dark greens and maroons of my wardrobe fitting?"

Joanna scrunched up her nose. "I suppose they are fine, but you may wish for Amelia's input as she is much better with such aesthetics. I do believe you would be quite fetching in whatever she recommends."

"Joanna." She used her stern tone, which she rarely used with anyone but her horses. "I am not looking to be courted, so whatever plot you have simmering in that smart head of yours, you must burn. I am not marrying again. I am a widow and the *ton*—Oh, no." She pushed her chair back and rose. "I can't go to London, ever." Dread, anger, and a deep ache filled her.

Joanna rose as well. "Mariel, what is it?"

She could see the women whispering behind her back even as the circumstances filled her head. "The *ton*."

"Yes, what about them?" Joanna moved closer and grasped her hand. "Why would they stop you from coming to London with us?"

"Marcus." She swallowed hard. "He's alive. Everyone will expect that he would seek me out, ask me to honor our betroth-al."

Joanna hesitantly shook her head. "That was four years ago.

I'm sure they have forgotten."

She cocked her head and raised her brows.

"Very well, they haven't."

She stepped away from her sister. "Can't you see it? The pitying looks, the whispers, and if Marcus were to court a young woman?"

Joanna frowned as she started to pace again. "I see what you mean. And what if you both are at the same recital or ball? It would be awkward."

"Awkward?" Her eyes began to sting. "It would be heart-breaking. Even if I could hide all my anger and hurt, they'd know."

"Or make up a story."

She took two more steps back at the thought, bumping into the sideboard as the pain of his betrayal washed through her again. "I couldn't. I just…" Though she tried to hold it in, the ache was too new and two tears tracked down her cheeks.

Joanna stopped, her hands curling into fists. "He should be horsewhipped for what he's done to you."

A part of her agreed, and for a brief moment, the thought of lashing out at the man she'd loved with her whole heart had her tears stopping. But she was and would ever be a lady. "I'm afraid no such punishment will be visited upon him."

"It's just wrong that you must suffer while he continues with his life as if nothing untoward has occurred."

For the first time, she agreed with Joanna's sentiment about the state of society. It did seem unfair that she must fade from society at the age of a score and six as if she were a matron like her mother. The feeling of resentment that bubbled up was so foreign that it made her uncomfortable. Despite having two sisters who had stretched society's patience and even secretly went beyond the pale, it had never been her way. "I need to ride."

"That is an excellent idea." Joanna strode around the table toward her. "And I need to confer with James on our trip to Town. There must be a way to protect you."

Before she could object, her sister left the room. Too off-balance to focus on her sister's plans, she ascended the staircase, anxious to don her riding habit and be on Xeres' back. He always wanted to go his way and at his pace, the perfect horse for riding right now.

For some reason, she wanted to fight for control.

CHAPTER THREE

"DRATTED DESIGN." MARIEL released the thread for the fifth time in less than an hour and pulled it out. She'd barely completed one peony on her embroidery loop, her lack of attention frustrating her. Setting the loop on the settee next to her, she stood. Perhaps being alone wasn't in her best interest.

She'd thought her ride early in the morning with Xeres would have settled her nerves. But her agitation had not decreased. Turning to the portrait of her sister, she looked into the happy and contented gaze of Belinda. That was what she needed to find again, and she was well aware of why she'd lost it. "It's time I searched out Joanna to discover what plans she has surely made."

Giving the portrait a wave, she headed for the old ballroom. It had not surprised her that Joanna and James had had the massive room changed into a large library and lecture area. Only they would need the largest room in a home for learning. Then again, their aunt's old home was now a school, which she had no doubt had the quality of Oxford, only its students were women of the aristocracy.

Upon entering the cavernous space with a multitude of sectioned spaces for various subjects, she halted. "Joanna, are you about?"

"I am." Joanna's voice came from the left as did her footsteps once she stepped off whatever rug she trod upon. "I was just researching a constellation that one of our students was interested in." Her sister came around a set of mahogany book presses, a book in her hand. "One problem with running a school is that all my students expect me to know all the answers." Though she rolled her eyes, she grinned happily.

"I imagine it would also be enjoyable to learn from your students, would it not?"

Her sister halted in midstride. "You are correct. Why didn't I think of that? I can allow them the research and have them teach *me*. It would give them a confidence I know some of them do not possess." She strode up and hugged her. "You, dear sister, are as smart as Socrates."

She felt the heat rise in her cheeks. "Hardly. I am observant and logical, no more and no less."

Joanna laughed. "Not to mention humble, gracious, kind, and oh, so proper. Perfect qualities in a wife."

Before she could object, her sister winked. "Do not worry, dear sister. I would much rather you breed horses."

At Joanna's full laughter, she relaxed. Her sister's teasing meant she'd not pursue either avenue.

A gleeful look filled Joanna's gaze. "Of course, you could stay here and take classes."

"Classes? I thought The Belinda School for Curious Ladies is closed."

"It is, but I have two instructors who are spending their summer here. One teaches physical defense and the other has expertise in managing estates."

"Physical defense? Truly?" Joanna had talked about teaching her girls how to physically defend themselves last year when they were in a coach with the duke and were set upon by drunken bullies.

Her sister nodded. "Yes, physical defense. These young ladies never know when they may find themselves at the mercy of a highway man. As Francis Bacon wrote, knowledge itself is power."

"I don't see myself having a physical altercation with anyone, but perhaps I could come back when your school is open again and learn a bit about estate management. I do not fancy being a sole pupil." She shivered. "As the oldest, I experienced enough of that before you were old enough to attend the tutoring sessions."

"If I recall, you always made me answer the questions."

A fond memory whispered through her mind at the young Joanna fairly standing up with excitement when she had the answers. "It was far less me making you and far more you being eager to show what you learned."

Joanna blushed, a rare occurrence. "I admit, I never could keep my knowledge to myself." She held her hand out to indicate the entire former ballroom. "And now I get to share it with so many young female minds."

"Aunt Mabry would be quite pleased, I think. Not only are you married, but you have made her home a haven for learning. But for me, I will retire to Thornwood this season. Have you decided when you will journey to Town? As I will need to make my own arrangements to return to Thornwood."

"I could not bear the thought of you back at Thornwood without any of us in residence. Whatever would you do?"

"I would do what I do anywhere else. I would ride, sew, and perhaps even design a new look for my rooms. It has been near on ten years since mother allowed me those dark green colors."

Joanna tucked the large leather volume under her arm. "That is all very nice, but you can do that after the season. I can't imagine attending any event without you."

"Please do not jest. You've attended many a lecture, recital, and play without me. And you have your gatherings to orchestrate with your students. You will be far too busy to notice my absence. I believe—" She halted as Joanna squeezed her arm and looked beyond her.

"Yes, Harrison."

"Your grace. Lady Beaumont has a caller."

Joanna nodded regally. "Thank you, we will be right in." As

soon as the butler left Joanna frowned. "I did not realize it was that time of day already. Who do you think it is?"

Though her stomach flopped over like a fish out of water, Mariel shrugged. "Maybe it is Lady Burchall. She does like to spread the latest gossip."

"Oh, that could be." Excited to hear the latest rumor, Joanna quickly set her book on the closest table then linked their arms. "Shall we see what she knows?"

"You mean, what she thinks she knows?" Mariel smiled at her sister, loathe to remind her that they really had no idea if it was Lady Burchall.

As they made their way to the parlor, her instincts rose. Lady Burchall would not call on her specifically. This was Joanna's school. Her step slowed. The only person who would call on her here was the one person she never wished to see again.

"Mariel, what is it? Are you feeling quite yourself?"

She shook her head. "Perhaps I should go upstairs and lie down."

Joanna stopped. "Of course. I will tell your caller…oh."

Even as Joanna surmised what she had, a figure stepped into the entryway from the parlor, a figure in black pantaloons and gray tailcoat. "Lady Beaumont."

Her breath caught at the sight of Marcus. Part of her wanted to run, but a stronger part of her wanted to rail at him. It was that new, strange part that had her lifting her chin and meeting his gaze. "Lord Blackmore."

"Would you like me to have Harrison escort the lord out?"

At Joanna's question, she shook her head. "No, that won't be necessary. I am quite curious as to why Lord Blackmore is here." She strode forward, brushing past Marcus as she stepped into the parlor. Not in the mood to sit, she stopped next to a wingback chair and turned to face him.

He strode back into the room, standing near the window across from her. Something told her he wished the room were larger so he could be farther away from her. Yet, he'd come.

Why?

Joanna moved to her side.

She turned her head to face her sister. "If you don't mind, I'd like to hear what the viscount has to say in private."

Her sister's brows lowered as she looked to Marcus. "Are you sure?"

"Quite sure." Though she had no idea why her legs weren't shaking. Instead, anticipation filled her just like it did before sending a horse over a rock wall.

"Very well. Harrison will be nearby if you need anything."

She gave her sister a curt nod and watched her leave the room. Though Joanna may be tempted to listen near the archway, she would respect them. After her sister disappeared, she looked at Marcus again.

It was lighter in the pale blue parlor and his black hair and attire stood out in foreboding contrast, but she felt no fear. Her feelings were as jumbled as the day before, but a strange calm had descended upon her as if she'd been waiting for this moment since she left him yesterday. "I expect you have a reason for calling. I highly doubt it is to become better acquainted with me."

His countenance revealed nothing nor did he blink. "I have come to offer my apologies for my behavior yesterday."

Though she had no expectations for the reason for his visit, an apology was a surprise. "Why?"

He pulled down on the tailcoat as if wearing it were unfamiliar, which wasn't true. "My behavior was not acceptable. I can only offer that it was the surprise of your visit when Gibson had strict orders to inform all callers that I was not in residence."

Did she hear him correctly? "Then you blame your poor behavior upon me."

"No." His answer was quick and for the first time since he'd stepped into the room, he appeared less than sure. "The fault was mine. I merely wished to explain myself and assure you that had I met you here, I would not have behaved so."

This restrained Marcus was an entirely different man than the one she'd fallen in love with. They had been so different. He, the second son of a viscount, enthusiastic, and quite impulsive. His emotions strong and quick. She'd been polite and reserved and like a horse to a herd, she'd been attracted to him. This man before her was not him.

Resentment built. "It would have been highly unlikely for you to have met me here since you hid the fact you were alive for three years. When had you expected to tell me, or was there no expectation for that?"

He stiffened even more, if that were possible. "My brother's demise took that decision from me."

At the mention of his loss, her heart ached for him, but her mind refused to give him any sympathy. "If not for that unfortunate occurrence, I can only imagine that I would have never known of your miraculous rise from the dead."

His lip curled up for a moment. "No one would have."

He hadn't planned to tell his family he was alive? She couldn't quite believe him. "But now, everyone knows. If I go to London for the rest of the season, I will be an object of pity because of you, so I am regulated to staying away."

"I do not see why you would be an object of pity simply because I have had the misfortune of not dying."

At the irritation in his voice, an imp inside her shouted in triumph. It was a side of her she didn't know and couldn't seem to rein in. "Then allow me to explain. As you may or may not recall, we were betrothed when you left to fight Napoleon. That you are back and there has been no indication that you plan to honor that, you, in effect, have thrown me over."

His brow furrowed and he didn't say anything at first.

A tiny flame of hope flickered deep in her heart. Would he consider honoring their old marriage settlement?

"Then I must apologize again, for I had not thought of how my return to society would reflect upon you."

As her hope was dashed, her imp took over. "An apology does not help my circumstances."

His gray gaze narrowed. "What would you have me do? I cannot undo what has been done."

She must have understood Joanna's rants against the unfairness of society and the way women were treated far more than she realized because his answer sent a lightning bolt of fury through her. "What you could do is honor our betrothal."

"You married. *You* broke our betrothal." His gray gaze turned ice cold.

"I married because you died. You have no excuse because you have appeared alive, and I am already a widow." She didn't know if there was any legal means to force him, but she didn't want to force him. She didn't even want *this* Marcus Stratton. He had grown into a different person altogether.

He shook his head, his brow lowered in puzzlement. "Are you saying you still wish to marry me?"

"Oh, my, no. Of course not." She ignored his affront as he pulled back his head as if slapped. What she wanted was the Marcus she'd fallen in love with, but he no longer existed. He truly had died on the battlefield. So what did she want?

Even as she searched her heart, a devious idea formed that had her taking notice. "This is what I propose, since you have so graciously issued an apology for your behavior yesterday, I would like your cooperation in saving me from public pity."

For the first time since he'd entered the room, his shoulders loosened. "How can I do that?"

"By putting it about that we are once again betrothed and allowing me to break it." Now that the idea was stated, she rather liked it. It would be a fitting punishment for him having hidden away from her for so long. Now, if she could just find such a simple solution to heal her heart.

CHAPTER FOUR

MARCUS TURNED AWAY from Mariel to look at the view afforded him by the window. He did not wish her to see his confusion over her proposal. She still appeared as beautiful as ever, which made it difficult to guard his heart, even though her more mature personality had changed her. While his ego was affronted at the thought she would publicly end their relationship, he did understand why. But for such a ruse to work, they would need to be in each other's company and he had little faith in his ability to keep his feelings hidden. On the other hand, it would solve his immediate problem with his mother and allow him to have time to design a succession plan before telling her that he would die a bachelor. It would also stop the myriad young women anxious to become his viscountess. In essence, it would benefit him far more than her.

He turned back to find she'd taken a seat on the pale blue arm chair near the fireplace. "If we were to put forth such a lie, we would need to be seen together at a few events to make it plausible. Though you say society will look upon you with pity, they will also look on the fulfilling of our old betrothal as unusual."

She grasped the arm of the chair. "Yes, I suppose that's true. A few appearances among those who would be in a position to further our ruse would be needed. Of course, we can tell our family the truth."

"No." Unconsciously, he took a step forward. "I mean, if our family members know, their actions could give us away."

Her green gaze left his as she contemplated his words.

No doubt she didn't like his suggestion. The Mabrys had always been a close family and keeping a secret would be difficult for her, but their relationship must appear authentic.

Finally, she looked at him and a sly smile lifted one side of her lips more than the other. "Since I am the keeper of secrets in my family, it would be no burden to hold this one. But what of you? You have only your mother. Can you resist taking her into your confidence?"

The relief he felt had him relaxing his shoulders. "Compared to keeping her in the dark for years about the falseness of my death, this will be a secret easily kept."

"And you accept that I will end it when I see fit?"

He couldn't have her ending it too soon. "So that I may react in a befitting manner, I suggest we have an agreed upon date."

"That is a valid point. The season in Town is well underway and my father expects it to end mid-July. As it is March, I would think if we travel into London soon, we could end this farce by mid-April."

He started to nod then thought better of his agreement. "I would insist on a couple outings here in Northampton. As you noticed, there are a few women here who had hoped to become my wife. If we are seen together, and it is made known we are planning marriage, then they will move to other possible bachelors. That would, of course, delay our travels to London."

He hadn't been unaware of her sudden intake of breath at the word marriage, but she recovered quickly. "Are you sure you wish to ruin your chances with your neighbors' daughters?"

He shrugged. "There are plenty more prospective brides in Town, so I have no fear when I am ready to take a wife that I will find someone worthy." He'd never uttered such a blatant lie in his life, but his instinct was telling him it would only be the first of many in the coming month or so.

"Then I can agree to that." She studied him as if to find a chink in his armor. "I suppose I can throw you over at the end of April. Is that acceptable?"

By the way she spoke, it sounded as if they were planning an outing, not a carefully orchestrated courtship and ugly parting for the benefit of society. He gave her a curt nod. "That is acceptable. But I must insist on knowing what reason you will give to society for denying my claim."

She cocked her head and raised her brows, the gesture so familiar that it threatened his hold on his countenance.

"There are so many to choose from. I will have to think upon it and inform you when I decide."

A chill coursed through him, and he held himself rigid. "Be sure that you do."

She stiffened, her back straightening and her shoulders lifting. "Then we are agreed." Rising from the chair, she stepped closer to him, the scent of orange blossoms filling his nostrils, triggering memories of dancing with her. "I will await your invitations."

He held his breath to avoid another whiff and gave her a nod in acknowledgment before she regally swept from the room.

Finally breathing in, his senses were once again assaulted by her scent. He closed his eyes and a long-buried memory of kissing her in the hidden Greek temple in the wood at Ravenridge filled him with longing. Opening his eyes, he fisted his hands. The next six weeks would be sweet torture. Though his mother's dreams motivated him to agree to such an outlandish façade, it was Mariel herself that deserved his cooperation. He owed her this. If it would ease her, he would do it, and hopefully in the process show her it was for the best that she forget about him, even if he would go to his grave thinking of her, as he once thought he had.

Turning on his heel, he strode to the entryway and collected his hat from the butler, before jogging down the grand steps of Silver Meadows and into the phaeton led by Legend and Lore, his matched pair of thoroughbreds. Clicking them into action, he headed back to Ravenridge, anxious to tell his mother. She would, no doubt, tell everyone she knew once she arrived in London, which would pave the way for his and Mariel's acted betrothal.

In very little time, he'd pulled up to the stables and stepped down from the conveyance. Anthony met him and held the horses.

"Where's Mr. Clancy?" His stableman was always waiting for him.

"Your mother has him setting up the coach for her. Something about one more visit to the village."

"Of course. She always brings a gift for her aunt."

Anthony's eyes widened. "You have a great aunt?"

He chuckled as he removed his gloves. "I do. The women on my mother's side of the family live forever. She only just lost her own mother last year. Would you mind getting a groom to stable the horses?"

"I'll do it." Anthony grinned. "I'll take any excuse to stay out of the house."

Immediately concerned, he frowned. His mother only tolerated Anthony because he requested that she be polite, but she could make things uncomfortable for the man. "My mother has not made you feel you need to leave, has she?"

"If you mean has she said something or in action made it known she no longer wishes me within sight? The answer is no. However, if you mean because the house has turned into a carnival of moving pieces and chatter? Then yes. I sought the solace of a few nickers and the calmness of your stable. I do believe I was in danger of being packed in a box and sent to London!" Anthony gave an exaggerated shiver before setting to relieving Legend of the harness.

"Now *that* I completely understand." He started for the house then halted. Though they had agreed not to tell their families, Anthony needed to know. "You did not ask the result of my visit."

"No, I didn't. It is not every day a peer must apologize to a lady. I thought it best not to inquire." He led Legend toward his stall.

"Actually, we came to an agreement."

Anthony closed Legend's stall and came back toward him to unhook Lore. "Is it a beneficial agreement?"

He smirked. There was something about the way Anthony asked questions around the topic being discussed that reminded him he'd been a Bow Street Runner before joining the fight against Napoleon. He assumed Anthony was gentry from his manners, but he rarely talked about his past. But that was a topic for another conversation. Was his agreement with Mariel beneficial? "I believe so. We are continuing our betrothal."

That caught Anthony's attention. "I'm confused. Did you not just say yesterday that you wished Lady Beaumont to marry another?"

"I did indeed. However, this is not real. This will only be for six weeks and then she will throw me over, so as not to be pitied by the ton."

"And that gives you time to contact your heir so you can be truthful to your mother."

Anthony's keen mind was just one of the characteristics he liked about the man. "Exactly."

Anthony unhitched Lore from the harness. "Do you know who's next in line?"

"There is a cousin on my father's side. For once, I won't need your help on that."

"I don't mind being of assistance." Anthony walked Lore to his stall. Opening it, he patted the horse on his rump and the gelding entered. He looped the horse collar over the horse and set it through the ring. Finishing, he headed out of the stall. "I should know in a few days if the man you saw in the village last week is from our former regiment."

He'd all but forgotten about that incident. If he hadn't had such a well-trained horse, he could have found himself on his backside or worse, with a broken neck. "I didn't expect your investigation to be so quick."

Anthony grinned. "I am nothing if not thorough."

That was quite true, and he was thankful once again for having a man of Anthony's character not as his former lieutenant but as a friend. "Your talents are invaluable."

The man winked. "I know." Laughing, he moved off in search of a groom to tend the horses.

Continuing to the house, Marcus took the steps to the side door two at a time, pleased to be able to give his mother good news, even if only temporarily. As he stepped into his study, the sound of servants talking and walking about could be heard outside the doors to the room. Once his mother was off and in London, he could begin his farce and make it clear to the woman he loved that marriage was out of the question for him, even if he had to tell her the truth…or rather the part that was fit for a lady's ears.

He opened the door to the corridor and quickly stepped back as two footmen carried a large trunk. Once they passed, he strode down the hallway where Gibson oversaw the chaos. "Is Lady Blackmore upstairs?"

"No, sir. She's in the parlor having ice cream." The man's expression didn't change but there was a slight uplift to his tone that clearly revealed he thought Lady Blackmore's activity unusual.

Their new butler didn't know his mother well…yet. "Thank you." He turned before Gibson could see him smile and strode into the parlor of pale blue. It was his mother's favorite color.

"Ah, there you are, Marcus. Wherever have you been? Were you hiding from all the noise like you used to when you were a boy?"

He shook his head, amused that she'd relate him to the innocent child he used to be. But since he was her only family left, he was happy to indulge her. "If you mean was I hiding under the sideboard in the dining room, the answer would be no. I'm afraid

I cannot fit under there anymore."

She looked askance at him, a secret smile on her face. "And you know this to be true because you have tried?"

He laughed. "I shall endeavor to try at the very first opportunity."

She grinned and raised her cup. "Would you like some parmesan ice cream? I do believe this is cook's best yet."

He waved her off, but took the straight back chair next to her. "I have news for you. I just called upon Lady Beaumont."

His mother stilled, her spoon in midair. "Why did you do so? She broke your heart." She set the cup down, clearly not happy.

He hadn't realized exactly how much he would have to explain. "It appears I was incorrect."

"How were you incorrect? It was only a year before we heard of your untrue demise and she was married within the month."

"I know. I assumed she'd married for love." He didn't want to let his mother know of the financial constraints of the Mabrys. That was too titillating for her to keep to herself. "She knew she would never love another and so took the first offer to allow her sisters the opportunity to find their own husbands."

"Oh." His mother sat back quietly, clearly thinking about what he said.

It was one of the characteristics he loved about her. She could be quite calm in the midst of upheaval.

Finally, she nodded. "That does sound like Lady Mariel. She is always thinking of others. Does she still feel the same way about you?"

"Yes." It was a lie, of course. Mariel made it very clear that she was furious and even worse, had no interest in him except to avoid being pitied.

His mother cocked her head and studied him. "And do you still love her?"

Now *that* he could answer truthfully. "I do, with all my heart."

His mother's face brightened as she quickly understood the

possibilities of his revelation. "Marcus, don't make me wait another moment. Are you saying you have chosen her again to be your wife?"

The hope in his mother's gray eyes, so much like his own, twisted his insides, forcing him to take a deep breath. "Yes. She has agreed to a betrothal once again."

"Oh, I'm so pleased!" His mother clasped her hands together as her eyes filled with tears.

A stone settled in his stomach at the knowledge his mother would be devastated once again. He should tell her the truth and be done with it, but explaining to his parent that he couldn't have the grandchildren she so desperately wished for wasn't something he was ready to do. She deserved a little happiness, even if it would only be for a short time.

Reaching into his pocket, he pulled out a handkerchief and handed it to her. "I hope those are tears of happiness."

"Oh, my, yes. Lady Mariel is just so perfect for you. She's the epitome of a lady. She's kind, well-versed in all the duties of her station, and a marquess' daughter. Even more importantly, she loves you. Why, I'd swear she practically worshipped you before you left."

He chuckled, not at his mother's description, but at the fact Mariel could hardly stomach him now.

"Oh, dear, the house is almost ready to move to London. I was planning on leaving tomorrow."

He was pleased that she wouldn't see he and Mariel interact right away. "There's no need to change your plans. You can be the first to break the news in Town."

His mother's eyes lit with delight. "I will definitely do so. And my first call will be upon Lady Wakefield. I always did admire Lady Mariel's mother. I couldn't imagine having to marry off four daughters." Her smile faltered. "Or rather, three daughters."

"Very good." He rose. "I will leave for London in another fortnight."

"But the season is half over. Surely you will want to leave

sooner." His mother lifted her spoon again and pulled the cold treat into her mouth.

"I have decided it would be best to stay here a bit longer. Since Lady Beaumont is residing at Silver Meadows right now, we can attend a few public events here in Northampton to be sure our neighbors are clear that I am no longer available as a husband."

His mother's eyes turned shrewd. "That is very strategic of you. If you wish to let it be known you have chosen a bride, then I suggest attending service at the parish church. Once you two are seen there, you will no longer have ladies fluttering about you."

"Mother, you are truly inspiring."

She waved off his compliment. "Hardly. I simply know how these mothers think." She gave him another searching look. "You are sure you still want Lady Mariel, I mean, Beaumont?"

"I have never wanted any other."

At his mother's pleased smile, he turned and strode from the room. There had to be a special place in hell for sons who lied to their mothers, and he would no doubt end up there. But for now she was happy.

CHAPTER FIVE

MARCUS GLANCED OVER the aisle at the pew across from he and Mariel. Two young misses, who should be attending to the vicar's reading from the New Testament, looked at him and frowned as they spoke in whispers, far too quiet for him or the vicar to hear. He hoped the other ladies attending church also noticed he had escorted Mariel into the pew.

A tap on his thigh had him bringing his attention back to her. She scowled at him, and he quickly pretended an interest in the words coming from the pulpit. She didn't realize how difficult it was to pay attention to the church service with her sitting next to him. Her scent and appearance were enough to distract him from just about any task. But listening to the vicar drone on and on made it hard to focus on anything but her.

Finally, they stood to recite the Apostles' Creed. Though he tried to keep his concentration, hearing her voice had him tripping over the words which garnered him another disapproving look from her expressive green eyes. Upon finishing the recitation, they sat again, her lavender skirt brushing against his legs. If they hadn't come to church under false pretense, he would have enjoyed her presence next to him, but the experience was more like torture.

Part of him found the entire situation humorous, but when he'd chosen the Sunday service as the first place for them to make a public appearance in Northampton, he'd done so purposefully. What better way to make it clear that he was very serious about his attentions to the Lady Beaumont. He had no doubt that by the time they left the service, everyone in church would know whom he'd brought. That there was no special occasion for his presence made it that much more impactful. Now, if the service would end, they could be on their way.

Though Mariel was a widow, he'd been surprised that her acceptance of his invitation made clear only she would join him and no other. They had always been so careful to ensure her reputation remained as pure as she. He'd want it no other way. The change in her position reminded him that she had shared with another what had been meant for him. Even as the old anger surfaced, it dissipated. It hurt that they would never know the intimacy they'd expected. He had to be satisfied with the sweet agony of being near her.

Finally, the vicar ended the service, and he rose. After pulling down on his black tailcoat, he offered his arm to Mariel. Ever the lady, she gracefully took it as she exited the row, but before they could turn to exit the church, the vicar accosted them.

"Lord Blackmore, what a wonderful honor you do me by joining us today." The young clergyman couldn't be more than a score and ten, a significant change from their last vicar, who appeared on death's door for over ten years.

"Mr. Elkins, I wished to meet you sooner, but taking on my new position as viscount has taken all my time."

"Oh, I am most sure. I would very much like to call on you. I believe there are some improvements we could make here in the parish."

He swallowed a groan, anxious to change the subject. "May I present my betrothed, Lady Beaumont. She is the sister of the Duchess of Northwick."

The young man's eyes rounded before a too-large smile filled his narrow face. "My lady, it is an honor."

"It was a lovely service, Mr. Elkins."

The young man blushed. "I will hold your praise close to my heart. I have been here such a short time, I have only heard how I am not up to par."

"They just need to become accustomed to you. Do not despair." She smiled before making her voice louder. "I know not of the past vicar, but I do know that I thoroughly enjoyed your sermon."

Marcus was not unaware that Mariel did so to influence those in the parish. Her kindness toward the man was very typical of her character and one of the reasons he'd fallen in love with her. She'd opened the world to him while a young, selfish man. If not for her, he never could have appreciated his friendship with Anthony.

"Thank you, my lady. I will take your words to heart." Mr. Elkins turned back to him. "My lord, there is one item that does need your immediate attention."

Keeping in mind Mariel's kindness, he nodded. "Of course, please feel free to call on Thursday. I will be happy to entertain all your suggestions."

The man glanced at Mariel then back at him, clearly uncomfortable. "It actually would be best if you could come with me now."

Surprised by the request, he looked about wondering if they were in danger and if it was a ruse to get them to safety, but scanning the church, he found it still filled with all the parishioners. Why had they not filed out yet?

"My lord."

At Mariel's low-voiced appeal, he turned back and lowered his head. "Yes."

"Might I suggest we follow the vicar. Not only would it take care of his immediate need, but it would also help us avoid a crush."

Enlightenment dawned. The parishioners remained to greet them on their way outside. "Mr. Elkins, Lady Beaumont and I would be pleased to accompany you." He made sure his voice carried.

For his effort, Mariel gave him a small smile of approval.

He should have known. It wasn't the crush she hoped to avoid, but she wished to make Mr. Elkins appear important. As they followed the man to a door near his pulpit, he whispered in her ear, "Your judgement is as always impeccable."

She didn't respond in any way, but he noticed she took a deeper breath, her chest in the somber grey dress rising beneath her white shawl.

The vicar took them through a small study of sorts and directly outside into the sunlight—and the graveyard.

He was not particularly fond of graveyards and taking Mariel into one had not been the plan for the day at all. "Mr. Elkins, why have you brought us here?"

Mr. Elkins stopped and clasped his hands. "My pardon, my lord. I…" The man once again glanced at Mariel.

Always observant, she nodded at the vicar. "Mr. Elkins, would you prefer to confer with Lord Blackmore in private?"

Relief shone in the man's eyes.

Now he was more than curious. "I prefer that you remain with me."

She gave him an irritated look, but he would not be gainsaid. Something was afoot and he may need her keen insight.

Mr. Elkins' shoulders drooped. "This way."

They followed the vicar through the graveyard toward a gravestone that had much digging around it.

Mariel gasped and halted.

Once again, he scanned the area for a threat, but there was no one about. "What is it?"

She pointed to the stone with the disturbed earth, where Mr. Elkins had stopped and faced them.

He read the stone.

Lord Marcus Stratton, b. 1782 – d. 1814

A chill ran through him accompanied by an unreasonable

anger. "Why is this here?"

Mr. Elkins clasped his hands again, his thin eyebrows lowered in consternation. "The former Lord Blackmore had it commissioned and placed here. He told me it was for his mother."

Some of his irritation abated. That would be something his brother would do. "But why is it still here?"

"We are in the process of removing it." He glanced toward Mariel once again.

Looking at her himself, he found her paler than a mountain top in winter. "Come." Turning her away from the headstone, he walked her to a small bench that faced the opposite way. "I will just be a moment."

She gave him a silent nod, but did not meet his gaze.

Angry with himself for not heeding Mr. Elkins' concerns, he strode back to the man. "Now tell me, why has this not been removed?"

No longer constrained by Mariel's presence, Mr. Elkins became quite forthcoming. "My lord, I've never encountered such a situation. I did not know if you wished to save the stone or—"

"Save the stone?" His voice rose in his astonishment. "Why would I save the stone? I'm not about to die three years ago."

The man cringed. "No, of course not. That's not what I meant. It doesn't even have to be for you. The carver can change anything on it."

Something about seeing his name and the year of his demise printed on the stone made him feel as if death lurked nearby to take him. "I'd as soon have it destroyed into pieces so small, they'd break beneath my feet."

Mr. Elkins clasped his hands yet again. "I understand, my lord. If that's truly what you wish."

"Oh for g—my sake. Out with it, man."

"On occasion, there are people who cannot afford such a luxurious stone, and this one would do for an entire family."

He stared at the man in awe. He wished to use the headstone for a family who had yet to die? "Fine, use it that way, but get my name and those dates off it by next Sunday or I will personally come here and destroy it."

"Yes, my lord. Thank you." Mr. Elkins' smile of pleasure was so incongruous to the situation, he could no longer stomach the conversation. Without another word, he turned on his heel and strode toward Mariel.

MARIEL PRESSED HER hand to her chest, the ache at seeing the headstone still sharp inside her heart. In her pique over Marcus being alive, she'd forgotten to be grateful he wasn't dead. That she could talk to him, argue with him, even be rude to him, was only because he was *alive*. How churlish of her to not appreciate that simple fact.

Tears welled in her eyes that she could have been so quick to condemn the man she'd loved. He had been carefree when he'd courted her. Now he was cold and hard. Gone was the spontaneity that drew her to him, so unlike her well-ordered planning. He had changed, but she never asked why. Now, she wanted to know.

"Mariel, I'm sorry you saw that."

At his voice, she looked up, his visage blurred by her tears. "Why are you alive?" It wasn't the question she'd wanted to ask, but it was the first to come to the fore.

He immediately looked away, stiffening. "As I said, I believe that would be due to an error on the part of the military." His gaze met hers again, his eyes unreadable. "I suggest we remove ourselves from this dreary place. It is far too morbid for a Sunday outing."

The new part of her wanted to remark on the sun shining and the pleasant temperature, but she clamped her lips together and rose from the bench. "Of course." Taking his arm again, they walked in silence out of the graveyard under an archway filled with vines and tiny buds. As they strolled along the side of the stone church, she heard voices over the sounds of the birds. No doubt many of the parishioners had tarried outside to intercept them.

As they rounded the corner, she found her guess to be correct. That Marcus hesitated in his step made it clear he hadn't been as aware. He must have been deep in thought.

Baroness Burchall approached them immediately and the chatter of more than a dozen people immediately quieted. "Lady Beaumont, it's so lovely to see you again."

She graciously took the hand extended toward her, hoping to impress upon the other parishioners that Lady Burchall was a dear friend of the family, though that was only partially true. It was, after all, about appearances. "It is always a pleasure to be in your company. Did you enjoy the service?"

"Oh yes. It's a breath of fresh air to listen to a young man's voice."

Mariel held her smile by force of habit. The older lady had been complaining about missing the former vicar just two days prior. "I agree. Our vicar is quite young as well, and brings much energy to the sermon."

The older woman had already stopped listening as she turned her attention to Marcus. "My Lord Blackmore, it is so good to see that you are in residence now."

"It will only be for a short while, but it was necessary that I might reclaim my betrothed." His arm tightened as if truly wishing she were his again.

She ignored the pleasurable feeling that imperceptible movement caused her. He'd made it clear he had no interest in renewing their relationship and only pretended because she'd made him feel guilty. At least that spoke to the fact his values were still in place.

"What wonderful news!" Lady Burchall clapped her hands together, her voice becoming louder. "How proud your mother must be that you have captured such a darling...woman." Lady

Burchall turned to her. "Congratulations my dear. You must be so pleased that he came home to you."

Mariel hadn't missed the hesitation in the baroness' statement. What had she been about to utter? Had she thought to say *young* but thought better of it? Or had she planned to say *marquess's daughter*, which would bring undue attention to the fact that had the betrothal been real, Marcus would be marrying up. She was just pleased that the older woman had refrained. "I am very grateful that my lord survived the war."

Lady Burchall's countenance immediately grew somber. "Oh yes, such a horrid event. I'm so glad it's over. Not being able to travel to the continent because of that little man was so inconvenient."

This time, the pressure of Marcus' arm was much stronger, and he immediately responded. "Well, I'm sure Wellington had that in mind when he turned the tide. Now, if you will excuse us. I promised Lady Beaumont I would return her to Silver Meadows in time to aid the duchess in a task that needs two sets of hands."

"Oh my, yes. I do hope the duchess doesn't require you to engage in her lessons. You are such a fine lady."

At the insult to her sister, she swallowed her retort, but it was harder than normal. What was wrong with her? "Her ladies are all in London for the season, so you need not worry that my sister will taint me in any way." She snapped her mouth shut as the words slipped from her lips.

At Lady Burchall's widening gaze, Marcus smiled. "Yes, I told Lady Beaumont that the duchess really should leave the painting to Lady Amelia."

The older woman wagged her finger. "Oh, it is not Lady Amelia anymore. She is the Countess Sommerset now." The woman smiled as if she'd been responsible for the match.

"I stand corrected. Countess Sommerset." Marcus gave the baroness a slight bow before turning his head to look at her. "Shall we?"

"Please." Waving a quick farewell to Lady Burchall, she

walked with Marcus to his phaeton, the chatter resuming behind them.

After handing her up, he settled in next to her and clicked the reins.

As soon as they were out of hearing, she turned toward him. "Thank you. I don't know why I said that."

Marcus' mouth quirked up on one side. "I thought the woman was going to have apoplexy. Did you notice how red she turned?"

She batted his arm. "Marcus, that wasn't humorous."

He shrugged, a grin on his face. "I think it was. She insults your sister and expects you to be polite about it? She's lucky you and your sister don't give her the cut direct. I would."

Now *that* was the old Marcus. Quick to judge and act. A warmth filled her, but she pushed it aside. "It would serve no purpose. Northampton is too small to be so insulting."

"Something Lady Burchall should learn."

She sighed. "I've found the older people are, the less they bend." She pointed to a large oak tree ahead on the road. "It's like that tree up ahead. The older and bigger it grows, the less it bends. Trying to teach it to bend would be a waste of one's time."

He glanced at her before returning his attention to the road. "How do you know so much about people?"

She shrugged, then smirked. "Perhaps my sister has influenced me more than I know."

He glanced at her again. "Then you must still be young like yonder sapling." He pointed to a tree barely as high as they sat.

She swallowed a laugh. The man had lost his powers of observation if he believed his own words. "Not so. I'm quite sure that Lady Burchall refrained from calling me a *young* woman because of the fact I am no longer."

The horses slowed as Marcus pulled back on the reins and faced her. "You are not so old."

She cocked her head and raised her brows. "Not only am I a widow, but I am on the shelf."

"A score and six is not so old. I am thirty-two and that is far older."

That he remembered how old she was, thrilled her. Did that mean he'd thought of her over the last two years while he hid? "But you are a man. Being of an age as a man is quite the thing. My husband was quite older and yet one of his requirements was that his wife be no more than a score and five."

Marcus studied her so avidly that she looked away, uncomfortable with such focused perusal. Did he look for her age?

"How old was your husband?"

Though the question was evenly spoken, the final word *husband* seemed to have a particular tone to it, as if he hated that particular word. If that was so, he'd best overcome his aversion to it for he would be expected to wed very soon. She thought back on her marriage, something she rarely did. George had been older than her father. "Lord Beaumont was about three score. It wasn't something we discussed."

Marcus turned away.

Though she couldn't be sure, it sounded as if he'd sworn under his breath. That was also a common habit he'd had before he left for the war. It was good to see that some of his former self remained. Which begged the question, what had changed him so?

Belinda, who had gone to the infirmaries while she lived, had spoken about men who had lost limbs, were scarred about the face, or looked at the walls all day. But Marcus had no such injuries. Except for being more muscular, he looked as he had before he left. But there was a coldness about him that hadn't been there before. Could that be the war?

He lifted the reins again. "Though your husband was old, you are not, and can easily find another to marry."

She did laugh at that. "Oh, no. I'm never going to marry again. Though I enjoyed running a household, there is much too much about the station that I do not like at all." She couldn't help the shudder that ran through her and she wished he'd clicked the horses into a trot again.

His head whipped around to stare at her, his gray gaze intense. "Did he hurt you?"

Heat rose in her cheeks at the question. George had been a kind husband, but his nightly visits to her bed had been uncomfortable at best and painful at their worst.

"He did!" The words were growled. "If the man wasn't dead, I'd call him out."

Confused by his anger, she set her gloved hand on his arm. "There is no need to think ill of the dead. Lord Beaumont was a good husband. He did not beat me, if that's what you think. He married me in the hopes of getting an heir. Unfortunately, I disappointed him in that, which is another reason I will never marry. Who would want a wife who is barren?" Despite the pain that admission brought, she managed a small smile.

He didn't say anything for a long time, just stared at her as if he were trying to puzzle things out.

But she didn't want him to know what it had been like. No one knew. She turned back toward the road, setting her hand in her lap. "Besides, I'm quite happy to be a widow. I can do as I please within the bounds of society and enjoy my family and friends. With our supposed betrothal, I will even be looked upon as twice lucky and later, after it ends, I will look for a home just for me."

Marcus finally flicked the reins and set the horses to moving again. "And what will you do in this home of yours?"

His voice was no longer angry, but neither was it friendly. In fact, it sounded as if he thought her idea silly. Insulted, she latched upon Joanna's idea from the other morning. "I'm thinking of breeding horses."

His eyes widened and a surge of triumph filled her.

Why was shocking him so fun?

"I see."

Disappointed he hadn't argued with her, she kept silent, not a little miffed. What did he mean by asking what she would do in her home? She would do what any other widow did. What did his mother do?

As Silver Meadows finally came into view, she couldn't help asking the question that had been on her mind since confronting him mere days ago. Not knowing if they would have the privacy to discuss it at another time, she steeled herself for his reaction. "Why did you not seek me out when you returned to England?"

His jaw tightened, but he didn't look at her. "I told you. I discovered you were a widow. I saw no reason to disturb your life."

The Marcus she had known wouldn't have thought twice about storming up her parents' steps and demanding her presence. Had he indeed changed that much or was there something else? Her heart hitched. Or was there *someone* else? The Mariel he'd known wouldn't dare ask, but she was far beyond playing coy with him. "Was there someone else you had hoped to marry?"

He slowed the phaeton as he brought it before the grand steps to Silver Meadows. When it came to a stop, he finally looked at her. His gaze was unguarded and for the briefest moment she saw pain. Was it heartache for someone else?

Then, as if remembering where he was, his expression changed. "Hardly. I've had no time to be social, which has allowed me to agree to your proposal. Do you think I would do so with another waiting for me?" It was quite clear he was insulted.

Not wanting to part on such a sentiment, she waved off the footman who'd come to assist her down. "No, I apologize. I simply search for the true reason you have been in hiding. I meant no slur on your character."

He gave a curt nod, but did not reiterate that it was her widowhood that had kept him away, which made her think she was correct, there had been something else.

"Were you wounded then and recovering?"

His hand tightened on his thigh. "I was. I believe that is why my family was notified I had died. My injuries were many."

Concern had her lifting her hand, but at his stern visage, she set it back in her lap. "That is understandable. Thank you for telling me." She waved to the footman, who helped her descend. She turned back to thank him for the outing, but didn't get the chance.

"I have been healed well over three years now and living in England the past two. You will hear from me soon." With that, he set the horses in motion and turned them to exit the long drive.

She stood with her mouth agape. Well over two years? In other words, he could have contacted her then. He could have let her think he was unable to contact her, but he made a point to let her know he *chose* not to. She closed her mouth and put her hands on her hips. It appeared that the older Marcus Stratton was far more rude and uncaring than the younger.

Dropping her hands, she turned and ascended the steps to the house. His attitude made her want to be rude in return. It was as if he wanted her to hate him. She paused just before reaching the door. Why would he want her to hate him? Having no answer, she continued into the house.

CHAPTER SIX

Marcus tapped his middle finger on his desk, not seeing the morning paper he'd been reading. He couldn't stop thinking of Mariel and her revelations of just two days before. All this time he'd held his resentment about her marriage like a fortification around his heart to keep him from wishing for a life he could never have, but now, she'd hit him with a cannon ball and left a gaping hole in his defenses.

Abruptly he stood, no longer able to sit and crossed the room. How could he continue with their false betrothal when he now knew she'd spoken the truth when she stated she only married to help her family? Was that why she'd worn his necklace through-out her marriage? Had she pined for him even then and into widowhood? If she had been true, he didn't have the strength to resist her.

But he had to find a way. She deserved to have the children she desired, the children he couldn't give her. He doubted she was barren. She wasn't the first young wife to not deliver children to a much older man. Most likely, it was Lord Beaumont who had no seed left to give by his age.

He stopped in mid-pace. Was that why she blushed when he'd asked if her husband had hurt her? As much as he hated to, he tried to imagine an older man in bed with Mariel, a man desperate to sire a son to carry on the line. Had he cared about her at all? The answer was swift and sure – no. "Devil it." His fingers curled into his palms. Did her family realize the sacrifice she had truly made for them? Again the answer came quickly. Mariel would never let anyone know of her pain. Fury rose hard and strong for the dead Lord Beaumont. The man had ruined her in his need for an heir and in the end failed at his goal.

Purposefully, he uncurled his fingers and rolled his shoulders, the muscles around his old bullet wound protesting his stiffness. If he wasn't careful, his chest would soon start aching as well as his left arm and thigh. Forcing himself to move, he continued his pacing.

He could be making assumptions, but his gut told him he was correct or close to it. Mariel would never speak of it, but she didn't have to. For the hundredth time, he wished he hadn't seen what his men had done. Only in ignorance could he have survived whole. But war could take more than flesh and blood, something he'd never considered.

A knock at the door had him pausing. "Yes."

Anthony stepped inside and halted. "Why do you look like you wish to kill me?"

He rubbed his thigh. "Memories, nothing more."

"Did you have another nightmare last night?"

"No. Just wishing for things to not be as they are. Come in."

Anthony strolled forward, sympathy in his blue eyes. "I have the information you've been waiting for."

It took him a moment to remember what task he'd set his friend to this time, but his mind wouldn't leave his uncomfortable situation with Mariel. "What have you discovered?"

"It's him." At his blank stare, Anthony elaborated. "It's Cobby. You were right, though how you saw the man's face that clearly while fighting to hold your seat on Merlin is beyond my comprehension."

"Fighting Merlin is second nature. Damn horse is like riding a tempest, and he's as fast and strong as one. How were you able to confirm it was him? He was listed as deceased like the others."

Anthony strode further into the room and sat on the arm of a wing-backed chair, a habit of his. "Since he was one of the two we could find no headstone for when we returned, and the other died at sea, I decided to return to the village immediately that night. I was told at the pub that a man fitting the description of *my brother* had been seen with a woman named Kitty."

"You convinced the patrons that Cobby was your brother?"

"Me poor, addle-minded brother, who had gone off to war and hasn't been the same since."

Anthony had an uncanny knack for convincing people of the most outrageous stories, even if this one was far closer to the truth. Only a man of addled-wit could have done what Cobby and his friends had done.

Forcing the image away that threatened to come into his mind and give him his blasted nightmares, he focused on the issue at hand. "Then you have confirmation that not only is he alive, but he was in the area."

"No. I have confirmed that Cobby tried to kill you."

"What? That makes no sense. I never had the chance to report those men after being wounded." Actually, he hadn't been in a shape to do anything besides try to breathe. "And until now, we thought them all dead. Why would he want to kill me?"

"I'd rather not contemplate what's in the mind of the likes of him." Anthony shook his head. "It could be anything from him thinking you reported them as you said you would. Or to him, it could be simply wanting to finish what they'd started since he's the last."

Despite the threat on his life, an old anger burned again in his gut. "It appears I'll need to take care of the last of my own men after all."

"Wait." Anthony shot to his feet. "Think about this. You have made it known that Lady Mariel is once again your betrothed. Going after Cobby could put her in harm's way."

"Exactly. Which means I must get to him first. Find out everything you can about his whereabouts. I plan on arranging an execution, and I won't make the same mistakes he and his comrades made."

"But—"

He held up his hand. "I will not be dissuaded. Whatever funds you need are yours. Find me Cobby before he can strike again."

Anthony shook his head. "I'll do what I can." With that, he left the study.

Marcus turned his gaze to the window, but he didn't see the landscape before him. Instead, the vision of the French farmhouse filled his head, the screams of the women inside echoing through the wood, stopping just moments before he stepped on the porch and opened the door.

Squeezing his eyes shut, he shook his head. He didn't need to see it again. He didn't want to. What did he have to do to get rid of the nightmare? "Mariel." He spoke her name, by sheer will, forcing himself to think about her in church, sitting beside him attentively listening, her sweet scent filling his nostrils. He opened his eyes and his breathing slowed as he once again looked upon the drive to Ravenridge.

She was his salvation, and he must push her away.

Seeing no alternative, he returned to his desk. He needed to respond to Madame Fontaine. She'd finally asked for his assistance, and he was pleased to aid her. Sitting, he pulled a paper from the left side drawer and dipped the quill in the ink. The old woman had found him on the battlefield after his men had left him to die. She'd saved his life until Anthony had come looking for him. He'd always told her to call upon him for anything. Though he'd set a regular allowance for her, her request for passage to England was the least he could do.

Though they had kept a correspondence going over the last three years, he'd refrained from adding anything about Mariel. By the time Madame Fontaine arrived, Mariel would no longer be in his life. Finishing his shorter than usual letter, he pulled another sheet of paper out and dashed off quick instructions for his solicitor. He'd just affixed his seal to the second letter when a knock sounded followed by Gibson.

"My lord. You have a caller."

He glanced at the clock. What gentleman would call upon him so early? It was not yet midday. "Is he in the parlor?"

"*She* is in the stables."

He rose at his butler's answer. Despite the warning of his own head, his chest filled with anticipation. He didn't have to be told who it was, but his butler expected the question. "Who is in the stables?"

"Lady Beaumont." Gibson didn't hide his distaste at the situation. The man was new, hired only two years ago, so was unaware of Mariel's relationship to his family.

Still, it angered him that the butler would think he had a right to pass judgement on Mariel, who in his estimation was the perfect lady. "Gibson, Lady Beaumont is not only a widow, but my betrothed. I expect her to be treated with respect."

The man's eyes widened, clearly ignorant of that, and his reddening neck proved his embarrassment. "Of course, my lord. Please pardon my assessment of the situation. After turning away so many young ladies and their mothers, I expected one had made bold trespass."

Now that Gibson explained himself, he understood the man was simply being protective. "Lady Mariel and I were betrothed before I left to fight. She is an excellent horsewoman and has come to see which horses still remain here at Ravenridge. She is as apt to arrive at the stables as the front door."

"Yes, my lord." Gibson quickly bowed and exited the room, his whole face having turned quite rosy.

Though he'd explained away Mariel's visit, he was as shocked as Gibson. Had she meant to send a note and forgot? It was not like her. She planned everything two days or more ahead of her intended outing, dinner, or event. Also, it was highly irregular for a woman to visit a man's stables. The more time he was in her company, the more he discovered she wasn't the same woman he'd left four years ago. The question was, how did he feel about that, and what to do about it?

Quickly, he strode from his study and ascended the stairs two at a time. If Mariel was at the stables, it could only mean one thing. She'd ridden over from Silver Meadows, and he planned to take advantage of that to determine if her interest in riding was still as keen as it had been. Her statement of a few days ago came to mind. *I'm thinking of breeding horses.* He had thought she'd made it to shock him, but now he wondered.

Within minutes, his valet had helped him don his riding clothes, and he was taking the path to the stables. Before he reached them, Mariel's laugh floated to him from the open doors.

"Mr. Clancy, you jest. A sheep? No. A goat perhaps."

His stableman's chuckle followed. "My lady, to be truthful. It was a pig."

Again, Mariel laughed.

He missed that sound. How many nights had he lain awake listening to it in his memories? He hadn't heard it in years, since the day he'd left for the war.

He stepped through the open doors just as she spoke.

"Has Lord Blackmore made the creek jump since he returned to England?"

"Not that he has shared." Mr. Clancy sighed. "He's not been about riding much since coming home."

He strode toward them. "That's because I've not had the time. Taking over the family has come with many responsibilities."

Mr. Clancy waved his excuse away with his hand. "Bah, that never stopped you before."

"Good morning, Lord Blackmore." Mariel rose from the bench she sat upon, her forest green riding habit accentuating her eyes and slender waist. She'd always been perfectly proportioned, but the riding habit style called out her slender build.

He forced his thoughts away from her physical form, or as far as they would go. "Good morning. I was surprised to hear that you had come to call, in the stable no less."

She brushed a bit of dust from the sleeve of her fitted jacket. "It would not have been proper to call upon you in the usual fashion since your mother is no longer in residence. But I did need to remove myself from the chaos of my sister moving her household out to London today. So instead, I simply came to see my old friend here." She held her hand out toward Mr. Clancy.

The old man's chest puffed out in pride. "That's right. She came to see me, she did. Who said it was you she wanted?"

He was well aware that she wouldn't want him if she discovered how damaged he truly was. He took no affront, having grown up with Mr. Clancy teaching him about the fine beasts in his stable. Besides, the stableman couldn't keep the twinkle from his eyes, even if his gray beard hid his smile.

He grimaced. "I'm afraid Mr. Gibson was under the impression that the lady wished for a partner to ride with."

Mr. Clancy looked to Mariel. "Be that so, my lady?"

She crossed one arm over her stomach and settled her other elbow on it to lay her hand on her cheek as she pondered. "I had not thought quite that far, Mr. Clancy, only that I wished to see you."

Mr. Clancy leaned in as if whispering, but he spoke very clearly. "Well, the lad got all dressed up for you and would be mightily disappointed were you to ride away without him, I'm thinking."

"Only disappointed you say? Not stricken with grief?"

At Mr. Clancy's shake of the head, Mariel sighed. "Very well, I suppose I must ride with yonder lord then."

Though the banter was much like what they used to engage in when they were still young and innocent, Mariel's undertones now were deadly serious. She'd made it quite clear that she still harbored ill feelings toward him for not contacting her immediately on his arrival home. Now that he understood her true circumstances, he felt like a heel. "It would be an honor. I saw that you brought Atalanta today." He turned to Mr. Clancy. "Saddle up Freesia. She's the only one fast enough to keep up with Atalanta.

"Good choice." Mr. Clancy nodded proudly then strode off to do as bid.

He held his arm out toward the wide open double stable doors. "I would like to be reacquainted with Atalanta. Shall we await my mount out of doors?"

"Of course, just be careful around her. She does bite."

Her warning held multiple meanings, of that he was sure, but he still admired the sway of her hips as she passed by him. He may not be able to act on his inclinations, but he could still very much admire the woman he loved. If he didn't miss his guess, her hips were a bit rounder, a trait he found quite enticing. Finally moving to follow her, he contemplated where they should ride. As he stepped into the sun, he found her petting Atalanta along her neck. "Is she still the fastest of your horses?"

"She is, though she doesn't have the stamina of Zephyrus." She looked at him as she shrugged. "I have not raced them, of course, but for a short race, she has the speed to win."

"You mentioned breeding horses the other day. Are you thinking of breeding racers?"

She moved her gaze back to the horse. "Not exactly. I had thought to breed for different characteristics, maybe different temperaments, or different capacities for trainings. I have not thought it through yet. First, I must find a small home with a large stable." She smiled crookedly while still looking at the horse. "It is a unique combination that may not exist." She finally glanced at him. "But that's a common dilemma for the people in my family."

While he remembered her parents being unusually loving and her sister Joanna being strangely focused on books, he wasn't sure he would call them odd. "I do not think your family so far from the norm. After all, there are other finishing schools for young women."

Her secret smile lingered. "It's not a finishing school, and with Amelia selling her paintings, if I were to breed horses, I fear the ton would shun us all." She shook her head. "No, I will have to keep it a secret. Maybe I should search in Scotland for such a place to spare my family."

Her usual self-sacrificing mode of thought irritated him. While courting her, he thought it charming and exactly what he wanted in a wife. But now, knowing how she'd wed, he wanted her to be happy doing what she pleased. He stilled at the thought. Her happiness had become his primary concern. When had that happened? When he'd come home broken and battered? No. Later, when he discovered his injuries were far deeper than he'd known. It had been the driving force that had sent him into hiding.

"Lord Blackmore?"

He shook his head, startled from his reverie by her voice. "Yes."

"I asked if your southern path was still kept cleared."

"Yes, it is. My brother kept all the riding paths cleared for me."

Her brow furrowed. "So your brother knew you were alive? I thought you said no one knew."

Too late, he realized his error. "No one but my brother. But even he continuously tried to persuade me to tell my parents."

"Why didn't you? Was hiding from me so important that you hurt your parents?"

Now he looked like the worst son. He should be happy she thought ill of him, but his very being rebelled at the idea. "It was far more complicated. Once I was healed and was sure that I would live beyond a few months, I did meet with my father. He decided not to tell my mother as she had been so distraught by my death." He didn't explain that his father saw no need for her to know about him since the Stratton line wouldn't continue through him.

"I see." She turned away, clearly not happy with him.

He didn't want her to be disappointed in him. He'd done everything right, yet it felt as if he'd done some horrible wrong for fate to deal him such a terrible blow. He reached out his hand to touch her, but dropped it as Mr. Clancy walked Freesia out of the stable. "Here you are, my lord. She's itching for a good run, she is. Better show her who's in charge."

He strode past Mariel and took the reins, his frustration communicating itself to Freesia. "Don't I always?" The mare stepped back and he forced himself to focus on his animal, stroking her and taking deeper breaths himself.

"That be true." Mr. Clancy ambled over to Mariel. "Need a hand up, my lady?"

He couldn't help watching Mariel mount into the side saddle. Her grace and confidence proving her abilities had not lessened over the years. She caught him watching and shook her head. "You dally, my lord. I shall see you at the head of the southern path." Then with no warning, she set Atalanta into motion.

Not to be outdone, he mounted. "Come, Freesia. We can catch them." He flicked the reins and they were off, cantering around the gardens until they hit the open field where he gave Freesia her head. The full out race restored his humors especially as they gained on Mariel.

Memories of chasing her across Silver Meadows burst upon him. She'd ride out straight then pull up behind trees, a statue, or some other object, and he'd lose her for a moment. Just long enough for her to race off, her laughter coming to him on the wind.

Now there was no laughter, and she pulled ahead a full length, but they neared the path and would need to slow. But she was hell bent on reaching the opening before him. "Mariel!" He shouted to warn her about the low hanging branch, but she continued on, plastering herself to her horse's back at the last moment, avoiding injury.

"Fool woman." Not taking any chances, he slowed Freesia and ducked beneath the branch, half expecting to find her lying on the path ahead, but as he entered the forest, she was nowhere in sight. She couldn't have taken the path at such a speed, could she?

CHAPTER SEVEN

H ER HEART RACING with her near-miss, Mariel smiled, her horse racing down the path she remembered. Coming around a corner in the tree lined trail, a tree up ahead lay across it. "Come Atalanta. Let's jump that minor obstruction." Their pace was perfect and as they sailed over the tree trunk, she felt as if she were flying. Exhilaration far beyond words pounded through her veins. Landing perfectly, Atalanta raced on.

Despite her complete joy in the ride, she took care of her horses and slowed Atalanta to a trot, well aware that there was a fork in the path up ahead. Was the old Grecian temple to the left, or right? Trying to imagine it in her mind, she slowed as she reached the spot. She could wait for Marcus, but her irritation with him couldn't be erased in a simple ride through the wood. Making her decision, she took the left path and walked Atalanta along it, allowing her mount to cool down.

Just as she thought she may have to turn back, she spotted her destination through the trees and followed the path around to the overgrown circular structure. Dismounting, she left her horse loose to find what she could to eat and walked to the old temple. Years ago, when Marcus had first shown her the marble temple, it had been bathed in sunlight, but the trees had grown up around it, leaving it to the smattering of light that made it through the leaves. The vines had been left to run amok, up the twelve marble columns and over the top.

The leaves on the vines were yet small, and she walked up the three steps of the base and between two columns. "Oh, my." The beauty from inside was breathtaking. In a couple more weeks, the vine leaves would make solid walls of the circular structure, but now the forest light dappled the mosaic floor. Looking up, she grinned at the cupid painting on the domed ceiling. What would Amelia say about that particular piece of artwork?

"Mariel?"

Her heart raced at Marcus' call, but she quickly remembered this was no game of hide and seek where a kiss would be forfeited should he find her. They had left those days behind forever. He shouldn't use her given name. It made her remember how perfect it used to be. "I'm here, Lord Blackmore, in the temple." That should set the ground rules for their new awkward relationship.

There was a quiet thump as his feet hit the ground. She moved to the far side of the temple, but as he strode up the steps and came into view, a rush of memories filled her of the last time they'd been there, when her knees had buckled at the kiss he'd given her. It had been her first passionate kiss, not the chaste ones they'd exchanged quickly among the gardens.

His broad shoulders brushed the tiny leaves as he entered, like her, taking in the overgrown temple in a quick scan. "This has changed much over the years."

"Much has changed." She needed to put some distance between them. The temple suddenly felt far too small with the vegetation encroaching.

His gaze snapped to hers. "Yes, much has changed and grown."

She pointed upward, wanting him to look anywhere but at her. "Cupid appears to be the same." As she'd hoped, he looked to the ceiling.

A frown flitted about his brow. "The gods never change, nor does the pain, it would seem." He brought his gaze back to her.

"Why did you come here?"

She shrugged, not having an explanation. "It's more interesting than the other path."

He leaned against a column and crossed his arms over his broad chest. "I'm sure the pond would be equally as overgrown. My brother only kept the paths cleared. He never used them. There may be quite a bit of wildlife about the pond now. I'll have to have the staff work on these areas as well."

She didn't like the idea of such beauty being trimmed back. "I see no reason to disturb such natural beauty, do you?"

"Were you not the woman who complained about a vine growing on the bench in the garden at Silver Meadows one summer?" His brows had risen with his question.

Her cheeks heated at the memory. Not because she felt her comments at the time were inappropriate but because of the reason for making them, which were to take his gaze from her mouth. Licking her lips, she turned toward the vine closest to her and touched a small leaf. "I was not so concerned with the pretty vine as I was of your intentions."

A soft chuckle floated to her across the small space. "You were observant even then and quite right to turn my attention to something else."

The old feelings of love and caring seemed to grasp onto his words and floated to her with his voice. She couldn't resist her curiosity to look at him. What she saw was the old Marcus, who flirted and loved with as much energy as he took a jump over a hedge. He was here and yet he wasn't. "Will you ever tell me what happened to you?"

His countenance immediately hardened. "It is far better not to know."

Frustrated with the cat and mouse game they seemed to be playing, she set her hands on her hips. "Well, not knowing is far worse. All I know is the man I loved left with promises of marrying me, then died, then came back and went into hiding specifically to keep me from knowing he was alive. You do not want to know what reasons I have in my head. I'm hoping they are far worse than the truth."

He didn't respond. Remaining perfectly still, he just stared at her with no feeling, as if he were a marble statue.

But he wasn't. He was flesh and blood and completely infuriating. She threw her arms upward. "Fine. I'll think the worst." She tried to tamp down her anger. She never had a problem remaining calm and proper, but this was too close to her heart. Actually, it *was* her heart. She lifted her left hand and poked it with her right index finger. "I'm guessing you fell in love with someone else and have a child you don't want me to know about."

His eyes widened.

"No?" She poked her hand again. "Then it must be that you committed a crime and you were hiding from me and everyone to avoid detection until you could kill the one person who witnessed it."

His brows furrowed.

"Fine, it's not that." She poked her hand and this time held her finger. "Then it must be that you have been with so many women that you can't stomach the thought of being with me too."

All expression left his face.

Drat it, she was close. Her heart skipped a beat. "So, it's just me you cannot bear to be near." The sting of tears just made her angrier. "This pretend betrothal must feel like hell to you."

He moved so fast across the space that she sucked in her breath as he clasped her shoulders.

"You can think anything of me, even the direst of deeds, but never think that." His gray eyes appeared darker and the truth of his words caused her to shiver.

Stubbornly, she ignored his claim. "Then you must love another."

"Damn it, Mariel, will you listen to me?"

"I've been listening, but I don't hear anything."

He took a deep breath before one hand moved from her shoulder to cup her face. "I can never love another."

His whispered words made no sense. If he loved her then why hide? She shook her head.

"You must believe me." He lowered his head and his lips brushed across hers like the sweet kisses she remembered.

It had been so long, and she was so confused, she ignored her racing questions and latched on to the feel of his lips. Raising on her toes, she kissed him in return.

"Mariel." He whispered against her lips before he took her in his arms. His lips moved across hers, begging entrance to her mouth.

Unable to deny him, she let her eyes close and opened to him, tasting him again for the first time in four long years. Her senses reeled with memories even as her heart beat for him. As his tongue touched hers, her knees weakened and she grasped his arms.

The kiss ended far too quickly as he pulled his lips from hers. "I cannot give you what you deserve."

She opened her eyes as his breath caressed her lips. "I don't understand. All I want is you as my companion, and a home, a place I belong." She implored him with her eyes to overcome whatever kept him from her.

Instead, he stepped back as if he didn't want to, but had to. "Don't you want a family, passion, laughter?"

"No." She shook her head. "I just want love. I cannot have a family and…" She grimaced, "passion is not for me nor is laughter a requirement for happiness." She shrugged. "I do not require much to be content."

His gray gaze studied her as if trying to understand something beyond her words, but there was nothing more. After George had died, she had realized her happiest times had been with Marcus. Since she thought him dead, she'd been content be with her family, but then Joanna and Amelia married and she'd begun to contemplate a home of her own. Nothing more.

"But you deserve more." His softly spoken words slid over her in a soothing, comforting tone.

"I do not believe I deserve more than any other woman in my circumstances. That you are alive was far more than I thought possible, but even now I wish for more, but do I deserve it? I don't think so. I have already been granted far more in life than many."

He turned away.

Confused, she remained where she stood, thinking about what he said and how he reacted. Then a cool chill filled her as his circumstances became clear. She should have understood sooner, but now with his father and brother gone, he needed an heir. She could not provide him with that. That had to be why he fought his feelings for her. That he had assured her of his feelings healed some of the hurt. He had to do what he had to do. She understood that. She didn't like it, but she now understood.

Though Joanna would surely rail at society's dictates, she did not. They were necessary for the continuance of civilization. No doubt he'd stayed away knowing she was a widow, thinking as he had that she had loved her husband. Then when he became viscount, he couldn't contact her because he had to have an heir and she'd provided none for her husband. That Marcus even agreed to their pretend betrothal was proof that he loved her, putting off his own duties so she would not be pitied.

Her heart swelled. He was sacrificing so much for her and she kept wanting more. Instead, she must not make demands of him that he couldn't fulfill. That she could enjoy his company for a little while longer would have to be enough. She couldn't think about the end of April. She would live only in the present. Joanna had told her that the sentiment was from a poet named Horace, who called it Carpe Diem. She didn't know Latin like her sister, but understood it meant to make the most of the time she had.

A calmness filled her as her plan emerged into existence. Planning always made things easier, and she'd done none of that since hearing that Marcus was alive. In fact, she had acted much like the old Marcus would have.

"What do you think about so diligently?"

At his question, she found him watching her, his expression once again devoid of expression.

"Why I'm planning, of course." She gave him a grin. She was tired of the new Marcus and she would bring back the old one before they parted.

The corner of his mouth quirked as if he wished to return the grin. "I should have guessed."

She chuckled, her heart feeling better, even if it would be for so brief a time. "Yes, you should have." She strolled past him to the column nearby and touched one of the vine's leaves. "Do you think when it is full summer that this temple will be completely enclosed?"

"I do." His voice gave no indication of what he was thinking.

She faced him, leaning her back against the column. "How dark it would be in here. I'm glad we became reacquainted with it before that occurred."

His brow wrinkled slightly as he contemplated her words. "I imagine many an animal will enjoy the coolness of this temple come summer."

"True, but now it is filled with promise as opposed to a *fait accompli.*"

His right eyebrow rose, a movement she hadn't seen him make since before the war. "I would think for someone who enjoys planning that the final product or production, as it were, would be more valued."

She shook her head even as she pushed away from the column. "Not at all. The joy is in the process. The end means there is no more, no hope, no anticipation. It is done, finished, over. I will always opt for the process."

Stifling a laugh at his surprise, she slipped through the column and out into the wood. She spotted Atalanta and moved between the trees to reach her. Taking the mare's reins, she walked her back toward the temple to use a step for mounting.

Marcus stepped out. "Allow me to help."

Gladly, she stepped into his cupped hands and found her seat. "Thank you." She thought about racing away, but enjoyed watching him move Freesia to a more open area and mount up. Marcus on a horse would always make her heart flutter. It must be because they were two of her favorite things.

Turning Atalanta, she walked her onto the path again, intending to return the way they'd come.

"Wait." Marcus moved Freesia in front of her. "I wish to show you something."

Curious that there could be anything to show her that she hadn't already seen on the property, she nodded, turning Atalanta around to follow him.

He walked them further into the wood. It seemed to have grown thicker, not the trees but the underbrush, and she didn't see a path anymore. Finally, he halted.

She brought her horse up to stand next to his and stared. There was a round stone pond the size of the temple made from the creek that ran through Ravenridge. The large trees stood back a good twelve feet, but the underbrush had encroached upon it. "This is beautiful. Has this always been here?"

"Yes, since my father's time."

She looked at him, but his gaze rested on the pool. "You never showed me this before."

"No. It was my brother's and my place to enjoy as boys, and later to talk in private as men."

She placed her hand over her heart. That he would share this with her now that his brother was gone meant so much. "I can see why you two enjoyed your time here."

He glanced at her before pointing across the pond. "There are large boulders on that side that serve as steps, and we would swim about here when much smaller. We alone kept the plants away. That so much has grown here tells me he didn't keep it up after being notified of my death."

Though he spoke evenly and clearly, she was aware of his

deep pain from the droop of his shoulders. She could understand such a loss. "I imagine he could not bear to come here then."

"Just as I have not come here since his passing." He straightened up. "I thought you would enjoy seeing it. It will soon be overgrown completely. There is no longer a need to keep the forest from taking it back."

"Not even for your children?" Surely, he would wish to show them.

"No." He avoided her gaze and turned Freesia around. "We can access the field from here. We are near the eastern edge of the wood."

She hadn't understood how much Marcus' brother's passing had affected him. But it made sense since he had been as close to his brother as she was to her sisters. When Belinda died, she'd thrown herself into keeping the house as her parents mourned. Then she'd felt the need to step into Belinda's shoes as best she could to ease the loss for her family. But every night for more than a year, she'd cried herself to sleep. Eventually, much like her sisters, she'd taken to talking to Belinda in private. She hadn't been as open about the wound to her heart, but Belinda would understand.

"Here we are." Marcus led them out onto an open field, beyond which looked like the tilled soil of one of his tenant farmers.

"Which way is the Ravenridge stables?"

He pointed to her left. "That way, but we need to ride along the Raven's Ridge to avoid the marsh."

He'd never taken her to the Raven's Ridge before, most likely because she always had a groom with her and their rides were much shorter and much more sedate. She appreciated that he respected her change in status from virgin maiden to widow. There was much to be said for being a widow, something she was quite sure her sisters wouldn't understand, nor would she want them to.

They cantered up a gradual incline with trees at the top. As they drew closer, they slowed to a walk, and she could see it was exactly that, a single line of trees. Even before they crested the hill, she could see the ravens perched in the sprouting foliage. "You've never shown me this before."

"I wasn't sure how you would feel about it. Many are nervous around ravens."

"Nervous? I'm not sure why. Then again, many are nervous around Zephyrus. I imagine strong, beautiful beasts can be intimidating."

"You are a very unusual lady." He had stopped and was staring at her.

"I told you, the Mabry family members are unique. My strangeness is well hidden." She gave him a crooked smile, not sure if he was happy or unhappy that she fit in with her family so well.

Eventually, he relaxed and smiled broadly. "Then you will truly enjoy the view from the ridge." He coaxed Freesia into moving forward again.

Atalanta fell into step with the other mare, not willing to be left behind. But as they reached the ridge line, she forgot all about her mount and sucked in her breath. Before her was the northern areas of Ravenridge, but she could see well beyond them to Silver Meadows. "I had no idea Ravenridge sat so high."

"It's not as high as it seems." He pointed beyond Silver Meadows. "See, that's the top of the village church steeple."

She covered her brow with her hand and squinted. Basically, Silver Meadows sat in a small valley, but it was so gradual as to not be noticed. "No wonder it has the morning fog so often that gave it its name. It sits lower than these hills."

"Look, I believe your sister is leaving." He pointed toward the large house beyond the wood that covered the border of the properties.

She focused on the grand drive and could see a coach leaving through the stone columns that marked the entrance. It would be lonely now at Silver Meadows without her sister, but she would soon follow to London.

"Are you ready to return to the stables?"

Marcus had moved Freesia closer. If she wanted to, she could touch him, but she refrained. "Yes. Now that Joanna is gone, I will need to take charge of the house until I leave. Thank you for showing me this."

For a moment, the old Marcus appeared again, his lip quirking. "I wanted you to enjoy the ride."

"Oh, I have." And learning so much more about the man she'd thought she knew. Obviously, there was much more to him, and she planned to discover every nuance before their pretense ended.

They started down the gradual hill, heading for the side gardens, the stables still to the left.

A shot rang out and something whizzed past her and buried itself in the ground before them. Atalanta reared, and she held on, her leg around the pommel gripping hard to keep her seat.

"The stables! Run for the stables!" Marcus' shout was hardly needed as Atalanta lunged forward, settling into a full out gallop. As they sped across the field, another shot rang out and fear blossomed in her belly. "Fly like the wind, Atalanta."

It wasn't until she'd raced through the gardens and had the stables in sight that she realized there were no more shots. Looking behind her to confer with Marcus, she found herself alone. Her heart lurched. She turned her mount around to race back.

"What's happening?" Mr. Clancy ran toward her with another man.

"It's Marcus. We heard shots as we descended Raven's Ridge. He must have gone to investigate."

Mr. Clancy exchanged a quick look with the stranger then took hold of Atalanta. "Here, let me help you off your poor mount. I'll have her walked while Anthony finds my lord."

She looked to the other man, but he had run back into the stable. Her feet had barely touched the ground before the man called Anthony galloped past them on a beautiful Irish Hunter.

She watched him race up the hill, her gaze scanning the ridgeline for Marcus.

A hand on her arm had her turning to Mr. Clancy.

"Come inside the stable. His lordship will have me drawn and quartered if anything happens to you."

She looked back up the ridge, but now no horse was in sight.

"Don't worry. Anthony will make sure my lord comes back to you in one piece. He always has."

At that, she finally turned as Mr. Clancy walked Atalanta around to the stable doors. She stepped to the side of the building to see him handing the horse over to a groom with strict instructions. Instructions she approved of.

"Come. I have a little something that will settle your nerves." He held his arm out toward the open doors.

She followed the older man, who despite his bushy gray beard and slightly curved back, walked with vigor. She stepped into the stable and allowed her vision to adjust before taking a quick look outside again, but the ridge was out of view. Continuing inside, she took her seat again on the bench against the wall of a stall.

"Here you go, my lady. Just take a sip at a time. I don't want my lord to find you tipsy when he returns."

She sniffed at the tin cup he handed her. "Scotch?"

He puffed out his chest. "I think not. That's good Irish whiskey, that is."

She hid her smile as she took a sip. The liquid burned as it slid down her throat, but the warmth that filled her afterward did calm her nerves. "Who is that man, Anthony?"

Mr. Clancy poured himself a bit of whiskey and sat on a hay bale opposite her. "Don't know much about him. What I know, I like."

She took another sip then put the cup aside. Any more and she'd be asleep before Marcus returned. *If* he returned. She didn't want to think that way. He'd just risen from the dead. She returned her attention to Mr. Clancy. "What do you know?"

Mr. Clancy took a second swallow then held the cup with both hands. "I know if it weren't for him, the lord wouldn't be alive or here in England. It was that young man that took it upon himself to go looking for Lord Blackmore. His name is Anthony Taylour and he served under the lord. After a battle when the other men in his company said the lord had died, Anthony went back to look for the body, but it wasn't there. Weeks later, when Anthony left the war, he went back again to look for my lord and found him at an old French woman's farmhouse."

"Was he badly injured?"

Mr. Clancy looked away. "I believe so, but he won't talk about it. Neither does Anthony. When his lordship was well enough to travel, which took almost a year, Anthony brought him back. That's all I need to know to trust that young man." He took another swallow of whiskey.

She glanced at her cup, but decided against the temptation. The longer it took for the two to return, the more nervous she became, but she would not give in to it. "Do you think it could be a poacher?"

"Aye, it must be. Why else would there be shooting so close to Ravenridge?"

She shook her head. "Not close, on the grounds, and not a very good shot from the earth before me that was hit."

Mr. Clancy's hand stilled with the cup halfway to his mouth. "The shot came close to you?"

"Right in front of us."

Mr. Clancy set the cup down and rose.

"What is it?"

"They're coming back."

She listened for horses but there was only silence. "I don't hear anything."

Mr. Clancy grinned as he pointed to the floor. "Not hear, feel."

She stood as well, trying to feel what the old man said he felt, but she didn't. Maybe it was her shoes. Quickly, she followed him to the entrance of the stable, very aware that he did not step out even though they couldn't see anyone yet.

For a few moments, they both scanned the field Marcus would need to ride through to reach the gardens.

"There." Mr. Clancy pointed to the north instead of the south where she'd come from.

Shading her eyes, she finally saw them. At the sight of two horses, relief threatened to buckle her knees, and she quickly leaned against the stable doorway. They didn't ride fast, so she could only assume that all danger had past.

As they rode in, she couldn't help comparing the two. Marcus had a much better seat on Freesia and his movements were in complete unison with his mount. It had been one of the first things she liked about Marcus, his riding ability. Once she discovered he understood horses and took the utmost care of them, she was half in love with him.

The two men came to a halt before the stable and jumped down.

Mr. Clancy frowned. "Did you find the miscreant?"

Marcus shook his head. "We caught sight of him, but he was already too far away to catch."

"Do you think it was a poacher?" She scanned his body making sure he'd come to no harm.

"A poacher?" He paused. "Most likely. We do have deer in that wood."

"Well, he was a terrible shot."

Mr. Taylour laughed before starting to cough. "I'll get a groom to walk these two." He strode past her and Mr. Clancy, a smile lingering on his face.

"We best get you home."

At Marcus' statement, she returned her gaze to him. "I can ride home just fine."

He walked up to her, hooked his arm in hers and turned her back into the stable. "No. That poacher could take another shot thinking Atalanta is a deer. He's obviously half-blind. You can use my coach."

She looked into his gray eyes and found they had turned hard. "Obviously, you will not be argued with."

"Correct."

"Very well. But if I'm going home in the coach, then I'm having another sip of whiskey, or two." Pulling her arm from his, she stalked over to the bench, picked up the cup, and purposefully threw back the rest of the contents. The burn was harsher than she expected and she wanted to cough, but she refused, her eyes watering instead.

"See, my lord. I told you there was more to her than you know." Clancy laughed before setting two grooms to harnessing horses for the coach.

In no time at all, she found herself on her way back to Silver Meadows, her horse tied to the coach, Mr. Taylour driving, and two footmen on the back. The liquor not only calmed her but she desperately wanted to sleep.

Finally, she made it to her bedroom at Silver Meadows, ready to collapse on the bed in her riding habit, but she stopped just in time. On the bed was a book with a letter. She moved the letter and read the title, *The Education of the Feminine Species*. "Oh, Joanna. I don't have time to read one of your books."

Setting the book and letter on top of the table next to her bed, she dropped onto the mattress and within seconds fell into sleep.

CHAPTER EIGHT

MARCUS PULLED ON the sleeves of his tailcoat as the coach rumbled toward Silver Meadows. After sending Mariel off the day before, he and Anthony visited everyone within riding distance, peer, and commoner alike, and Cobby was nowhere to be found. Though he allowed Mariel to believe the shooter was a poacher, he'd seen the telltale light brown hair pulled back in an old-fashioned queue. There was no one else it could be. There was no one else who wanted him dead. He could no longer ignore the obvious.

Now his priority was to keep Mariel safe and London was the perfect place. A shooter in London would be far too obvious. Though his father had been killed by a thief, it had not been a man with a gun. In fact, if his father hadn't resisted, he probably wouldn't have been hit on the head with a hammer. But that was his father, too arrogant to think someone would dare rob from him. It was such an unusual occurrence, especially not far from Cavendish Square, he could imagine his father's disbelief.

In London, Mariel would be in coaches with her family, or walking about crowded streets, shops, and theatres. She would be safe until he could catch the man who had committed the most unspeakable crime under the guise of war. Being in London would make it more difficult to tract Cobby's movements, but with Anthony and a couple of well-paid men, he'd find him and meet out his just punishment.

The coach pulled up before the grand stairs of Silver Meadows. Pleased to see that no one else was calling quite this early, he calculated he had at least thirty minutes before anyone would arrive, if they arrived. With the duke and duchess gone and most of Northampton already in London, there were few people about beyond Lady Burchell.

As he was shown into the parlor, he hoped Mariel had received his note. He was well aware she did not like changing plans, but being in public again in Northampton was out of the question. Gravitating to the window, he viewed the fine lawns of the large estate. He had to acknowledge that it was a fitting place for a finishing school. When he heard footsteps on the staircase to the upper floors, he turned toward the open parlor doors.

Mariel swept in wearing a lavender day dress that gave a light glow to her skin. She held out her gloved hands. "My Lord Blackmore. What a pleasant surprise. I had not expected to see you again so soon."

At her formal greeting, he looked beyond her to see a footman standing by the doors. At least the duchess had taken her butler with her. "I admit Lady Beaumont, I have been quite anxious to see you again." He squeezed her hands.

She looked to the footman. "Please have tea served."

The footman gave a short bow and headed off.

Mariel let go of one hand and walked him to the arm chair next to the settee. "I received your note." She kept her voice low. "I can only assume something is amiss."

It hadn't occurred to him that she would think so simply because he wished to speak in private. "Not at all. I simply wanted to discuss our plans." He kept it vague, not wishing to begin until the refreshments were brought.

She dropped his hand and floated down onto the settee. "Of that, I'm glad to hear. Did your men find the poacher?"

He shook his head as he sat in the chair perpendicular to her. "There was no sign of him, but I put out word that he was spotted, so I doubt he'll make that mistake again."

"Any man who can't tell the difference between a deer and a horse should be forbidden to hunt." She paused, her green eyes looking about as she thought. "Unless, of course, he was aged and cannot see well. In that case, his family should see to him."

Only she could find a sympathetic reason for someone almost shooting her. Even as he thought of how close the first bullet had come to hitting her, his chest tightened. "I'm relieved that you were not injured."

"Me? I'm glad Atalanta wasn't injured."

He suppressed a grin. Any other woman would have fainted on the spot, but Mariel was most concerned about getting her horse away from danger. She truly was remarkable.

"Have you heard from your mother? Has she settled into your house in London?"

He didn't want to discuss his mother, but it was a safe subject for now. "Yes. I received a letter from her just yesterday. She wants to plan a ball for us."

Her eyes widened. "Oh no. You mustn't let her."

"Do not worry. I convinced her it was more proper for your family to do the honors first."

She clasped her hand around the index finger of her other. "That was the perfect answer. I will, of course, put my family off any grand ideas. Joanna was skeptical when I told her you had committed to our betrothal. In fact, she mumbled something about writing up a new marriage settlement." She cocked her head and raised her brows. "You will not want to sign any new contract my dear sister creates. Ever since our old solicitor beggared us, she has taken tight reins on our financial affairs."

"Your sister? The duchess?" He knew the woman read a lot, but to handle the affairs of one family, never mind two, would be too much.

Mariel waved off his comment. "Not to worry. Joanna adores numbers, and according to the duke, is better than he at them. She did write Amelia's betrothal agreement, and Amelia and the

Earl are quite happy with it." She turned toward the doors as the footman returned with the tea service.

Once the man left, Mariel set about pouring them tea. Not once did she ask what he preferred and as he lifted the dark liquid to his lips, he found it exactly as he liked it, a bit of sugar and no cream.

She gave him a shy smile. "Is it acceptable?"

Acceptable? It was perfect. Everything about her was perfect, and no one seemed to notice but him. That knowledge irritated him. "Very." Taking a second sip, he set the tea cup down and stood.

At her look of surprise, he laid his finger against his lips then quietly moved to the doors. Looking about and seeing no one, he quietly closed them. When he turned to her, there was a slight flush in her cheeks.

He strode back and sat next to her. "I know this is slightly untoward, but I did say I wished to speak to you in private."

"So you did." Her voice was hushed as if she expected a romantic interlude.

That hadn't occurred to him, but it should have. She was still a woman in her prime and she would assume that if he wished for a private meeting that it would not be entirely proper. Unfortunately, now that the thought was in his head, his body agreed.

Forgetting his true reason for being there, he cupped her cheek. "Do you know you were the one person I thought of every day while on the continent?"

Her lips parted as she took a sudden breath. "I have never stopped thinking of you."

What she didn't say was that even when married, she'd kept him close in her heart. Suddenly, he wanted to erase whatever experiences she had with her late husband. He wanted her to feel love and pleasure…and fulfillment. He could do that for her. He could give her that gift at least.

Lowering his head, he brushed her lips with his.

She gave a soft sigh as if she'd been waiting for his touch. It was all the encouragement he needed. Moving his hand to the back of her neck, he nibbled at her lips, before nudging them. As she opened to him, he swept his tongue inside and tasted all that was Mariel.

Her arms wrapped around his neck as she welcomed him, one hand rifling through the hair on the back of his head. Her tongue tangled with his before slipping by and into his mouth, starting a fire in his gut. He wrapped his other arm around her waist, pulling her closer. He wanted to taste all of her.

Her mouth became more demanding as if she couldn't get enough. He welcomed her passion and slid his hand up her side to cup her breast.

She broke their kiss and pushed him away.

Dropping his hands, he stared into her startled gaze. "What's wrong?"

"You touched me." Her utter surprise was clear. "I thought you said you loved me?"

He frowned, completely confused. "I'm not sure I under-stand."

Her face heated, but she didn't look away. "Touching my body is to have children. I told you, I cannot have them. There is no reason to touch me."

Quickly, he tried to make sense of what she said, his instinct telling him it was vitally important that he understand. "But you kissed me."

"Of course I did." She shook her head at him as if he were daft. "I love you."

Her explanation didn't help. "So kissing is good between people who love each other, but touching a body is for procrea-tion?"

Her whole body relaxed at his words. "Yes."

Bloody hell! Unable to sit there, he rose and walked to the window. What had her husband taught her? That copulating was only about having children? A new thought came to the fore. Without looking at her, he spoke over his shoulder. "Did your husband ever kiss you?"

"Of course not. I told you, it wasn't a love match."

His fingers itched to curl into his palms, but she watched, and he didn't want her to know of the fury burning inside him. Beaumont had done far more damage than anyone knew. Even she didn't know. The whole situation reminded him of a mare he'd saved from an irresponsible dandy. She'd been abused and neglected. It had taken him over a year to undo the damage, though she still shied from loud noises.

"Marcus?"

He needed to get his emotions under control. Taking a deep breath, he slowly exhaled before he turned to face her. "I apologize. Your thoughts on the subject of intimacy are new to me."

She gave him a soft smile. "I'm sure they are. You have never been married."

Her condescending tone was so ill placed, he rubbed his hand over his face to keep from smiling at her naiveté. "Perhaps we should discuss my thoughts on our journey to London." Which would allow him a distraction until he could contemplate his new information on Mariel.

She picked up her cup of tea and took a sip. "I have already started planning my departure. It won't take me as long as my sister to be ready as I don't have an entire household to move yet. Have you decided what public venture you wish to pursue before we remove to Town?"

He walked back to the chair he'd originally taken and sat. "Having seen Lady Burchell at church last weekend, I don't believe we need to be seen in public again here in Northampton."

She raised her brows. "Truly? You think the baroness will ensure everyone here knows of our betrothal?"

"I do. Have you had any callers since then?" He had no doubt people would come to judge her to determine if she were worthy of their local viscount.

"I had two yesterday, but I was not at home."

No, she was at Ravenridge with him being shot at. "What of before that?"

"I did have three callers the day before, but as I was out riding and my sister still in residence, I didn't think anything of it. From what I understand, all callers were told she was not receiving. I imagine she was quite busy ensuring all staff and household goods which needed to be moved to Haven House were ready."

As he expected. His mother was right. Going to church did spread the news quickly. "Then I would suggest being available for callers today and tomorrow at the least. How soon can you be ready to travel to London?"

She tapped her index finger on her palm multiple times as she thought about his question. Finally, she returned her gaze to his. "I could be ready in two days."

He should have known she'd be so efficient. "I think we should wait three days. If you can be ready then, we can travel together."

"In separate coaches, of course."

He coughed to hide is surprise. He should have known she'd want to arrive in London in proper fashion. "That is agreeable."

"I will be ready. Would you like more tea?" She reached for the pot.

His inclination was to leave immediately as his purpose for calling on her had been fulfilled, but as he glanced at the mantel clock, he delayed his departure. Picking up his cup, he swallowed the rest of the now cold tea and handed it to her. "I would, thank you."

As she poured, he strode back to the parlor doors and opened them. The footman stood to the side. "You should expect callers for Lady Beaumont soon."

The man gave a quick nod.

Walking back into the room, he strolled over to the window and grinned. In the distance, a coach approached the entrance to Silver Meadows. Yes, very soon.

"Here you are." Mariel's words had him turning.

He accepted the tea before taking his seat again. "Now, it's time to play our assigned parts. If I don't miss my guess, you are about to have a caller. I, of course, will only be able to stay for a brief time, but I look forward to hearing everything that occurs. Are you ready to play the betrothed couple again?"

She set her cup down and met his gaze. "I am. I find it much easier than I anticipated it to be." She cocked her head. "Perhaps that's because you've stopped growling so much."

"And you've stopped yelling at me." He raised his brows, waiting for her acknowledgement.

She shrugged instead. "I suggest we call a truce for the rest of our charade. Would that be acceptable to you?"

"Yes." He held his cup aloft to acknowledge their agreement before taking a sip. It might be easier to play at their betrothal now, but what did that portend for the ending of it?

CHAPTER NINE

London

AFTER BEING IN Town for three days, Mariel opened the last chest to be unpacked. There was something invigorating about being in Town for the season. She hadn't realized she'd missed the activity in the streets and the people calling upon her mother. It would be much harder pretending to her family than to strangers, but having this time with Marcus meant that much to her.

Lifting Joanna's letter and book from the chest, she set it on the bed. She'd planned to leave it at Silver Meadows, but the maid must have packed it. Curious now, she picked up the letter and moved to her dressing table. Breaking the seal, she read.

Dearest Mariel.

Since you have embarked upon the journey of betrothal and matrimony again with the man who has always had your heart, I thought you would enjoy this book. I'm sure that you know much of what is between these pages, but I have it on good authority that even the most knowledgeable person can find something new. My only wish for you is your unending happiness.

And if Lord Blackmore dares to break your heart again, I

promise retribution.

Your loving sister, Joanna.

Stunned by the last sentence, she read it again. Love and something akin to nervousness filled her. Surely Joanna wouldn't do anything untoward once the betrothal was broken. After all, it wouldn't be Marcus who would break it. But what if Joanna didn't like the reason?

Uneasy now, she folded the letter, then rose and brought the book to her dressing table. If she had left the book at Joanna's school, Joanna would have been very put out.

Thankful now that her maid had packed it, she clicked the small latch and opened the cover to put the letter inside. The first two pages flipped over with the cover and as she reached to set them back, her gaze fell upon the third page. *The Illustrated Pleasures of Seduction.*

She blinked and read the title again. "This doesn't make sense." She closed the book and read the cover. *"The Education of the Feminine Species,* by Lord Ancil Rutherford." That's what she'd thought it was. Opening the book again, the first two blank pages fell back and once more she was staring at an outrageous title. The book must be faulty. Putting her thumb against the bulk of the pages, she opened the book halfway through.

Her breath caught. The image sketched on the page showed a man's head between a naked woman's legs. Why would he be there unless…heat filled her. He must be examining the woman for her ability to have children. Had Joanna surmised as she did that she was barren?

She closed the book again and reread the correct title. Her sister must want her to understand her condition. Joanna had always said that it was better to know the worst than to remain in ignorance. Though the thought was admirable, the problem was no longer an issue, unless… She stared at the book. Could there be a cure? Was that what Joanna referred to by saying that even the most knowledgeable person could find something new in the volume? What if that were true? What if she could find a way to conceive? If that were possible, Marcus could marry her. But how would they know until he…she shivered. Maybe creating life wouldn't be as uncomfortable with a man she loved.

Stubbornly, a small glimmer of hope flared to life and a new wave of love for her sister swept through her. She would have to study the book carefully. Rising, she set it on the table next to her bed. She would do so in the evening, but as it was almost time for callers, she needed to meet her mother in the parlor.

Checking her reflection in the looking glass, she tucked a stray lock of hair back into place then brushed a wrinkle from her forest green dress before walking to the door. As she descended the grand stair of Craymore Hall, a new lightness settled about her.

She'd just reached the bottom step when her mother came to the entry from the corridor.

"Ah, there you are, Mariel. Do you think your dashing officer will be calling today?"

"I'm sure he will. But remember, he's a viscount now."

Her mother waved off the comment as she strolled into the parlor, her favorite blue day dress that matched her eyes perfectly swishing with her gait. "Officer or viscount, that young man has always been quality. I'm so pleased that you and he will finally have the wedding you've been waiting for."

Not sure why, she felt the need to point out that she'd already had a wedding. "You mean a second wedding."

Her mother sat in the armchair covered in a pretty ivory cloth with small roses and green vines that matched the walls exactly. Lady Wakefield held out her hand. "I'm sorry. You're correct. You did so much for us by marrying Lord Beaumont."

She took her mother's hand. "I was pleased to do so."

Her mother squeezed her fingers even as she shook her head. "I would have happily lived in a cottage if I thought you weren't treated well."

She released her mother's hand and sat upon the settee. "I

know, Mother, but I wasn't treated poorly, and I had my own household to run."

Her mother studied her as if to be sure once again that she had not suffered being married to Beaumont. Though she had repeatedly said as much, her mother never seemed completely satisfied.

It was time for a change in topic. "Have you heard from Teddy?" Her melodramatic cousin Teddy was off on the continent to mend his broken heart.

Mother picked up the embroidery loop that lay on the side table next to her. "No, but his father told us last night that he should come home."

"Already? Is he over Lady Elsbeth then?"

Her mother grinned. "I believe so. According to your uncle, Teddy has asked three other women to marry him and they have all said yes, including one who is already married."

She widened her eyes in shock, but then again, it was Teddy they were discussing. "Was he in his cups?"

"I do believe he was. Your uncle said Teddy left Paris under the cover of night."

She had so hoped that Teddy would mature on his adventure, but it appeared that had not occurred. "You could always send Joanna over there to bring him home."

Her mother chuckled even as she started to work her loop. "That's true, though I fear the duke might gainsay that."

"He could go with her, but maybe they should wait until Lady Elsbeth is married. Then Teddy will *have* to look elsewhere."

Her mother gave her an odd look, but didn't say anything.

It wasn't hard to surmise that her mother was thinking about her love for Marcus and how even when she thought him dead, she'd still loved him even while married to another. Would he have let her know he was alive if she hadn't married? Though the question begged for an answer, its relevance no longer mattered.

Just as she was about to ask after her mother's good friend

Lady Dulac, the parlor doors opened and in swept her younger sister Amelia, now Lady Sommerset. Though more petite than herself, Amelia's presence always turned heads, whether she wore the charming yellow dress that matched her hair or if she wore somber gray. Joanna referred to her as a sprite. It fit her, especially with her round blue eyes and secret smile.

"Mariel, you must tell me, is it really true? Are you to be married to Lord Blackmore after all?"

She grinned as she rose and gave Amelia a hug. "Yes, it's true." She smiled to belie the lie.

Amelia immediately sat on the settee and forced her to join her by pulling her down. "You must tell me everything."

She looked to her mother, who shook her head. Facing Amelia, she explained quickly. "There's not much to tell. I asked him why he didn't let me know he was alive, and he said it was because he'd learned I had married and thought I had fallen in love with someone else."

Amelia crinkled her upturned nose. "Lord Beaumont? How could he think such a thing? Your husband was old, wrinkly, and very squat. He reminded me of a frog."

She barely suppressed a snort at her sister's perfect description. It must be her artistic way of looking at everything that painted such an apt picture. "Lord Blackmore wasn't familiar with Lord Beaumont. Do remember that my late husband was a marquess and Lord Blackmore merely the second son of a viscount at the time."

"I suppose." Amelia didn't appear entirely convinced. "So once he discovered that you had married to save us from destitution, he asked you to marry him again?"

She should say yes, but the new part of her couldn't resist telling the truth, or as close as she could come to it. "Actually, no. I asked him."

To her right, she heard her mother gasp, and Amelia's eyes grew wide before narrowing. "I don't believe you."

She couldn't help the laughter that bubbled up and she let it out. "Don't be so shocked. It's not like we don't love each other or hadn't planned to marry. It's just that I have waited long enough." Which was far too true.

Amelia's gaze softened. "Then I'm proud of you. And of course, he said yes. This is so wonderful. You are the one that always said love was more important than anything. I never truly understood until Andrew."

Their mother cleared her throat. "I do believe I may have mentioned that."

Amelia rolled her eyes before smiling. "You were definitely the first, Mother. And then Joanna with all her philosophers and poets, but Mariel showed us what it truly meant."

Again their mother cleared her throat. "Would you like to think about that further?"

A smile tugged at the corners of Mariel's lips, but she kept it at bay. Amelia appeared completely perplexed. Finally, her younger sister's eyes opened in understanding. "Oh, you mean you and Father. Yes, that's true, but you're older."

It was Mariel's turn to gasp, but at the twinkle in her sister's eye, she understood she only teased.

"Young woman, married or not, you come over here and give your old mother a proper apology."

Mariel finally looked to her mother to find her not the least insulted.

Amelia rose and kissed their mother on the cheek. "I am truly sorry, Mother. You do not look old at all."

"Hmph." Lady Wakefield, whose chestnut hair barely held any white and whose wrinkles clearly spoke of years of smiles and laughter, was still quite beautiful. She waved her youngest back. "Fine. Now do call Channing and have tea brought. I'm sure we will be having guests now that Mariel has joined us."

Amelia headed for the open doors of the parlor just as Channing welcomed their newest visitor.

"Lord Blackmore."

Mariel's heart fluttered as if four years, a marriage, and a war had not taken place since Marcus had last come to call on her at their London home. Pretending to be betrothed was becoming far too easy.

"Channing. It's good to see you again."

"And you, sir. Lady Wakefield, Lady Sommerset, and Lady Beaumont are receiving."

She tried not to crane her neck to catch sight of him, but it would hardly be proper, so she settled for watching the doorway while gripping the side of the settee. His boot heels on the entry floor announced his arrival just seconds before he crossed the threshold to the parlor.

He took in all three of them in one glance, then strode to her mother. "Lady Wakefield, Lady Beaumont, Lady Sommerset, it is a pleasure to see you all again."

"And you, sir." Her mother smiled, but her gaze took in everything at once. "We are so pleased that you came home with no injuries."

Mariel caught the stiffening in his shoulders and neck, and she had no doubt her mother did as well. "I am lucky to have made it through my final battle. I only wish those of my family here had been as fortunate as myself."

Her mother shook her head. "We heard of your family's misfortunes. We are very sorry and hope you and your mother can find peace in the future."

"Thank you." He gave her mother a short nod.

"Please, have a seat and join us for tea?" Her mother's kind smile was quite welcoming and Marcus seemed to relax.

"Lord Blackmore, are you not pleased to find my sister here?"

At Amelia's question, she looked at her, willing her to face her, but she didn't, an impish smile filling her face.

Marcus raised his brows. "But of course she is here. We traveled to London together, in separate coaches."

Amelia finally looked at her, now with wide eyes. "You did?"

"Yes, I did. Remember, Amelia. I'm a widow." She gave her younger sister a stern look, since Amelia had been secretly seeing her husband before they were married and had risked her very reputation for the sake of art.

Their mother addressed Marcus. "I called on your mother as soon as I heard the wonderful news. We are going to the Burlington arcade on the morrow. Would you like to join us?"

Her mother hadn't mentioned the outing before now. Maybe she forgot.

"Actually, I was hoping Lady Beaumont would accompany me to Tattersall's tomorrow." He turned his attention to her. "Would that be of interest to you?"

"Tattersall's?" Excitement filled her. While her family had bought horses from them, none of them had ever visited. She'd never expected to see the premiere horse auction house in person. "I would very much enjoy such a venture."

Her mother frowned. "I suppose we can speak to your father about attending."

Amelia patted her hand before responding. "Mariel needs no chaperone. Her reputation is beyond reproach, and she is a widow after all."

She couldn't allow her sister to assume so much. "That may be true, but Tattersall's would require a chaperone."

"Truly?" Amelia looked past her to direct the question to their mother.

"Yes, truly."

She shrugged one delicate shoulder. "Then Andrew and I will attend with you. Father would find it a bore. That is, if that is acceptable to you, Lord Blackmore?"

He gave her sister a kind grin. "I'd be happy to have any of Lady Beaumont's family attend."

"Then it's settled. I will bring my sketch pad. So many beautiful animals in one place is an opportunity not to be passed by."

Surprised but pleased by her younger sister's offer, she gave her a genuine smile. "While you sketch, I can view those for sale."

Her mother interjected. "Mariel, certainly you don't wish to purchase yet another horse, do you?"

Marcus responded first. "I believe she'll need to purchase more than one if she wishes to breed a certain temperament."

"Breed?" Her mother's head snapped toward her. "What's this about breeding horses?"

Drat it. She should have never mentioned Joanna's idea. "It was something I discussed with Joanna before Lord Blackmore called on me to renew our betrothal."

Her mother looked to Marcus. "And you are accepting of this?"

Marcus grinned, looking like he did before he'd headed to war. "Accepting? I would encourage it. Lady Beaumont has exquisite taste in horses and is the best horsewoman I know. I believe she could breed the calmest horse or the fastest."

Heat filled her cheeks at his praise. As her mother opened her mouth to ask more questions, she turned her attention to Marcus. "Do you look for a new mount then, my lord?"

"I do. Though I do not need a fast horse. I'd prefer one that has been through the war."

That was an interesting requirement for a horse. "Do you not own one such a horse?"

"I do, but I would like another. Once having been through the chaos of war, a mount worth its mettle will hardly notice the busy streets of London."

She found it puzzling that he would compare war to the London roads, but he was far more knowledgeable on that score. Her mother turned the conversation to an upcoming ball.

As Marcus conversed politely with her mother and sister, she couldn't help wishing that the farce they perpetuated could be real. He appeared more relaxed and more of his old expressions came out, making it seem as if he'd never gone, but not quite. Often times she noticed a stiffening in his jaw around certain subjects and when he wished to change the subject, his shoulders straightened as if expecting resistance.

But the most significant change in him was how he covertly

scanned the room as if expecting someone to leap out at them from the shadows. Surely that couldn't be it, but it seemed like that was what he was about. If only she could know what he'd experienced while away from her.

As he answered a question her mother put to him, the parlor doors opened and Lady Dowling walked in. The woman was of an age with her mother, but appeared far older and lived upon gossip. Her daughter was currently one of Joanna's students and the opposite of her parent, preferring books to people.

"Lady Dowling." Her mother rose to take the woman's hands.

Marcus stood and offered his chair.

The woman turned toward him after greeting her mother. "Why Lord Blackmore, what a pleasant surprise to find you here at Lady Wakefield's. I had not heard that you had arrived in Town. Are you here for the season?"

"I am. It is a pleasure to see you again. It has been many years, I believe."

The older woman sat. "It has. You really must come to Town more often." Lady Dowling looked directly at Mariel. "Now you have good reason to be here, do you not?"

Marcus gave the woman a perfunctory smile. "Indeed, I do. My lovely betrothed is here." He moved to stand next to her. "Wherever she is, I will be close at hand."

Lady Dowling sighed. "Young love. It is so reassuring to see. I only wish my own daughter could find a match soon. We are halfway through the season and still no one has shown an interest."

Mariel hated to see young ladies pressured into marriage. Her parents had always wanted their daughters to find love, and they had, even if hers would never be her husband. "I'm sure there is a young man about who will see all the wonderful qualities of Lady Sophie. They simply haven't met yet."

"That's quite possible. Getting her to an event takes days of preparation."

Before Lady Dowling could elaborate on her complaint, Marcus stepped around the settee and into the middle of the parlor. "Lady Wakefield, I fear I must take my leave of you as I have many more calls to make now that I'm back in London."

"Of course, Lord Blackmore. It was so very good to see you."

He turned to her. "I look forward to our outing tomorrow."

"As do I." She gave him a small nod, belying the quickening of her heart as she anticipated spending time with him again.

After he strode out, Lady Dowling launched into every rumor she'd heard about Marcus. Mariel forced herself not to comment on the most outlandish ones the lady mentioned.

Amelia tapped Mariel's leg. "Lady Dowling, I heard that Lord Fellingham has run off to Gretna Green with Lady Anna."

"Oh, my." Lady Dowling's eyes rounded. "Lady Anna? I don't believe I know the young wanton."

Amelia nodded before launching into an elaborate story about the desperately in love couple, which if Mariel wasn't mistaken, was completely fabricated. It wasn't long before Lady Dowling left to spread her new piece of gossip about Lord Fellingham and Lady Anna.

She turned to Amelia. "Thank you." She cocked her head and raised her brows. "But do you think the upturned mincemeat pie on the villain Lord Montague wasn't beyond the pale?"

Amelia placed the back of her hand on her forehead and reached out with her other. "Oh, but it was a horrific sight. I thought for sure he had soiled himself."

Even as she shook her head, Mariel laughed. "I can see you've remembered the play Joanna would have us perform at Christmas time. She would be proud."

Their mother cleared her throat. "I do worry though when Lady Dowling starts repeating that terrible love story, that others will see it for what it is and it will come back to us."

Amelia waved her hand. "Do not worry. Her daughter will set her straight before long, and maybe she'll learn her lesson." She scowled. "I couldn't sit here and listen to her say that Lord

Blackmore had been a highwayman and only came out of hiding because of his brother's death. And then to insinuate he'd caused the poor man to take ill! Mariel, I don't know how you could sit there so calmly."

She grasped her sister's hand. "Because I have a sister like you."

"Yes, you are so lucky to have one fun sister and one stodgy sister."

"Amelia." Their mother's tone made it clear she didn't appreciate the aspersion cast upon Joanna.

Amelia gave a one shoulder shrug and rose. "I best be on my way. So many people to tell about Lady Anna." She laughed before waving to her mother as she reached the parlor doors just as they opened.

Lady Dulac entered, her mother's good friend, and soon the two were chatting about the next ball.

But a ball was the furthest thing from her mind. She kept thinking about the book Joanna had given her. What if it had the cure to her barrenness? What if theirs could be a true betrothal? Glancing at the clock, she tried not to fidget. Sometimes being a lady, even a widow, and a betrothed one, could be so trying.

※

CHAPTER TEN

MARCUS STROLLED TOWARD the courtyard at Tattersall's, Mariel on his arm. She didn't say anything as they followed Lord and Lady Somerset, but her observant gaze took in everything. When he'd suggested such an outing, he hadn't known she'd never been to the premiere horse auctioneer in all of England. He'd assumed that with such fine mounts, she had chosen her own horses from seeing them, not reading about them. Now, he was eager to see her reaction to the establishment, and most of all, the choice of horseflesh.

Just as they entered the courtyard with its four-columned fountain in the middle, a groom walked a horse toward the covered walkway to their right.

"Oh, Andrew. That's a beauty. I must sketch him." Lady Sommerset took a step in the direction of the horse then suddenly turned about and approached them. She had her ever-present secret smile, which he found very unusual. In truth, Marcus found talking to the couple, each blond and far too happy, a bit uncomfortable. She glanced about then lowered her voice. "I've arranged for our coach to come for us in a couple of hours." Then she grinned widely before joining her husband and hurrying off toward the first horse she'd seen.

Mariel's brows rose then turned toward him. "It would seem that my chaperone has made other plans."

He couldn't be more pleased, his opinion of the younger couple improving. "I promise, I will take the utmost care with you."

She looked askance at him. "Why do I think there is more meaning behind your words than I know?"

"Because there is?"

Her eyes widened before she laughed. "Marcus, you are a tease. We are in public with a preponderance of horses. I doubt even you could be anything but a gentleman."

She made a good point. He gave her an exaggerated sigh. "Then I shall be on my best behavior, but only for you."

Tapping his arm lightly, she returned her gaze to the crowd of men talking, walking about, or viewing the horse her sister had spotted. "And for my family and your mother and—what is he doing?"

He reluctantly moved his gaze from her excited profile to the area she nodded toward. Beneath the columned walkway, where a long line of men stood, a groom walked an Irish Hunter past them. "He's letting the buyers see the horse in motion before it goes up for auction."

She snapped her head around toward him. "They're selling horses today?"

"Yes, every Monday. Would you like to purchase one?"

Her brows knit and her gaze moved away as she gave the idea consideration. She shook her head. "No. I would rather learn all there is to know about buying at auction, so I might come back in the future more knowledgeable about the proceedings."

Her answer didn't surprise him. She was not the type of woman to act on impulse, always in control, always having a plan. It was this calm about her that had originally attracted him to her, that, and her horsemanship. "Then I suggest we tour this fine establishment so that I might teach you all that I know, though to be honest, it's been a few years since I was last here."

"That may be true, but that still means you have far more experience than I do. I can't explain what a pleasure it is to be here and learn all there is to learn."

Her words, though delivered with a confidant smile, sent a chill through him. He *did* have much more experience in both life and death, and even in wishing for death. An overwhelming need to protect her filled him and he scanned the crowd, looking for threats.

"Marcus?"

"Yes." Was that a groom or someone who didn't belong?

"What's wrong?"

The man he'd been watching moved around a corner and came out with a horse. Seeing no threat, he gave Mariel his attention once again. "Nothing is wrong. Would you like to see an auction or the stables first?"

"I think the stables. Are they very large? How many horses are housed there? Do they come from all over England? Are they for riding or for coaches? Oh, maybe there are some from working the fields?"

He swallowed a chuckle at her enthusiasm and turned them in the direction of the building, happy to move her away from the crowd. "The horses come from all over England but also beyond. The only horses sold here are for riding or for coaches. Yes, the stable is large. It can hold over a hundred animals."

Her step faltered, and she gripped his arm. "Over a hundred?"

He gave a soft chuckle. "Yes, but they are usually only here a few days before being purchased and the stables aren't always full. There are also carriages and hounds for sale." He could tell she was no longer listening. Either the subject was of no interest, which could be the point, or it was that she'd caught a glimpse of the building.

"It is good to see how my horses have come to be mine. Not all, of course."

He led her toward the large open doors where he could see only a few gentlemen milling about and more groomsmen. "Did Zephyrus come from here?"

She shook her head without moving her gaze from the stable

entrance. "No. I purchased him from a lord who didn't want him."

"Why wouldn't he want such a magnificent beast?"

She halted as they stepped onto the brick floor of the building, her gaze sweeping the stalls. "He said the stallion was uncontrollable and since he wasn't fast enough to breed race horses, he didn't want him."

She'd never told him that. Even now, barely paying attention to her own story, she didn't see how surprising it was that she could ride Zephyrus easily. She was his perfect mate. Why had fate been so cruel? What had he done in his youth to deserve losing such a woman?

"This is quite impressive, not just in size but in how well kept it is. I can see why people feel comfortable buying from here." As if drawn to the animals, she started forward again. "What a beautiful Arabian. She will be well-liked." They moved to the next stall where a young gray gelding with black spots stood watching her. "This one has a lot of spirit. Do you think it's a race horse?"

"I would expect so." He enjoyed horses, but watching her study them and draw conclusions was far more interesting. He could tell she was excited by the way she held her head and the quick movements of her eyes.

"Oh, isn't she pretty?" She stopped them before a Thorough-bred. "She looks young."

"I agree. She'd make a good horse for a well-bred lady."

They continued on, Mariel commenting on each horse. Her knowledge and intuition were equal to his own and her observations very astute. They came to an empty stall, and she halted. "Now this one is truly spectacular."

He frowned as he scanned the empty space. "What do you mean?"

"Just look at his lines. He has a grace, even standing still."

Truly puzzled now, he turned her toward him. "Mariel?"

She chuckled. "He is the horse of my dreams. He can be

whatever I wish."

"Ah, I see. And do you wish for a stallion?"

"No, one is enough. I would like a gelding who is affectionate and of happy disposition."

He raised one brow. "You sound like you wish for a dog."

"I suppose it does sound that way, but I don't want a dog. They are too small. Each of my horses have a dominating characteristic. One is headstrong, one is fast, one is a great jumper, one is a true lady, and one is unpredictable, but none are affectionate."

Did she long for affection? Did she even know she did? He wanted to give her that, the horse of her dreams, and more.

"I could spend the whole day in here. The scents, the sounds, the animals, the—oh." She crinkled her nose.

He looked around her into the next stall to see the large horse inside had just relieved himself. He chuckled. "You did say you enjoyed the scents."

She pinched her nose. "Some are better than others."

At the sound of her voice, he laughed. "Then may I suggest we remove ourselves from the vicinity and make our way to the auctions?"

Letting go of her nose, she hooked her arm in his again. "Yes, please."

Still smiling, he walked them down the center of the massive stables. He had thought Mariel unchanged, but he was discovering new sides to her daily, and he enjoyed every one of them. She'd always been sweet, but never forthright. She'd been witty, but not outright funny. There was so much more to her now, or was it that she was allowing him to see more?

"Wait."

He halted at her command. "What is it?"

"That horse. I wish to see it."

He moved them closer to a Thoroughbred unlike the others, it stood against the back wall, its gaze on them, but not moving.

Marie set one gloved hand upon the stall door. "We mean

you no harm." Her voice was soft and soothing as she spoke to the gelding. "What is amiss that you look at us so?"

The horse didn't move, not even a swish of its tail.

"You poor thing. You're so beautiful. No one should treat you so poorly." She moved her gaze from the horse to him. "He deserves a better owner. He doesn't know it, but his sale will probably save his life."

Shocked by her words, he studied the horse more carefully, finally noticing what she had. Scars. An age-old anger simmered in his gut. There were two incidents he would not let go unpunished, the mistreatment of horses and the mistreatment of women.

She turned back to the horse. "I promise you. It will be better when you leave here."

Her belief in mankind humbled him, but he was not so naïve. He glanced at the horse's name as they turned away. He couldn't leave now without ensuring the animal had a better owner.

As they exited the stables, they strolled back into the court-yard. He led her past the fountain and to the far end of the covered walkway on the right where an auctioneer had just finished a sale. He brought her just under the cover, but not too close to become a part of the proceedings.

A horse was led up the walkway and made to stand near the front of the auctioneer, but they couldn't see it as they stood in the back. The crowd of men shifted slightly forward. As the bidding started, Mariel's head moved as she sought out each bidder, her body leaning forward. When the winner was called, she let out a breath. "How fascinating. I'm not sure I would be very good at buying a horse in this way. I'm sure I would either spend too much or bow out too soon. Just watching it left me a bit breathless."

"Shall we move closer to see the horse auctioned? As long as you can refrain from bidding, you may find it more interesting."

"More interesting than watching a man standing above this crowd of hats and seeing random hands go up?" She widened her eyes as if that had been incredibly exciting.

He'd never known her humor to be sarcastic, but it was quite funny and yet pointed. He liked it. "Yes, well, I thought to keep you from spending a fortune, but let us make our way toward the front so you can see the next horse."

She gave him a wicked grin. "I do believe that would be lovely."

Enjoying her more every minute, he directed them through the crowd which loosened after the final bid was called. Some would remain but others would look to examine more potential purchases. As they neared the center, he halted. "What is your sister doing here?"

Mariel looked at him quizzically. "She came with us. Remember?" Her expression turned to true concern. He could almost read what she was thinking that he'd been shot in the head and had lost his mind.

He straightened his shoulders even as they approached Lady Sommerset who was seated directly across from the auctioneer before the space where the horses were shown. The earl stood behind her. "My lady, how is it that you have come to be in this coveted position?"

Lady Sommerset looked up at her husband with that secret smile of hers before facing them. "It was no easy task, I assure you. I requested a seat from a groom, who did my bidding, but when he put it against the wall over there, Andrew moved it here. Immediately, there was an uproar."

That was no surprise. "Did they request that you move?" Taking permanent space before every horse shown was considered poor etiquette.

"Not at all. They demanded it. Can you imagine?"

He glanced at her husband who obviously found the entire episode amusing.

"Of course, I refused. How could I possibly sketch a horse perfectly if I'm over there?" She gestured toward the wall where presumably they had set her chair.

"Oh, dear, Amelia. What happened?" Mariel's concern for her sister reminded him that they were unfamiliar with how Tattersall's operated.

Lord Sommerset couldn't seem to hold back. "Tattersall himself came out to see what the fuss was about."

"Yes." Lady Sommerset nodded. "And when I explained to him what I was attempting to accomplish, he was so excited that he has commissioned a number of sketches. Not all today, of course. But since I'm here, I have done a few of the crowd and auctioneer."

He was stunned by the entire event. Perhaps Mariel had been correct in stating that her family was odd, but he had to admit, it was the type of eccentricity he quite enjoyed. "Your sister would like to see an auction take place. May we join you for the next one?"

Lady Sommerset nodded. "Of course, just stand to the side so I might have a clear view of the horse."

Mariel leaned in, the scent of citrus filling his senses. "She tends to be a bit demanding when it comes to her artwork. Let us stand over there." Her breath against his jaw had him suddenly remembering they would have his coach to themselves. He hoped she didn't want to stay much longer. He valued every moment with her until they parted.

They moved to a spot where they could both see the horse and her sister. Another was brought from the stables, the young mare who appeared to preen with all the attention. Again Mariel leaned in. "She would not do well in my stables. Zephyrus expects all other animals to praise him, even the local rabbit family." She chuckled as the auctioneer started the bidding.

As with the last auction, her hold on his arm tightened as the bidding intensified. It was all very gentlemanly, but voices definitely raised and murmurs floated through the crowd when a large jump in price was offered. He caught Lady Sommerset watching them more than once, but between the auction and Mariel, he didn't wonder much about it. Finally, the auction was called and the new owner patted on the back for his good fortune.

Mariel leaned heavily on his arm as she let out a breath. "Now that was much more exciting. I'm sure that pretty horse is going to be spoiled, which is exactly what she wants."

He wanted to spoil Mariel just as much. He shouldn't allow himself to become accustomed to having her on his arm, yet he patted her hand upon it. "I'm glad you enjoyed it. There is something else I'd like to show you today, if you are willing to take a short ride with me."

"A ride to where?"

"Now, it wouldn't be a surprise if I told you."

She nodded. "I like a surprise. Let us tell Amelia we're leaving, then."

"Of course." He led her back to her sister. Wishing to talk to Lord Sommerset, he scanned the area nearby. The blond man, who always wore tans and browns, was easy to find. He leaned against the back wall, arms folded. After conferring with the man, he waited for Mariel.

When she had finished her conversation, he offered her his arm and they strolled toward the exit.

She practically floated alongside him. "Amelia already has at least a dozen sketches. She even did one of you and me."

"She did?" He led her through the final arch that announced the entrance to Tattersall's. "How could she do that?"

"Oh, my younger sister is quite adept at catching people unawares. She sketched us while we were watching the last auction. I didn't see her looking at us."

So that's why she kept looking at them, sometimes squinting her eyes. He'd thought she'd judged him and found him lacking. Obviously, he wasn't very good at reading faces. "I noticed her watching us, but had no idea she sketched us. Was it good?"

She halted just feet away from the coach, forcing him to stop.

"What's wrong? Did you lose something?"

"Marcus, Amelia not only exhibited at the London Academy, but she is also a sought-after artist with paintings in over a dozen homes just here in town. Of course the sketch of us is good."

Not expecting such a staunch defense of Lady Sommerset, he found himself taken aback. "I apologize. I did not mean to give an affront. I admit I am not used to being in the company of artists, only amateurs." He grimaced. "And those works have been less than…"

"Wonderful? Acceptable? Adequate?" She cocked her head as she thought about another description.

"Hardly. If forced to choose a word, I would have to say distasteful, perhaps even torturous to look upon."

She patted his arm where her hand rested. "I believe you exaggerate."

Thinking back to a letter with a sketch enclosed left by one of his mother's callers at Ravenridge before Mariel arrived and their betrothal was announced, he shook his head. "As I burned the image I received, I cannot show it to you, but be assured that my forehead was twice its real height, my lips pursed like a woman's, and my nose so large as to appear to be two."

Her eyes rounded before she grinned. "I do wish you had saved that. I've never seen a man with two noses. Are you sure?"

Enjoying her glee, he replied honestly. "It was quite a sketch. I'd never seen four nostrils on a face before. I can only be thankful that it was so far removed from my actual appearance, that if anyone were to have come across it, they wouldn't have associated it with me."

Mariel laughed, the sound enveloping him with warmth. "Now I know you exaggerate. No mother would allow her daughter to make a gift of such an ill accomplished drawing."

He started them toward the coach again, anxious to be alone to enjoy her company. "I do not think any parent was consulted in this gift as it was folded up inside a letter. Which now that I think upon it, the folds may have contributed additional angles that added to the overall grotesqueness of the image."

"Now, I truly wish I could have viewed such a horror." Her lips twitched upward. "At least you can be thankful it wasn't a sketch of your horse. Can you imagine how many legs it might have?"

He slapped his free hand to his chest and lifted his chin in exaggerated affront. "You unfairly wound me to think that saving my horse the embarrassment of disfigurement on paper is more important than my own visage."

Her lips widened into a full smile and she pulled her arm from his and rested her gloved hand against his cheek. "Since the true visage is so pleasant to look upon, I could easily forget any sketch."

His heart thudded in his chest, and he captured her hand against his face. To look upon her face every day had been his dream and he yearned to have her beside him always. Unable to pretend otherwise, he struggled with telling her, finally swallowing the words. Instead, he stayed with their present situation. "While I would enjoy nothing more than to continue to view your lovely visage, I propose we be on our way."

She gave him a quiet nod, and he took her hand from his face and helped her into his coach. He gave his coachman instructions and quickly joined Mariel inside, sitting not across from her, but next to her.

Though her eyes widened, she did not shy away. Her growth from young maiden into a woman called to him on a more primal level than he could act upon. As soon as the coach moved forward, he took her hand. "Do you think your sister would paint a portrait of you for me to have?"

He felt her pulse race beneath his fingers and a slight blush filled her cheeks. "I would be honored, but I do not think the future viscountess would appreciate it."

How he wished to tell her there would be no future viscountess. There would never be another woman in his life. At that realization, a deep sadness filled him and along with it a need to claim what happiness he could.

CHAPTER ELEVEN

MARIEL STARED INTO Marcus' mercurial gray eyes and her breath hitched. There was a deep sorrow there and a desperation that drew her in, wishing she could save him. Without meaning to, she found herself leaning forward. "Marcus?" Her voice came out in a whisper, barely able to get the word past her tightening throat.

He didn't answer. Instead, his lips pressed to hers and instinct told her what he needed was her. The thrill of that knowledge didn't mean she understood exactly, but she was willing to comply. Wrapping her hand around his neck, she parted her lips, inviting him in.

Immediately, his tongue swept inside her mouth as if he'd been starving for her taste.

To be so loved made her toes curl in her shoes and she grasped his hair, silently letting him know, he was welcome to love her.

There was a hunger in his kiss that she hadn't experienced before. She didn't understand it, but the feeling was heady. He needed her, loved her beyond anything. She loved him too. Tangling her tongue with his, she tasted him, her belly tightening, so when his mouth left hers to kiss her throat, she could do no more than let her head fall back and allow him free rein.

His mouth moved to her collarbone, causing shivers to race

across her skin. Her body seemed to be melting, even her dress felt loose. As his kisses moved lower, an ache started between her legs. It was strange but not painful. For some reason she wished her clothes were off, which made no sense.

Then his kisses trailed down to her bare breast and she opened her eyes just before his mouth latched onto her nipple. The spike of pleasure that shot through her made her gasp and though she'd meant to pull his head away, she held it to her, hanging on as her body was awash in exquisite feelings.

Now the ache between her legs grew more demanding and a strange moisture emerged. She must have a fever as she felt so hot. She wanted to say something, but then Marcus used his teeth and took her hard peak between them and rolled.

Her hips bucked of their own accord and she felt as if she were drowning. "Marcus?" She could barely hear her own voice, yet he halted.

"Yes."

Though embarrassed that his mouth was but a hairbreadth from her, she pulled gently on his hair so he would look at her. When his gaze met hers, she felt her cheeks heat. "What are you doing to me?"

One corner of his lips lifted. "I'm loving you, sweet Mariel."

Her nipples seemed to harden even more at his words and became almost painful. "I don't understand. I feel as if I'm falling but floating. I'm so warm."

He lowered his head to lick her hard peak, sending another shock of pleasure through her. He lifted his face again. "Does that make you feel warm and relaxed, yet tense at the same time?"

She nodded as it was easier than to try and talk.

"Then I'm doing it correctly."

Before she could ask another question, he lowered her so she lay against the corner of the swaying coach seat. In the process, her other breast was exposed. She should care about that, but she didn't. With Marcus, she felt safe.

As his mouth moved to her newly bared breast, she watched,

holding her breath, waiting for his touch. He didn't disappoint. His tongue shot out and encircled her peak before stroking is back and forth. As her limbs weakened, she let her head fall back again, unable to do anything but enjoy the pleasure of his kisses.

Her belly felt strange and she wanted something, but she wasn't sure what. It was nothing like wanting a favorite dessert or a new hat. It was as if her body wanted to feel. It wanted Marcus! Her eyes opened just as he took her peak between his teeth. Arching despite her own will, she moaned, craving his touch. She wanted his mouth everywhere.

That thought shocked her, and she tugged on his hair. "Marcus, stop."

Immediately, he sat up, hunger in his eyes as if she were a feast and he a starving man. "Did I hurt you?"

She shook her head. "I…I want…It's wrong."

He cupped her face between his palms and touched his forehead to hers. "Nothing is wrong between two people who love each other." He pulled his head back to gaze at her. "I know this is all new for you, but there is so much more I wish to show you."

"You do?"

He nodded. "I do. I want you to know love and passion. You deserve to feel the pinnacle of life. But I will always respect your wishes."

She pondered that. "Do you mean there is more to these feelings I'm having?"

"Much more."

It wasn't the words so much as his look as he said them that sent tingles racing across her skin.

"But we are almost to our destination. Allow me to help you adjust your dress."

Her dress?

As he moved off her, she gasped. The front of her dress was puddled on her lap. When had she slipped her arms from the small sleeves? Quickly, she pulled the material on and held it against her.

Marcus gazed at her as if he couldn't look away. "If you move over, I can secure your clothing."

Though heat filled her cheeks, she moved over and sat facing the side of the coach, while keeping one hand against the material over her chest.

He sat behind her and she felt her shift neckline tighten. Next her stays pulled against her and were secured before her dress no longer sagged. Without turning, she spoke to the coach wall. "How did my clothes loosen so much? Should I reprimand my maid?"

Marcus left the seat and moved to sit opposite her. "Not at all. It was I that released you from the bonds of so much fabric."

That the man was pleased with his accomplishment was obvious in the small prideful smirk he wore.

"And is that what they teach at Oxford? Or is that part of your military training?" She wasn't sure why it bothered her so much that he could relieve her of her clothing without her being aware, but it did.

Ignoring her pique, he smiled slyly. "Both."

She opened her mouth, shocked that he would admit so much to her.

"If you like, I can show you how to release me from my clothing."

"Marcus!"

His laughter filled the coach. "I see that it is fortunate that I have the skills for both of us."

Confused and not a little intrigued by his banter, she moved her gaze to the window, but her thoughts were not on the scenery. Ruefully, she recognized that he had reverted to the man she used to know, and instead of being excited by that, she'd been uncomfortable. When he used to steal kisses from him, she never wanted them to end. She still didn't, even though where he had kissed her was shocking. She still felt loved, almost worshipped. It was strange to feel so lost and without control while at the same time enjoying the pleasure of his mouth.

"Mariel?" His voice was soft.

She turned to face him. "Yes?"

"You know I would never hurt you."

But he would. He would destroy her heart when he was released from their betrothal and married another. "I'm not sure what you mean."

He leaned forward and took her gloved hand. "I mean that physically, I will only bring you joy, never pain." His gray eyes shone almost silver with their intensity as if he willed her to understand something she didn't.

Hesitantly, she nodded.

His face relaxed and he gave her a reassuring smile. "Good, because I want you to know all there is to pl—love."

Her heart warmed at his words. "I know so much already."

He let go of her hand and sat back, his smile gone though he continued to look at her. "No, you don't." He studied her as if looking for something, then seemed to come to a decision. "But I will teach you."

If he had said so with a smile, she'd know he teased, but Marcus made the pronouncement as if were as important as a new bill set before parliament. She wasn't quite sure how to feel about that, but any time she may have hoped to contemplate his meaning, was lost as the coach came to a stop.

"We are here."

"Here?" She took a moment to look out the coach window. Here appeared to be the country, but they had not ridden so far, had they?

Marcus alighted from the coach as his footman held the door open. "You will see much more out here." He held his hand out for her to take.

"Do you think so?" She let her voice drip with sarcasm before taking his hand.

He raised one brow at her quip, but didn't respond. Instead, he placed her hand on his arm and led her toward a very large structure that appeared to be stables but was almost the length of St. Paul's cathedral.

As they approached, a young man of maybe a score strode toward them, a large smile on his face. He looked vaguely familiar, but since she had no idea where they were, she couldn't possibly know him.

"Lord Blackmore. It is an honor to have you visit Clancy Stables." The man's green eyes danced with pleasure as he turned to greet her. "Lady Mariel. It has been so long, I imagine you don't recognize me."

She blinked. Recognize him? She started to shake her head when he spoke again.

"Do you not remember me, Lady Mariel? I so loved the honey cakes you brought me at Ravenridge."

At the sound of his words spoken in a high-pitched child's voice, she widened her eyes. "Tiery Clancy? Can it be?"

The young man laughed, the sound much like his grandfather's back at Ravenridge. "Aye, it's me, just a bit older. I'll be a full score in three more years."

Little Tiernan Clancy had been eight years old the last time she saw him. His father had moved the family closer to London by the following year. She thought it had something to do with racing horses. Suddenly Tiernan's welcome made sense. She gestured with her free hand toward the massive building. "Is this yours?"

He laughed again and a faint blush rose in his cheeks. "No, my lady. It's my father and uncle's. I just oversee the training."

"Is your father about?"

At Marcus' question, Tiernan shook his head. "He will be terribly sorry he missed you. I hope I will do as a guide."

"That's perfectly fine."

She looked up at Marcus. "There's training done here?"

His smile was back, his whole body relaxed. "Yes. Tiernan's father and uncle became horse jobbers and in just a few years have a very successful enterprise."

Unfortunately, his explanation didn't help. "And a horse jobber does what exactly?"

"A horse jobber lets out trained horses for the season."

Still not sure what he meant, she was about to ask a follow up question, but Tiernan jumped in. "That's right. We rent them to many aristocratic families who don't want to bring their horses to London. We also lend them to the gentry and a few merchants as well. We train and match pairs for carriages of all kinds as well as provide individual mounts."

She hadn't realized that some people didn't bring their own horses to Town. She glanced at the large building again. "It appears your father is very successful."

Tiernan beamed with pride. "Aye. We all help. Would you like to see?"

Marcus chuckled. "I hope you do, because this is what I wanted you to see. Given your interest in horses and possibly horse breeding, I thought you might like to see the Clancys' business."

Her heart filled at his thoughtfulness and unusual thinking. Bringing a woman to a business of this sort was not common. Even Tattersall's had very few women who attended, yet here was Marcus offering her experiences she could only dream about, if she knew they existed. If she didn't know better, she'd say he was using their fake betrothal to apologize for staying hidden. Surely, that couldn't be it. He did not apologize for hiding.

Tiernan opened his palm toward the stables. "My lady?"

She looked from him to Marcus, whose brow furrowed in worry. "I would love to." She faced Tiernan. "Please, tell me everything there is to know."

At the young man's toothy smile, she started forward, rather excited to discover this other world within her world but completely unknown to her until now.

Marcus leaned in and kept his voice low. "Be sure to ask how they train the horses if you wish to see a young man excited to be alive."

She nodded to acknowledge his remark just before they entered the massive building.

"This is where we house the carriages, coaches, phaetons, and curricles. We train the matched pairs on them daily, so having an area to harness them up out of the weather is helpful. We drive them out every day no matter if it's stormy or sunny, so they get used to all conditions. Of course, after training here, we do bring them into our stables in Town to get them used to the noises and traffic there. We'll have to walk down further to see the horses."

As Tiernan explained everything from the horse collars to the feed, she noticed everything, most especially how neat it all was. Mr. Clancy at Ravenridge kept those stables spotless, or as spotless as possible with horses about. It appeared it was a family trait.

Tiernan moved to the side and held his arm out. "These horses in this section are the ones who are being trained. The ones further down are the ones that are let out, though with it being mid-season, we only have a few matched pairs available."

Tiernan moved forward again, looking back at them after empty stall after empty stall was passed.

She could tell he was quite excited. "Are these all out being trained?" She motioned toward the last empty stall before one that had a young mare in it.

Tiernan immediately spun around to face them. "Aye, they are. I have seven men I'm in charge of. I insist on my training regime." He shook his head. "Sometimes the older ones want to tell me what should be done, but I tell them if they do not follow my instructions, they can find another post. They don't realize I've got horse training in my veins."

Marcus explained further. "The way Mr. Clancy tells it, he can trace his ancestors back eight generations and every one of them was a horse lover."

She nodded, having heard the same from the old man. "I cannot say the same. I know not why I enjoy the company of horses so much. No one else in my family is that enamored of them."

Tiernan took a couple steps back. "These are the horses I train myself. They are for young ladies and gents. I train them differently as I like to have a horse for a lady who is used to the sidesaddle, though those mounts can also be ridden by men."

She let go of Marcus' arm and strolled toward the first stall. A lovely seal-bay thoroughbred mare stood there eyeing them. "She's still young."

Tiernan joined her. "Yes. She just started her training. She won't be ready for a couple of years yet."

The deep brown horse with the black mane, tail, and legs moved toward her. She backed away, not wanting to interfere with any training.

Tiernan gave the mare a pat. "She's a smart girl. Sometimes too smart."

She meandered past a few more stalls, the number far surpassing what was at Tattersall's' stables. Though he strolled behind her, she could sense Marcus observing her. She felt both safe and oddly excited by that. She halted as she came upon another empty stall, no doubt waiting for a new horse to be born or bought. She faced Tiernan, Marcus remained in her peripheral vision. "Do you train the horses to follow any particular commands for women that are different than for men?"

The young man frowned. "Different? I'm not sure what you mean."

She set her index finger in the palm of her other hand and held it. "Women on horseback in a sidesaddle might be in danger of wild animals or even unwelcome guests. I trained Zephyrus to rear and attack upon a certain whistle I make."

Tiernan's eyes rounded. "You did?"

"Yes. I did so because while riding, I may become separated from my groom or escort and so wanted to be sure I could depend upon my mount."

Marcus strode up to her. "Do you do that with only Zephyrus?"

She unlocked her hand and added a second finger to her palm before closing it again. "Of course. It was the only protective command I could get him to agree to. Now Atalanta, I taught her to run a person down while Xeres will throw things on command."

"Throw things?" Both men asked the question at the same time.

She grinned, thoroughly enjoying herself. "Why yes, though I cannot take credit for that particular talent. Xeres would do it all the time. I simply trained him to only do it when I give him the command. I command it every time we ride or I fear he'll revert to doing it all the time."

Marcus recovered first. "What kinds of things does he throw?"

She let go of her hand and waved in the air. "Oh, anything. Something on the wall of the stall, a branch on the ground, or one time, he lifted my hat right off my head while I stood next to him and threw that aside."

The two men looked at each other in disbelief.

She slapped her hands on her hips. "It's true."

When they looked at her but didn't say anything, she threw her hands up in the air and turned her back on them. Fine. If they didn't want to believe her, it didn't matter. She stalked forward, happy to leave them behind.

Tiernan quickly strode past her. "We just had a new foal. Would you like to see her?"

Still in a pique, but not willing to miss seeing the baby, she nodded and followed him to yet another section of the building.

Marcus fell into step next to her, but didn't say anything, which was fine with her. As they reached the large stall, she stepped to the rail, not worried about interfering in any training. A piebald mare stood in front of her, but she could see the legs of the little one behind her. "You're a wonderful mama to be so protective. I'm quite proud of you for bringing your little one into this world. Is she pretty?" She stared into the mare's eyes as she softly spoke.

The mare turned her head to nose her baby then moved around her as if to show her off. Mariel's heart beat a staccato in her chest at the precious piebald-colored baby, a tiny replica of its mom. It shook its head before nuzzling its mom for milk.

She could feel an itch behind her eyes as she watched the mare feed her little one. If she had any thoughts about breeding horses, they vanished. She could never do it without losing her heart every time there was a successful birth. The pain it brought her would be far too much.

Marcus' hands clasped her shoulders from behind. "She knows you mean them no harm."

She gave a short nod, her throat too tight to speak. Slowly, she turned away from the scene, dislodging Marcus' hands as she moved back the way they had come to compose herself.

"I can show you the training areas and the offices if you like?"

She didn't turn at Tiernan's words, nor did she respond.

"I believe we've seen enough for today." Marcus must have sensed her retreat. "I thank you for explaining so much. I'm sure we will be back, if your father would find that acceptable."

"Oh, yes sir. I know he will be sorry he missed your visit today. May I show you out?"

Marcus came to stand next to her and placed her hand on his arm. "No, we've kept you long enough from your work. Please give your father my regards."

"Yes, sir. It was a pleasure seeing you again Lady Mariel."

She turned with a smile on her face, happy to have someone else to focus on. "I enjoyed your explanation very much. You have grown into a very knowledgeable man."

Tiernan looked down as a blush crept up his face. "Thank ye, me lady."

Marcus whispered in her ear. "Come, before the young man develops feelings for you."

She snapped her head around ready to disabuse him of any such notion, but the twinkle in his eyes made it clear he teased.

She relaxed and allowed him to lead her forward, back the way they had come.

She kept her voice low. "It is a sad truth that I have attracted many a lad who to this day longs for just a look or word from me. I'm like the pied piper of Germany." She waved her free hand. "Only without those nasty rats."

Marcus laughed.

The sound pleased her down to her toes. It wasn't quite as loud and exuberant as when he was younger, but it filled her with happiness.

"Mariel, I can easily see you with a line of youth following you about wherever you go." He leaned in. "And I would battle every last one of them to keep you mine if I could."

She felt her cheeks heat, but she didn't look away. "I have no doubt you would win."

CHAPTER TWELVE

MARCUS, NOT A little confused, followed Channing down the corridor of Craymore Hall, the Mabry's London home. When he'd said he was calling on Lady Beaumont, the man had not led him to the parlor but past the main stairs. Could it be that Channing was going deaf?

It had only been two days since he'd taken Mariel to Tattersall's, but he wished to have as much time with her as possible before she ended their pretense. He was about to ask Channing where they were going, when the butler opened the doors to the library.

"My lord. Lord Blackmore has arrived."

Mariel's father, Lord Wakefield rose from his chair behind a large desk, a wide grin on his face. "Lord Blackmore. It is a pleasure to see you hale and hardy." The man's graying hair appeared mussed as if he'd run his hands through it multiple times.

He moved into the room. "Lord Wakefield, it is an honor to be in your presence again."

The older man stepped around the desk, strode forward with purpose, and clapped him on the shoulder. "Yes, yes. Channing, have Joanna join us please."

He was about to remind the older man that he was calling on Mariel, but didn't have a chance as he was ushered forward and offered to sit in one of the two wingback chairs before the desk.

Lord Wakefield took the other chair, his rounded belly making the perfect place for him to set his folded hands. "I must say, I was quite pleased to discover that you not only lived, but sought out my daughter straightaway."

Someone had obviously not told the man the true timeline, but he didn't feel impelled to do so since the betrothal would be broken in just a couple more weeks. Even as the thought filled his head, an ache started in his chest. He would never love another, but he could not put his heart before Mariel's happiness.

"We will get started as soon as Jo arrives." Lord Wakefield leaned on the arm of his chair toward him. "Tell me, was the battle truly bloody? How many men did you command? How did you fair at the surgeon's tents? I have so many questions. It is not every day a man brings a war hero into the family. I do so want to know what strategies your battalion officer chose for each position. Did he follow some of the ancient formations from Alexander the Great? He was called great for a reason as I'm sure you know."

Not having any idea what formation the ancient commander had used, he attempted a change in subject instead. "Is Lady Beaumont receiving today? I hope she's not ill."

"Mariel, ill? Hah. That young woman is never ill, and if she were, my Jo would make her better. Do you know that she saved my daughter Belinda?" The man crossed himself and for a moment the liveliness left him. "But she was too sweet for this Earth and left us far too early."

While he didn't remember Belinda, he did remember Mariel talking about her when first they met. "I am sorry that you lost your daughter at such a young age."

The older man looked away, and Marcus felt like a heel for unintentionally bringing the subject to bear. Maybe another distraction would help. "Is the Duchess bringing Lady Beaumont as well?"

Lord Wakefield turned back to look at him, his hazel eyes lost for a moment before his face lit again. "The duchess. Yes, I would have never expected Jo to marry a duke. Don't tell my wife, but I was secretly hoping she would never marry so we could continue learning together. Now, she is focused on her school and educating all the young women there. I can tell you, I'm quite proud, even if I have to share her with all of them."

"Father, what are you going on about?" The Duchess spoke from behind them.

He quickly rose and bowed. "Your grace."

She waved her hand, much like her father did. "No need for all that, Lord Blackmore. We are soon to be family after all." She continued past him to pull out the chair behind the desk and sat.

Confused, but assuming he would see Mariel soon, he resumed his seat.

"Now, has my father explained why we asked you to meet with us?"

He looked at the older man, who seemed to find everything else more interesting than meeting the gaze of his daughter. Seeing no help for it, he admitted the truth. "Only if discussing Alexander the Great's military maneuvers was your quest."

"Father." From her tone, she sounded like the man's mother. "How many times have I told you we need to do business first before learning more."

Lord Wakefield sat straighter. "Yes, of course. It was just that you arrived before I could explain."

She gave her father the side-eye before returning her attention to himself. "Lord Blackmore, I apologize. We have asked you to meet with us because I went over the betrothal agreement you made with my father and found some areas that I think could be improved upon. Since your relationship is your second with my sister, her having married thereby nullifying the former agreement, I suggested to my father that we draw up a new marriage settlement."

"Yes, that's right." Lord Wakefield nodded seriously. "I did not think I would be giving my daughter up twice, so it's important that she is well endowed."

With his chest tight at the ruse he played, he addressed his comment to Lord Wakefield. "My lord, I assure you no dowry is required."

The older man smiled before looking to his daughter. "See, Jo. I told you he would say that. He is a man in love indeed."

Though the lord's words were true, sweat began to trickle down the center of his back. Despite the fact that Mariel would be the one to end the betrothal, he felt like a criminal before the man's faith in him.

"That may be true, father, but a dowry must be accepted and Mariel's happiness assured." The duchess flipped over three pages with writing on them before running her finger down the next page where she stopped. "Lord Blackmore, I will of course let you read through the whole contract; however, my father and I have a few questions."

"Of course." He wasn't quite sure who he should be looking at. The first time he'd met with Lord Wakefield, the man had handed him the marriage settlement, asked him to sign and then offered him a scotch to celebrate. That time he'd signed without reading, perfectly happy to do whatever was necessary to marry Mariel. What a change in circumstances four years had wrought.

The duchess cleared her throat, so he focused on her. "What do you wish to know?"

"Do you intend to marry my sister this time?"

Affronted by the question, he sat straighter. "I intended to marry her the last time."

"Jo, what do you mean by that?" Lord Wakefield had sat forward as well. "The man was killed." He turned to him. "Obviously, you weren't killed. Was it a clerical error then?"

Mariel's sister clasped her hands over the documents before her. "Yes, Lord Blackmore. How is it that you were on the rolls of the dead? I was with Mariel when she saw your name. Was it a clerical error, or perhaps planned?"

Though the woman had every reason to be skeptical, his

irritation didn't lessen. "I was shot three times and left for dead on the battlefield." He expected the duchess to at least go pale, but her brows remained lowered and there was no such change in her complexion.

"Then how did you find yourself back in England, whole and hearty?"

It appeared the woman thought he'd hidden away from Mariel since the start of the war. "I was discovered that same night by an older French woman who was searching the pockets of the dead on both sides for valuables. Napoleon didn't care that his people suffered, so she kept her granddaughter and herself fed, clothed, and sheltered with what she found. Since I was not dead yet, when she went into my pocket, I woke from my painfilled doze and grabbed her hand. She offered to care for me in exchange for my help later. I was in no position to argue. Even as she dragged me through the wood, I lost consciousness due to the pain."

Though the lady no longer frowned at him, she was clearly not convinced. "Would it not have been smarter to wait for your men to find you?"

And there it was, the true reason for his horror. "My men knew I had fallen and were more inclined to report my death, since saving me meant the gallows for them."

The silence from the duchess was broken by Mariel's father, who it appeared had a keen interest now. "Had they committed a crime you witnessed then?"

He nodded, trying not to think of the crime even as the farm-house in the wood appeared in his mind. As he approached the small home, the screams inside suddenly stopped, sending a chill up his spine. "Yes, they had. I was on my way to report them when we were called into action."

"For them to leave their commanding officer to die, must mean their crime was significant." The older man's hazel eyes seemed almost as gray as his own now.

As much as he wished to keep the images at bay, they refused, filling his head. His body broke out into a sweat, even as a chill passed through him. He couldn't tell Mariel's family nor Mariel herself that he'd witnessed his men raping unconscious women, and Cobby in particular, raping a dead woman. He'd never be able to forget Cobby's grin as he noticed him in the doorway and told him he could take a turn. In that moment he'd sworn to bring Cobby and his followers to justice.

He hadn't realized the extent of his own disgust until he'd learned that Mariel had married, and tried to drown his sorrow in the best bordellos in Paris. No matter how many women he took to bed, despite how hard he became, the moment before he sunk into their bodies wishing for oblivion, the images and sounds of that night flooded him, and he lost all ability to perform. As the courtesans were paid, they did not mind, and he brought them to fulfillment in other ways.

"Lord Blackmore?"

Lord Wakefield's hand on his arm startled him, and he opened his eyes, not remembering he'd shut them. He stared at the man, whose sympathetic gaze offered comfort.

"I'm to guess it was a significant crime then."

He nodded, swallowing to force his throat to work. "It was horrific." He finally moved his attention back to the duchess. "I searched for all five men as soon as I was well enough to do so. Four have already met their fitting ends, but I still search for the last."

Lady Joanna gave him a brief nod, accepting his explanation. "And was this while on the continent?"

He glanced at Lord Wakefield, who was clearly unaware of the timeline. When he looked back at the duchess, she had her eyebrows raised in expectation of his answer. Obviously, she wanted her father to know everything.

Feeling as if he were on trial for a crime he didn't commit, he told the blatant truth. "I found two on the continent. When I came back to England, I found the other two."

The duchess set her hands down flat on the desk. "Here in

England. Yet you did not feel the need to tell Mariel you were alive?"

He rose to his feet, his anger no longer allowing him to sit. He placed both palms on the desk. "That's correct." He looked the woman in the eye, his tone deep. "I didn't contact your sister because I read of her widowhood while still abroad. It wasn't difficult to surmise that after a few short months of my absence, she had quickly turned to another." The old hurt rose in his chest.

Sitting back, the duchess didn't blink. "She married to save our family."

He stood straight. "What I knew was that she had married another. Why would I tell her I was back in England? She'd obviously had no feelings for me."

Now the duchess rose as well. "She never stopped loving you. When we read of your death, she stopped living. She was wasting away, not even eating. I told her she didn't need to marry and that I could eventually bring us back to comfort, but she needed a reason to live."

He understood Mariel's marriage may have given her purpose, but at what cost? She hid her scars from her family, yet had revealed them unwittingly to him. If she kept those a secret, it was not his place to divulge them. "That may be, but I did not know it at the time. As for any other questions, I suggest you ask Mariel as I'm finished here."

He turned on his heel and strode for the closed door. Opening it, he paused and faced the two family members who had thought to protect Mariel then and now. "You may send the marriage settlement to Blackmore House. I will review it and determine if it's acceptable. Tell Lady Beaumont I am sorry she was unavailable today."

Barely keeping himself from slamming the door, he closed it with a thud. Striding down the corridor, he heard women's voices coming from the parlor, but continued out the door once retrieving his hat. Not waiting for his footman, he pulled open the door of his coach and jumped inside, slamming it closed behind him.

He found his coach already occupied and his muscles tensed. "Who the devil are you, and what are you doing in my coach?"

The man sitting across from him was about his age with a trimmed black beard and mustache, with dark brows over green eyes. A light scar along the side of his right cheek gave him a sinister appearance and he was dressed head to toe in black.

"I suggest you send the coach to Blackmore House while we talk." The voice was gravelly as if the man had escaped the hangman's noose just in time.

Since they sat outside Craymore Hall and he didn't wish to endanger Mariel or her family, no matter how irritated he was with them, he used his walking cane to knock on the ceiling and they started to move. "There, now explain who you are and why you are here."

The man held his cane between his legs with both hands on the head. There was a large ring on one finger, but Marcus couldn't see what stone or signet it might contain.

"I'm here because I understand you search for a man by the name of Cobby."

Immediately, his interest was caught. "That is correct."

The man grinned, making the scar crinkle, giving him a maniacal visage. Then he lifted the hand with the ring, which proved to have a blood red ruby in it, and tugged at his beard.

As the hair pulled away, Marcus contemplated his options to defend himself. With the beard stripped away, he stared at the man. Why would the man disguise himself?

"Do you not recognize me?" The familiar voice held laughter as the man rubbed the scar until it made a large smudge on his face.

"Anthony!" Relief mixed with impatience. "What are you about?"

Anthony lifted his top hat and pulled the dark wig from his blond head. "I was gathering information among strangers, but after seeing their reaction to this disguise, I thought I'd test it with someone I know. You didn't know it was me. Don't deny it."

He shook his head, only now truly appreciating the lengths his friend went to for his benefit. "I would not deny it. I did not know you. But you are lucky you revealed yourself as I was about to pull the dagger from my cane."

Anthony's eyes rounded. "You were? Excellent!" He laughed, obviously very pleased with himself.

"Did you mean what you said? Do you have news of Cobby?"

His friend sobered immediately. "Yes, I do. He has returned home to Berkshire. He is aware that you are in London. My instinct tells me he is trying to figure out how to get to you. I doubt he's willing to wait until after the season."

Knowing where his enemy was had him calming. "Then I need to go there. It's time I eliminated the man from humankind. He is a danger to every woman he meets."

"No." Anthony shook his head. "He is well known in Berkshire and has far too many friends who would come to his defense. The man has a way of attracting others of his ilk. It's not safe. I suggest finishing here in London and then we can devise a scheme for drawing him out." Anthony held up the wig. "I could even disguise myself as you and you can deliver the pièce de résistance." The man flicked his wrist as if the conductor of an orchestra.

He felt like a horse biting at his bit, anxious to put an end to the threat Cobby was, but what Anthony said made sense. He had only a fortnight before Mariel would break their betrothal and while in London, they were safe for now. He had so little time left with her, and so much he wanted her to know before he set her free. Despite the pain in his chest from the thought of giving her up, it was the right thing to do. Someday, she would have the children, household, and stables she always wanted, and he would be content that she was happy.

A sudden thought chilled him. "How do we know Cobby will remain in Berkshire for the next fortnight?"

Anthony pulled the ring from his finger and dropped it in his pocket. "Because I have a man watching him. If he leaves Berkshire, we'll know."

Relieved, he finally relaxed back into the cushions of the coach. "I received word that Madame Fontaine has booked passage for herself and her granddaughter on the *Wind Sprite* and is due to arrive in England in a fortnight. See if you can secure lodgings for them in a respectable area of Town."

"She will not stay at Blackmore House?"

"No." He tensed as he imagined his mother being told a woman of the *bourgeois* class would be staying in her home. "She wishes to be in the center of the city. Blackmore House is too far if she is hoping to enjoy the entertainments of London."

Anthony studied him, obviously guessing there was another reason, but he didn't comment on it. "How was your visit with Lady Beaumont?"

"I didn't see Lady Beaumont. I probably should have had you watching the Duchess of Northwick. That woman interrogated me on why I didn't let her sister know I was alive."

"She did? Does she not know that you were severely wounded, left to die, and then heartbroken over her sister's marriage?"

He rubbed his left thigh. "She does now. She and Lord Wakefield also know that I had men I was about to report."

"You didn't tell them why, did you?" Anthony's eyes were wide at the thought. He was the only other person who knew, not because he had been there, but because he'd heard him in his delirium and again when he'd yelled out in his nightmares.

"No, I did not. To say it aloud would spread it like a disease. It is enough I must live with it and the ramifications of my injuries. As it is, I'm afraid my nightmares may return after talking around it today. Be sure no one is in my wing tonight."

"I understand."

As the silence grew, his mind started to wander back to that fateful day, but he refused to allow that. "I bought a horse for Lady Beaumont."

"You did? It seems there is much I've missed in a short time period. Tell me about it."

Thankful that Anthony was accepting of the change in topic, he proceeded to tell him of his time with Mariel while he was away.

Maybe if he could stay focused on her, he could keep his equilibrium. And maybe he could plan another opportunity to show her that making love was the ultimate pleasure.

⁂

CHAPTER THIRTEEN

MARIEL OPENED THE *Illustrated Pleasures of Seduction* and turned past the opening pages and dedication to the images of a naked man and a naked woman on facing pages. She always skipped dedications, finding them of little import. She had stopped on the facing sketches last night before deciding daylight would make it easier to read the explanations that went with the images.

If there was a way to cure her barrenness, she wanted to know. It concerned her that almost a sennight had passed since being with Marcus at Tattersall's. She'd expected to see him before the ball planned to celebrate their reunion, but he hadn't called.

She stared at the pages, unseeing. She needed to know if there was hope before next they were in each other's company.

Looking upward, she spoke to the empty room. "Belinda, I know you never talked about having children as if you knew you never would. Yet you always spoke about the games we played and how I would teach them to my daughters. If there is any guidance in this book to cure my barrenness, please help me find it." Closing her eyes, she remembered Belinda as a child as they acted, or attempted to act in one of Joanna's plays. Her sister's laughter was so clear that she opened her eyes looking for her. Shaking her head at her fancy, she gave the book her full attention.

From the title, she imagined that having pleasure helped with procreation. That gave her hope since she felt much pleasure when Marcus kissed her lips and other places on her body. She flushed at the memory of what he'd kissed in the coach. Having his love made her feel so different from her late husband. Now, she was anxious to learn more.

Settling herself on her armchair in her room, she cradled the book on her lap. The sunlight streamed in behind her, making the drawings very clear. She studied the man first. Her husband had always worn his night shirt, so all she'd seen of him was occasionally his skinny bowed legs. When he'd been drinking late into the night, he'd just unbutton the fall of his breaches, and she'd wake to find him between her legs.

The man in the sketch resembled Marcus, or how she would guess he looked without clothes, much more than George. The sketch was of a man of about thirty with dark hair and a smattering of hair on his chest. Did Marcus also have that? What would it feel like? The hair on his head was very silky and she rather enjoyed touching it. She'd seen a couple naked chests in her life, mainly by accident, but the sketch gave her a chance to study it. Unlike Amelia, she had not studied nude statues in Italy and unlike Joanna, she hadn't known how procreation happened until she'd married.

At that thought, she moved her gaze lower to study that piece of a man that made him such. She swallowed down the bile that rose in her throat. She was well aware of the flaccid state. George would call her a cold fish when his manhood didn't work as he wished, while she had always thought those times were a relief.

As she examined the man's legs, she knew that Marcus would have limbs that were much stronger. He was terribly athletic with all the riding he'd done as a young man and most assuredly as an officer. Would she ever see his legs? Even in the coach she'd seen nothing of him while he'd seen as much of her as her late husband.

Moving her gaze to the facing page, she found the image much more familiar. The naked woman sketched there had her hair down as if getting ready to plait it before going to sleep. Her breasts and waist and legs were very much like her own, except her hips were much more rounded than the sketch, at least from the few times she caught her own image in the looking glass after bathing. She generally avoided the sight as it didn't seem proper.

Turning the page, she found images on facing pages again, but this time they were enlarged sketches of the area between the legs. Shuttering at the male image, she focused on the woman and frowned. Could that be right? There were multiple folds and a peak that she wasn't sure she had. The identification of each area was clearly marked with a brief explanation. One such marking remarked it was a "pleasure point" and another marking simply stated "sheath, where the penis enters."

Anything about a man entering a woman's body gave her the chills and she quickly turned the page. Sucking in her breath, she stared in shock. It was a man procreating with a woman and they were both naked. Surely that couldn't be it. Had she not conceived because George and she had not been naked? More importantly, if she and Marcus were naked, could she become with child? She needed to ask one of her sisters. Joanna? No, definitely not. Definitely Amelia. But at the thought of her youngest sister's reaction to her question, she negated that idea. Hopefully, the book would explain everything.

A phrase from Joanna's letter floated through her mind. *I'm sure that you know much of what is between these pages, but I have it on good authority that even the most knowledgeable person can find something new.* Shaking her head, she whispered. "I am far more ignorant than you think. But it's time I learned more."

The only words on the page were "Before this." So she turned it to find a man and woman clothed with the man kissing the woman below her ear. Not a little confused, she read the caption. "There's this." It took her a moment to sort out what the author meant. It sounded as if kissing was indeed supposed to come before procreating.

Excited that she'd already learned of two reasons why she hadn't got with child while married, she quickly turned the page. As she read and studied, the couple in the sketches were slowly devested of their clothing, touching and kissing each other as they went. The author explained how the man could tell a woman was pleasured, which included hard nipples, short breaths, rapid heartbeat, and moans. She couldn't imagine herself moaning. George had told her she shouldn't make a sound, yet he grunted like a wild boar. Had he really known so little about getting a woman with child? Was that why at his age he'd been so desperate?

She had felt guilty that she'd been unable to fulfill her part of the marriage settlement before he'd passed, but now it was clear that neither of them knew what they were doing. She finally understood Joanna's zeal for teaching and learning. Did Marcus know how everything was to be done? Based on what he'd shown her, she was quite sure he understood, which meant the possibility of having a child was much better.

Happier than she'd been since Marcus left for the war, she turned the page, anxious to know it all. "Oh." She pressed her hand to her chest, but quickly dropped it as her arm brushed her own breast. The sketch now had the couple lying down, she on her back with her legs spread. He leaned on an elbow while his other hand showed a finger disappearing between her thighs.

Though she'd felt flushed before, her breathing now grew shallow and a strange moisture gathered between her own legs. A little worried she might be growing ill, she forced herself to read the page in case she'd have to put the book away for a few days. "If your woman is not wet and slick inside, then you need to stimulate more pleasure. Move your finger to her pleasure point and gently rub, while taking a nipple into your mouth as seen on the following page. The more moisture she produces, the more pleasure you both will have."

Feeling herself growing hotter, she wished her clothes off, which made no sense. Quickly, she flipped the page. The sketch was exactly as indicated. The written material stated that only when the woman was hot with need, was it appropriate to slip inside. Noting the page she was on, she closed the book and set it on the side table.

She was reacting like the woman in the sketches and Marcus wasn't even with her. She rose and opened a window. The slight breeze and growing clouds made the air feel cool against her heated skin. There was so much more to having children than she'd imagined. She walked to her dressing table and retrieved her fan, opening it and cooling herself.

Sinking onto the chair before her looking glass, she stared at herself as she continued to ply the fan. Her cheeks were flushed as was her chest above the neckline of her beige day dress. Was this the result of what the books called making love? She already loved Marcus. She obviously was able to feel what she was supposed to feel. No, she didn't like the idea of being "penetrated," but if they did it right, she could possibly give him an heir.

The idea, so new and exciting, had her rising. She must speak with him about her discovery, without giving any details, of course. She couldn't speak of such private matters as written about in the book, and if he already knew of them, then they could definitely have children.

A niggling doubt spoiled her happiness. Would he want to marry if he could gain an heir with her? She set the fan down. She couldn't bear for him to deny her again. She walked back to the window to close it when her gaze landed on the clock. She was supposed to be meeting her mother in the dining room to discuss the final details of the ball celebrating her betrothal, though not a betrothal ball.

Quickly, she turned on her heel and headed out of the room with a new hope burning brightly in her chest. They were only calling it a celebration among the family, since she'd already been betrothed, married, and widowed, but it would be the first ball she and Marcus attended together. She had been uncomfortable planning the false celebration, but now she would ensure every detail was perfect. She wanted Marcus to be proud of her abilities to entertain as well as ride. If everything went according to her plans, they could be married before the end of the season.

MARIEL STOOD NEXT to her younger sister, Amelia, who practically sparkled in a bright yellow gown. They quietly watched the dancers, her own gaze wandering to where Marcus stood next to his mother, looking very dashing in his black tailcoat, breeches, and white shirt. He'd been quite distant since arriving, which made her nervous.

After her sister informed her that they had spoken about a new marriage settlement, she'd expected him to call on her. But when three days went by, even her mother started looking askance at her. Finally, she'd written him to see if anything was amiss. The polite letter she'd received in return simply stated that his mother had him calling on her friends and he looked forward to her ball.

"You two make an aesthetically pleasing couple."

Amelia's sudden remark let her know she'd been caught staring, so she turned her head to address her sister. "Do you think so?"

"I do. You complement each other very well. I didn't think so before he left for the war, but you have both changed and now you make the perfect pair for a painting."

Amelia's views on how people looked together meant much to her. "I hope that means we will have a happy future together."

Her sister shrugged one shoulder. "Appearance is only that, but sometimes it's more, and I must say that emerald-green dress makes you shine."

She looked down at the bright color she wore. It wasn't her

norm, usually preferring a darker green, but when she'd seen the material a fortnight past, she purchased it on impulse. "That does make me feel a bit better. I thought people were just making an excuse to talk to me when they mentioned it, so they could find out more details about my betrothal."

Amelia laughed, her eyes alight with mischief. "I have no doubt they are using your beauty to get the latest *on dit* about you."

"I thought that might be the motivation, so I kept all details to myself." She grinned, pleased she'd been completely evasive and proper. Spotting the Earl of Sommerset leaving the room with their father, she gestured that way. "I believe Father has absconded with your husband. You may have to go looking for him when supper is rung."

Amelia waved her hand as if it were nothing for her husband to be leaving the ballroom. "He already told me he may disappear because father purchased a new book of Grecian statues."

"Statues? I though your husband collected paintings."

"Oh, he does, but ever since I created my masterpiece with his help, he's reading more and more about statues. I certainly hope he neither expects me to take up sculpting nor that he starts purchasing them. Lyonsmere already looks like a perpetual art exhibit."

That didn't surprise her since the earl had collected artwork before he met Amelia, and Amelia had been adding her own artwork to the collection. "You never did show us your master-piece you painted with him." She had a notion as to possibly why, since he'd had to pose nude for it, but surely Amelia would have added clothes.

A secret smile formed on her sister's face. "Nor will you ever see it. It is far too personal, but it is magnificent. I would prefer not to have my sisters and mother ogling the painting of my naked husband."

She widened her eyes. "You left him nude?"

"Of course, that was our bargain." Amelia looked askance at

her. "Have you not seen Marcus without clothes?"

"Of course not. It's not proper." She leaned in. "Not everyone gets to view their spouse before marriage. You are very lucky you weren't caught."

Amelia looked her in the eye. "Don't you wonder though?" She moved her gaze to where Marcus stood. "I imagine he is quite well made."

She sucked in her breath through her teeth.

Amelia raised her hand. "I speak from an aesthetical viewpoint only. I'm sure you will be pleased with his form." Amelia crinkled her nose. "He must be a sight better than Beaumont."

Since she hadn't actually seen her husband naked, she couldn't comment. But for the last few nights, her dreams had been filled with the sketches in Joanna's book, only the man in them had Marcus' face.

"Mariel, did you not see Beaumont nude?" Amelia's voice rose with her incredulity.

She quickly scanned their immediate vicinity and grabbed her sister's hand, giving it a tug. "Shh. There are too many people about."

"Well, I'm glad you never saw the man naked." Amelia controlled the volume of her voice. "I couldn't imagine bedding a frog like him."

Even at the thought of George naked, she shivered. If she'd seen him, would she ever wish to procreate again?

Amelia's hand in hers, squeezed. "You poor thing. I didn't realize what you lived with until just this moment. I'm very pleased that you will finally be with the man you love."

Her sister didn't let go of her, instead, she started to stroll, forcing her to join her. "Are you going to seek out your husband?"

"No, we're going to talk to Lady Blackmore. You haven't danced with the viscount all evening. It won't offend anyone's sensibilities if you happen to see if his mother is enjoying the ball you planned."

She did want to talk to Lady Blackmore, but even more so Marcus. She had hoped he'd seek her out, but except for when he entered, he'd not looked for her. Had he already found someone else? At the thought, her heart shuddered.

As they approached, she noticed Lady Dowling talking to him, her daughter simply staring. Her heart squeezed at the obvious admiration of the younger woman as she watched Marcus while he spoke to her mother.

Lady Blackmore observed their approach and said something to her son before smiling at them. "Lady Beaumont. Lady Sommerset. What a lovely ball. Lady Beaumont, your mother couldn't praise you enough for arranging everything. Was it your idea to offer multiple tables about the room with punch?"

She puffed with pride. "It was. I thought it would eliminate a crush after each dance."

"And so it has. I shall be sure to do the same at my next event. Then again, if I wait long enough, I'll be able to simply attend." The woman gave her a knowing look.

"I'm pleased that you think the idea worthy. I do enjoy planning such events." It was the truth. She just wasn't sure if she'd have a chance to plan another.

"Do you hear that, Marcus?"

She had felt his gaze upon her the moment Lady Blackmore spoke to them, but had purposefully kept her attention on his mother. Now that he'd been invited into the conversation, she allowed herself to look at him, wishing they could be anywhere but in the middle of the ballroom.

He smiled politely. "I do. Lady Beaumont has always excelled at planning."

Though his words were appropriate, there was no warmth in his voice. Something was wrong. "And I believe that you, my lord, are quite good at extemporaneous events, am I correct?"

He gave her a nod. "I am. Sometimes not knowing what reaction will occur due to an action makes for quite a bit of excitement."

From the look in his eyes, she could see he meant something beyond his words, but she didn't understand. "I must accept your knowledge on that score."

"I would much rather you experienced it." His gaze locked with hers, searching for something.

His mother replied. "Yes, well, look at how well that treated you. You went off—"

"Lady Beaumont." Marcus offered his arm. "Would you care to walk in the garden? I'm finding it a bit warm in here."

Not a little surprised he'd interrupt his mother, she simply nodded, biting her tongue that it would be no cooler outside. She placed her hand on his arm and allowed him to walk her toward the closest terrace doors.

Though Lady Dulac and Lord Hennings separately attempted to intercept them, Marcus side-stepped further conversation. That could only mean that he wished to speak to her about something important. She found herself beginning to perspire, and pulled her fan from her pocket, using it with efficiency as Lady Astor looked as if she would engage her.

Finally, they stepped out onto the terrace. The additional lanterns she'd had placed in the garden didn't leave many shadows just outside the ballroom doors. Marcus turned to their right and strolled out of the lighted area and into the darkness near the dolphin fountain, whose flow of water minimized the ballroom sounds. Suddenly, he halted.

She looked at him in question, having just enough light to see the frown on his face. "What is it?"

His lips parted then closed then parted again. Suddenly, she found herself embraced and her chin lifted. Again he opened his mouth, but instead of speaking, he kissed her.

Not expecting it, she lost her balance as his need for her communicated itself to her body and her knees went weak, his tongue sweeping into her mouth like a conqueror. Grasping him around the neck as much to keep from falling as to enjoy the kiss, she found all her doubts floating away.

As abruptly as the kiss started, it ended and he unlinked her hands from around his neck before stepping back. "I apologize."

It took her a moment to regain her balance both physically and mentally, and still she was thoroughly confused. "I don't understand."

His hand moved to his left thigh, kneading the fabric of his black breeches. "I know. I wish that I could explain."

Marcus had never had difficulties talking to her, so it must be something of great concern. The only subject that came to mind was the contract Joanna mentioned. "Is it the marriage settlement? You don't need to sign it." She didn't want him to obligate himself unless he was absolutely sure.

"Yes. No." He turned away to stare at the fountain in the darkness. Ambient light filtered through the garden from the upper story windows, reflecting off the patina of the dolphins as they forever leapt upward in abandon. "It is not the settlement." He whirled around to face her. "You do know that I was wounded and left for dead. I did not pretend to be dead. I was anxious to get back and marry you."

Her heart skipped a beat at his admission. "I know you were wounded. I didn't know you were left to die." The thought of him lying on a battlefield bleeding and unable to find help, made her want to cry.

He moved away again, back toward the fountain, clearly upset.

She stepped closer, wanting to comfort, but not knowing what he needed. Since he faced the fountain, she sat on the edge to look at him. "Why did you mention your injuries when I asked about the marriage settlement?"

He didn't look at her, his eyes focused on something else, perhaps in the past. "Your sister questioned why I was declared dead." He glanced at her.

"She did not tell me that. She doesn't know when not to pry."

A slight sneer appeared, but he turned his head away. "She was right to ask the questions she did. Unfortunately, the answers have caused my nightmares of the...war to return. They are disturbing and have kept me up most hours of the night. I didn't call on you to keep my ugliness away, but seeing you tonight..."

She held her breath, unsure what he would say.

For the longest time, he stared into the darkness, not moving. When he did move, it was to slowly rest his gaze on her, but not simply her eyes. His gaze roamed over her face as if memorizing it.

A chill ran up her spine. Why did she fear losing him when she didn't truly have him?

Finally, he spoke. "Seeing you tonight, I have realized that staying away made it worse." He lifted his foot onto the fountain next to her and cupped her chin. "You are the goodness I need to keep the ugliness at bay. I don't know what I will do when we part."

Anticipation filled her as she searched for the words she needed to tell him. Too impatient to phrase it politely, she blurted it out. "I don't think I'm barren."

He dropped his hand as a light chuckle floated through the air. "You don't? Why is that?"

She'd been thinking about it for the last few days and she was quite positive she was correct. "My late husband and I were doing it incorrectly."

He immediately sobered, his foot coming down to the stone pathway with a thud. "What do you mean?"

The tension radiating off him didn't make sense to her. It was as if he were horrified and furious at the same time. It was supposed to be good news. Maybe she wasn't explaining it properly, though how to talk about such a subject appropriately was a bit beyond her knowledge. "I mean that the way we procreated was not the way it's supposed to be done."

Instead of relaxing him, his body seemed to stiffen more and his gaze became piercing. "Did he force you?"

"Force me? No, of course not. It was my duty. But we didn't..." Heat filled her cheeks and she was thankful for the cover of darkness. "We didn't kiss or undress." Now she felt like sinking into the fountain water, but that was not possible.

Marcus sat down next to her and took her gloved hand. "So you didn't make love. You believe that's why you didn't produce a child."

She nodded with relief. He *did* understand.

Lifting her hand to his mouth, he kissed the back of her glove. "Mariel, I have always doubted your claim of barrenness, but while making love is the most enjoyable way to get with child, it is not required."

She stared at him in shock. "You haven't believed I'm barren? But I thought that's why you cannot marry me because you need an heir."

It was his turn to be surprised, his hand squeezing hers in response. "Not at all. It is because I believe you can still have children that I can't marry you."

Completely confused and not a little irritated, she pulled her hand from his and stood, pleased she could look down on him for once. "Then sir, instead of leaving me to conjure up yet another excuse, tell me why it is that we can't marry if I can give you an heir."

His shoulders fell and instead of looking at her, he spoke to the ground. "It's because I cannot give you children."

She froze, the truth filling in the missing pieces. He wanted her to have the family he knew she always wanted and because he couldn't give it to her, he would not marry her? For him to make such a sacrifice meant he loved her more than she knew.

Sinking down on the edge of the stone basin next to him, she took his closest hand in both of hers. "Marcus, I have always wanted a family, but I have always wanted you more."

His gaze lifted to meet hers. "But I could not live with myself knowing I took you away from motherhood. That would be far too selfish of me."

Her heart squeezed and her eyes stung with tears. "But I don't want to lose you. I may never have children anyway. I am old already and my heart has always been yours."

Instead of answering her, he brushed his lips across hers. "We best get you back to the ballroom."

"But—" His finger on her lips silenced her.

"You may be a widow, but your reputation is still important. I promise to call upon you in two days' time." He rose, taking her hand and encouraging her to stand.

If he wished to continue their conversation in two days' time, then she would be open to it. And if he didn't wish to resume their topic, she would anyway. Rising, she laid her hand on his arm, and he walked them back into the light of the terrace.

"Oh, there you are." Lady Blackmore stood on the top of the steps. "I was looking for you. It is almost the supper dance and I do believe you two should lead it off." She practically exuded excitement. "It's time everyone saw how well you two suit each other."

She was quite willing, but Marcus would need to ask her.

As they approached his mother, she started to think he wouldn't do as suggested, but when they were on the top step, he turned to her. "Lady Beaumont, would you do me the honor of allowing me to partner you for the supper dance?"

She smiled, her belly jumping with happiness. "I would enjoy that immensely, Lord Blackmore."

His mother sighed. "Perfect."

Marcus held his arm out to his mother. Once she took it, the three of them returned to the ballroom just in time for the dance.

As they lined up opposite one another, Mariel's mind was spinning with ways to convince Marcus that he was far more important than a family. She'd already lost him once, and she didn't plan to lose him again.

As everyone moved into position, the couple she and Marcus were with suddenly left their places, and the Duke and Joanna replaced them. Her sister leaned in. "I thought it best to show our guests that James and I approve of this match." Her smile was triumphant as she stood straight again and grinned at her husband.

It was no secret that Joanna and her husband often danced the waltz while at a ball, but they never danced the Quadrille. Looking at the duke, she could tell it wasn't his favorite activity, but he willingly did so for her sister.

Now if she could just get Marcus to do what she wished him to do. She'd have to ask Joanna how she managed it.

Joanna winked at her husband just as the first strains of music started and the duke's nostrils flared.

Mariel missed the first step, she was so surprised by the man's reaction, but a note in the book Joanna had lent her answered her question. Joanna had promised the duke they'd make love if he did this for her!

As she linked arms with Marcus, then separated back to her place, she grinned. It looked as if she'd be busy reading a certain book over the next two days, so she too could entice her man to do as she wished.

CHAPTER FOURTEEN

MARCUS HANDED MARIEL up into his phaeton, not unaware of her dress choice for their ride in Hyde Park. The shimmering pale blue and gold brocade pattern would turn many heads and was a reminder of how she'd dressed before he'd left the country. It even appeared to make her happier. She also wore a simple bonnet made of the same material tied beneath her chin with pale blue ribbons that matched. Mariel's quiet elegance had always made her stand out from other ladies.

Walking around to his side, he climbed up, taking the reins and nodded to the footman holding Legend and Lore. As soon as the man stepped aside, he set the horses to moving down the curved drive to the street. It had been only two days without her, yet upon waking, he found himself smiling, knowing he would be with her soon.

It was the perfect Sunday afternoon for a ride through Hyde Park in his open conveyance. The sun shone, the air was a pleasant temperature, and there was a slight breeze keeping the usual smells of the city at bay. They had very little time left together, and he intended to enjoy every moment with her. Though he'd planned to take her to see the latest art exhibit at the London Academy of Art, when the day dawned, it promised such fine weather, he'd sent a note earlier. "I hope you don't mind the change in our plans."

"Not at all. It feels so good to be outside after a whole year of gray skies. Though truth be told, I'd rather be about on Zephyrus." She leaned closer, a whiff of orange blossom floating past his nose. "Don't tell anyone though. It just wouldn't be proper for me to traipse about Hyde Park on my steed."

He glanced at her to find a teasing light in her eyes. "I promise it will be our secret among all the others."

"Oh, I'm sure there will be many more as well."

At her sly tone of voice, he looked at her, but she faced forward and all he could see was the edge of her bonnet. Focusing instead on driving the pair of thoroughbreds, he navigated around the more congested parts of the city to arrive at Cumberland Gate, the east end of the park. As he directed his team beneath the tall arch, there were already a number of people enjoying the day, some in coaches, some in open conveyances like his, and still others strolling the paths.

They'd just entered Rotten Row when Mariel sat forward. "Oh, there's Lady Astor and her daughter Elsbeth. Elsbeth is one of Joanna's students and Lady Astor is one of her teachers." She leaned in as if someone might hear. "Lady Elsbeth is the one who turned down my cousin, Teddy's, proposal."

He'd forgotten her younger cousin. His impression of him had been of a young man about town, more interested in wit than substance.

Mariel waved to the two ladies riding toward them in another open phaeton. "You met them at the ball the other night, remember?"

He'd met many people the other night, but doubted he'd remember them since his focus had been on Mariel the entire evening, even if he'd tried to avoid her company. He'd been an idiot to think being apart would help rid himself of his nightmare. Being in her very presence had soothed his spirit, and he'd slept soundly since.

Maneuvering Legend and Lore to the side, he pulled them up next to the ladies' now stopped phaeton.

Mariel smiled widely, proving she truly liked the two women and was not simply being polite. "Lady Astor. Lady Elsbeth. Do you remember Lord Blackmore?"

The older woman, dressed in a pale blue day dress, nodded. "Indeed we do. Lord Blackmore, what a lovely idea to bring Lady Beaumont out for a drive on such a splendid day. We rarely see her in the park."

He lifted his eyebrows in question at that news. "Then the park has been the worse for her absence. She is far more beautiful than the day."

All three women reacted to his comment. Mariel blushed prettily, while Lady Elsbeth sighed, and Lady Astor nodded with approval. "My lord, it is obvious that Lady Beaumont is better for your company as well." She glanced at her companion. "My daughter has no one to bring her about and so it is left to me. She'd rather have her nose in some geology book or be studying a rock brought over from the continent." Though the woman made it sound like a complaint, she was clearly proud of that fact.

"Lord Blackmore, my mother would have you believe that I dig in the dirt for such finds, but I assure you they are shipped cleaned and ready for examination. In fact, my mother and I were just discussing how to convince my cousin to allow us to visit the Dragon Caves in Spain, so that I might see for myself the intricacies of the stalagmites and stalactites."

He hadn't heard anyone speak of the Cuevas del Drach since he was at Oxford. Not sure how to respond, he was saved the effort by Mariel.

"Would you like me to make the suggestion to Joanna? I'm sure she'd approve and she has a way of convincing the duke to look at ideas in a new light."

Lady Astor laughed. "That is quite true, and in fact, we were just discussing that avenue."

There appeared to be a subtext beneath the conversation that he was not privy to. Still, he thought it unusual that Lady Astor would encourage her daughter to explore such a subject in another country, especially as she had just complained of the young woman's lack of husband prospects.

Mariel placed her hand on his arm, a movement noted by the two women. "Then we shall let you continue your strategizing, and if you need any help from me, please don't hesitate to call on me."

"We may very well come to you. Thank you."

As they said their goodbyes, he started the horses moving forward once again. "I don't understand why Lady Astor would encourage her daughter's pursuit of geological knowledge when she obviously wishes Lady Elsbeth to find a husband."

Mariel's hand which still remained on his arm was joined by her other hand as she held on to him, which was far too familiar in such a public setting, but which he was too pleased by her comfort with him to discourage her.

"As I said, Lady Elsbeth is one of Joanna's students. She has finished her first year of general studies and now will be pursuing her primary interest. This is how the Belinda School for Curious Ladies operates. With Lady Astor as one of the instructors, it is only fitting that she encourage her daughter."

He obviously hadn't truly understood the duchess' school. "That is a rather unorthodox educational objective for a ladies' finishing school."

Mariel laughed, the sound filled with happiness. "Oh, Joanna could never run a finishing school. She wouldn't know where to start. Her school is about offering women of the aristocracy a similar education to what men receive at Oxford or Cambridge. Of course, she is still only in her first year and it is highly experimental, but both the daughters and mothers seem to be quite pleased."

He had to ask. "And what of the fathers?"

"Why, I don't know what the fathers think, but since they are supporting their daughters' attendance, I can only surmise that they are pleased as well."

So this was what she'd meant about her family when she

labeled them as odd. "With your sister running such a school and your other sister becoming a celebrated artist, I'm surprised you do not wish to become a tightrope walker." He didn't mean his comment to be a criticism, but as Mariel released his arm and sat back to look forward again, it was clear she'd assumed it was so.

"I may not be as unusual and as interesting as my sisters, but I'm still very proud of them."

"Unusual? Mariel, you wish to breed horses. I would say that qualifies."

Her head snapped toward him and a slow smile spread her lips. "Actually, I've revised my ambition. Now I wish to train ladies' horses. It's obvious no one has accomplished that feat yet."

He raised his brow. "Only ladies' horses."

She nodded emphatically. "Yes, only ladies. There are plenty of men to train horses for their gender."

He thought to argue the point, but at the secret smile she sported, all thoughts vanished except that he wished to kiss her. Something he could not do on Rotten Row in Hyde Park, but he could once back at Blackmore House. "I have another surprise for you if you'd be willing to forego being seen together by the rest of the *ton*."

She wrinkled her nose, something she hadn't done when he'd first met her. "I never feel the need to be seen and would happily leave to discover whatever you have planned."

He grinned, anxious to see her face when he presented her with Hector. Hopefully, a kiss of gratefulness could be bestowed upon him then. "Then next we travel to Blackmore House."

Her eyes widened. "Blackmore House? Is that where my surprise is?"

"It is." He turned the phaeton half way down the lane and moved it in to return the way they'd come. "If you do not like it, you need not accept it."

"If it is from you, then I know I will like it. No one knows me as well as you do, except my sisters."

Her statement humbled him while at the same time was a

reminder that their time would soon be over. He would not break the betrothal, but he would have to insist she keep their agreement and do so. The thought was like ice thrown upon a fire, but he refused to dwell on what would be and enjoy what they had for now.

Unfortunately, it took longer leaving the park than he preferred as many seemed intent on stopping them and discussing the weather, the duke and duchess, the ball, and the latest gossip. Their arrival at Blackmore House would be so delayed that they would have little time before he must return her to Claymore Hall or her reputation could be called into question.

Taking the road beyond Hyde Park, he led Legend and Lore to the outskirts through open fields boarded by trees. A few stately homes sat not far from the road, some new, some older like his own. Finally, he turned his team left, up the short drive to Blackmore House. Passing the front steps, he stopped them before the stable, much smaller than at Ravenridge. Impatiently, he waited for a groomsman to come out and hold the horses as he alighted and helped Mariel down. After giving the man instructions on caring for the team, he walked back to her.

"Mr. Clancy is not with you in Town?"

Though his home was on the outer edges of London, he didn't consider it quite in Town, but as the city continued to grow, he had no doubt it would be soon. "No, he says travelling causes his bones to rattle, and as he is so valuable to me at Ravenridge, I do not insist."

She nodded in understanding. "You are very kind. I agree that a man of Mr. Clancy's talents should be accommodated."

Pleased she felt as he did, he offered her his arm. "Would you like to see your surprise?" Anticipating her reaction, he couldn't wait to bring her inside.

"I would indeed. Lead on." Her emerald eyes sparkled with excitement, making him wish he could fulfill her every wish.

Forcing himself to look away, he led her into the stable.

"My surprise is in here?" She looked about the eight-stall

building. "Quite an unusual place to keep a gift. Perhaps you are going to show me how to do something?"

At the seductive tone of her voice, his body reacted. That made no sense. Mariel knew naught of such things, even if she'd been married. He must stop thinking of her in that way.

He halted before a stall. "I purchased him for you as I could not imagine anyone else who could help him flourish." He held his hand out toward Hector, who stood at the back of the enclosure watching them, much like he had at Tattersall's.

Her eyes rounded as she viewed the horse then turned to him, her smile wide. "I can't believe it. Thank you. He is the most wonderful gift I've ever received." Rising on her toes, she took his head in her hands and pressed a chaste kiss on his lips before turning back toward Hector.

Her reaction was more than he'd hoped and had his heart tightening. He wanted to give her far more than simply a damaged horse, and yet she claimed it to be her best gift. Suddenly, he wanted to give her the necklace back that she'd thrown to the ground only two months earlier. But it wouldn't be right, knowing she was destined for a better life without him.

So focused on his own thoughts, he missed her entrance into the stall. She approached the horse slowly.

"He is not combative, just scared. He shakes when people come near." He remained outside the stall, wanting her to be the person Hector saw as his savior.

Mariel didn't respond to him, continuing to walk toward the now shaking horse. "Now, Hector. There is no need to be afraid. You and I will be fast friends soon. I hope you will shake with excitement knowing we are about to gallop across the fields of Thornhill. I have a pretty mare that I think you would like very much."

Her quiet voice was soothing, but the horse continued to shake. It was so obvious that even his own groomsmen had noticed it.

She now stood next to Hector and held her hand out near his

nose, but not quite close enough that he could smell it. Curiosity must have got the better of fear as he turned his head to sniff at her.

"I want you to always remember my scent." The voice remained soothing. "Then you'll know you're safe and loved."

Holding on to the stall gate, he found himself gripping it hard as he watched Mariel in her element. Right now, he wanted more than anything to simply take her as his wife and love her as much as he was capable. She already had his heart. And there was the rub. Because he loved her, he couldn't take away her dream of having a family. She would no doubt insist on her children sitting at the table with her as opposed to in the nursery like her own mother had. He wanted that. He wanted her.

He forced himself to let go of the bars and step back. As much as he wished it, he could not allow it. Maybe he should stop torturing himself and have her call off the betrothal this week.

"You are such a handsome horse. These scars just prove you are strong and a survivor. To me it makes you noble and I can only hope to be worthy of you."

He watched as she gently laid her hand against the horse's neck, her very words making it hard for him to swallow. It was as if she spoke to him.

The horse stepped back, and she dropped her hand. "I understand. Thank you for meeting me. I will see you again soon."

As she slowly walked toward the gate, he called himself a fool, much like the horse who was still wary. But unlike the horse, he understood where Mariel belonged.

Unlatching the gate, she slipped out and closed it. "I will see you soon, Hector."

The horse's ear twitched at the sound of his name, but otherwise remained where he was, though he no longer shook. Why did he feel like he was Hector?

Mariel strolled toward him, but didn't stop a few feet away. Instead, she looped her arms around his neck and pressed her body against him. "I want to thank you properly."

What he should do is set her back from him, but he was a man. He was weak and he was in love with her. Unable to stop himself, he wrapped her in his arms and lowered his head, powerless to resist the call of her lips.

As his mouth covered hers, she opened and her tongue thrust forward to tangle with his. Her uncharacteristic actions made him curious, and he allowed her free rein to explore. Being passive was not his strong suit, yet as his body reacted to her assertiveness, he didn't take control. But he couldn't help cupping her arse to press her closer.

When she broke the kiss, he loosened his hold, though he wanted far more. She pulled her hands down and he dropped his arms only to find her unbuttoning his tailcoat. He should stop her, but it was so unlike Mariel that he stood frozen in place. She pushed the coat from his shoulders and dropped it over the stall wall.

"Mariel, what are you about?" He kept his voice low, so as not to startle her.

"It's too many clothes." Almost frantic now, she unbuttoned his black shirt and started to pull it from his pantaloons.

He glanced toward the open doors of the stables, knowing any moment the groomsmen would return from cooling down the horses. Placing his hand over her two small ones, he effectively halted her movements. "Come. The stables are not the place."

At her unladylike grunt, he had to stifle a chuckle as he grabbed his tailcoat and took her hand to lead her outside into Blackmore House's back gardens. He brought her to the closest bench set among his mother's aurora blue delphinium.

She abruptly sat with a pout.

Dropping his coat on the back of the bench, he set his foot upon it. "Why do you look so disheartened?"

She didn't look up at him, and he had to lean down to hear her. "I must be doing it wrong."

He lifted her chin with his finger. "What are you doing

wrong?"

She met his gaze full on. "I was trying to seduce you."

His entire body seemed to heat at once, and he dropped his hand. "Why would you wish to do that? Our betrothal is only temporary."

Her gaze shifted for a moment. When it returned to him, her eyes appeared tear-filled. "Because, if we are not to marry, I want to know what it would be like to truly make love to the only man I will ever love."

His chest tightened seeing the truth in her eyes. He could deny her nothing, even knowing what would happen. He removed his foot from the bench and pulled her up by both hands, then he swept her up into his arms, carrying her toward the house. If he was going to bring her fulfillment, even if he couldn't join her, it would be in a bed. She deserved that dignity.

"Oh." Her arms wrapped around his neck. "Marcus, what are you doing?"

"I'm granting your request."

CHAPTER FIFTEEN

MARIEL FELT LIGHT as a feather, though she was anything but as the tallest of the Mabry sisters. Still, being in Marcus' strong arms, knowing she would soon discover the wonder that the book she'd read had described in too vague detail, had her feeling lighter than air.

As he strode toward the grand house, she couldn't help wondering which position from the book he might choose. Would it feel as wonderful as suggested? Would she be *ready* for him and would he know what to do? A niggling doubt wormed its way into her thoughts that it would end in procreating, which she'd never enjoyed, but to be with Marcus was all she'd dreamed about, so she'd accept it.

"Door, please."

At his request, she turned the knob and he strode in. With firm footsteps, he travelled down the corridor with her in his arms. She was about to tell him she was perfectly capable of walking when the butler appeared out of nowhere.

"Sir, can I be of assistance?"

Without even breaking his stride, he addressed his man. "Yes, Gibson. Have Cook wrap a piece of ice in a cloth and send it up to the gold bedroom." He looked at her then added. "Lady Beaumont has twisted her ankle and is feeling faint. Have smelling salts sent up as well."

Grimacing to stifle a smile, she hoped she looked as if she were in pain. Why Marcus kept trying to protect her reputation when she had no intention of ever marrying anyone else was beyond her. Now that she thought about it, perhaps a compromising situation would force him to wed her. Even as the thought occurred, she shoved it away. She wanted him to marry her because he wished to, not because he had to.

At least one question she had was put to rest. Though he couldn't have children, he must still be able to make love if he was so anxious to grant her request. At the top of the stairs, he turned right and strode down another corridor. He passed four doors before stopping. "Door."

She let go of his neck with one hand and turned the knob.

He pushed the door open with his foot and laid her on the pale blue brocade quilt on the bed.

She grinned. He'd not said a word about her dress earlier, but that was never his way to comment on mundane things, yet he'd obviously noticed. The room he'd chosen was covered in gold brocade wallpaper with pale blue accents throughout.

"Why are you smiling? You're supposed to be in pain." Though he scolded, his voice held humor as if he held back a laugh.

She cocked her head and raised her brows. "Unfortunately, or rather fortunately, I've never twisted my ankle before. Is it quite painful?"

He shrugged. "Bugger if I know."

She swallowed a laugh. "Should I moan?"

His own grin froze. "No, just grimace when I touch it."

"That should be easy to do."

He frowned at her, but she didn't elaborate. She wasn't about to discuss her past husband. Instead, she watched him slip off her walking shoe, his touch very light. He scanned the room before taking a pillow from an arm chair and placing it under her foot. "Should you close your shirt then?"

He looked down as if he'd forgotten she'd unbuttoned it.

Quickly, he refastened it. "I don't imagine my butler saw that since I had you in my arms."

Footsteps in the corridor had her looking to him for instruction. He'd always been so good at navigating sudden changes, but coming up with this story so quickly had her admiring his intellect even more.

He caught her gaze and lowered his voice. "Just close your eyes and when I touch your ankle, grimace."

She immediately closed her eyes, anticipating his touch. Instead of being wary, she found herself curious.

"Sir, I've brought the items." Gibson strode into the room.

She heard him until he stopped, which meant he wasn't very close as the rug beneath the bed covered half the room.

"Thank you." Marcus' voice was so much deeper. She'd always enjoyed listening to him.

"Should I send for a physician, my lord?"

She could imagine Marcus frowning, which made her want to smile, so she bit down on her lips in case Gibson was looking at her.

"No. A twisted ankle needs no physician. I tended many of them during the war. Our surgeons were too busy pulling bullets from the lads."

"Of course, sir. Here you are, then."

Neither spoke for a moment, then she felt a cold weight on her ankle. Forgetting it was coming, she hissed and grimaced.

"I'm sorry, Lady Beaumont. This will help the swelling go down. Once it's down, I will wrap your ankle and you can be on your way."

She nodded, but didn't speak.

The pressure on the cold cloth lessened before Marcus spoke again. "Is my mother home?"

"No, sir. She's still about shopping."

Marcus sighed heavily. "Very well. We will need to allow Lady Beaumont complete rest. Please ensure no servants are in the rooms in this wing and that they don't come up here until after Lady Beaumont has left. I don't want her to wake or the swelling will take much longer to go down and I must return her home before long. Can I trust you in this?"

As he'd spoken, she could hear both men's footsteps moving away.

"Absolutely, sir. You can depend upon me."

Marcus didn't say anything else as Gibson's footsteps retreated. She opened one eye to peek at the doorway. Marcus stood just outside looking farther down the corridor. Footsteps approached that were much lighter than Gibson's and she shut her eyes again. More steps sounded before Gibson spoke. "No one else is in this wing."

"Good man. I will send for my coach after Lady Beaumont wakes up. That will be all."

Once she heard Gibson leave, she opened her eyes and sat up. Marcus remained by the doorway, then left.

Confused, she pulled her foot from under the cold hunk of ice and swung her legs over the bed, intending to follow him, but suddenly he was there in the doorway, his own shoes in his hand. "I didn't wish Gibson to know I would be staying here."

His prideful grin had her chuckling. "Have you ever thought to go on stage? I'm sure you would be quite successful."

He strolled in, dropping his shoes on the rug before kneeling before her. He laid one hand on his chest. "My lady fair, art thou ready to undress and may I be of assistance?"

She put her hand under her chin as if giving it serious thought. "I suppose if you must." She dropped her hand and looked askance at him. "But I would expect to be able to aid you as well."

Instead of agreeing, he ducked his head and took her foot in his hand, easily slipping off her shoe. When he dropped it next to the other, she expected him to rise, but he remained where he was, finally meeting her gaze. "Do you know that touch can be as important as kissing?"

She swallowed, images from *The Pleasures of Seduction* floating through her mind proved his words. Silently, she nodded, both fearful and curious about what *his* touch would feel like.

"I'm going to remove your stockings."

Must you? She gritted her teeth to keep from saying the words. She already knew the answer. They had to be completely unclothed.

Luckily, Marcus didn't expect an answer. He took her foot and placed his hands on either side of it before slowly moving them up her leg. She froze, too fearful to move until tiny tingles flew up her thighs where his hands stopped to roll her stocking down.

She let out her breath in a whoosh. The strange disappointment she felt that his hands had only gone so far didn't make any sense.

When he cupped her other foot, she didn't steel herself against his touch, but allowed herself to feel. This time, as his fingers touched her flesh, warmth travelled from that spot to the place between her thighs. She found herself taking shorter breaths.

The new sensations were pleasant, and she thought to contemplate them when Marcus put one hand on each ankle and ran them slowly upward. Now, with no stockings to stop him, her tingles turned to sharp stabs of excitement.

His hands continued past where they'd gone before, and she found herself holding her breath.

"You are so soft." His eyes had closed as he felt her, the pleasure on his face enough to make her want to grant him anything.

Not sure what to say, she said nothing and his hands continued to the very spot she dreaded. All pleasurable feeling stopped, and cold, like that of the ice, filled her.

As if sensing her fear, he lifted his hands from her and brought them out from under her dress. "I'm acting like a randy boy instead of a man of much experience. Forgive me."

He rose before she could respond and pulled her to stand in

her bare feet. Cupping the back of her head, he stared into her eyes. "I am but a poor sailor listening to your siren call."

"No." The word came out on a breath, barely audible, so she cleared her throat. "No, you are the man I loved, I love, and that I will always love."

Though he shook his head, he pulled her closer and kissed her. It started gently, but within seconds, his passion for her communicated itself, and she pressed herself against him, wanting to get closer, again feeling that there were too many clothes. She broke the kiss to move her hands to his shirt, only to find her dress loose about her shoulders. "What?" She grasped it to her chest to keep it from falling.

He gave her a sheepish grin. "They say idle hands will do the devil's work, so I put them to good use."

Holding her dress against her, she lifted her chin. "Then use them to work at removing your shirt, since you've made it impossible for me to do it for you without losing my dress."

"No. I think you should do it." He grinned as if he had won some battle of wills.

She would absolutely not allow that. They had to remove their clothing anyway, and she still had her stays and shift on. So without warning, she shrugged. "Very well." And let go of her dress.

Marcus's grin faded as his eyes seemed to darken to a charcoal gray. His look sent a shiver of anticipation through her.

Forgetting what she was about, she couldn't stop watching his face as his gaze ran the length of her and came back to her eyes.

"You tease me." His voice was almost a growl, sending sparks of anticipation skittering over her skin.

She wasn't sure what he meant. What she was sure of was that she wanted to see him as much as he viewed her. Quickly, she unbuttoned his shirt again and rose up on her toes to push the sleeves back over his broad shoulders. As she continued to pull it down his arms, her gaze found a scar not far above his heartbeat.

Instinctually, she kissed it.

"Elle."

The soft-spoken endearment from years ago almost buckled her knees, and she found herself grasping his wrists instead of freeing them of the shirt. Titling her head, she looked into his love filled eyes, her own itching with tears.

He wriggled against her grip and she let go. In the next moment the shirt dropped and he held her against him, hugging her to him as if he couldn't believe she was there.

She understood. Part of her felt as if it was all a dream. Thinking him dead for so many years, she still had difficulty truly believing he was hers. Or rather, not quite hers. But his nut and leather scent filled her nostrils, and his warm heart beat strongly beneath her cheek. He was very much alive and in her arms.

"Is that better?" His words were whispered against her neck.

She lifted her head from his bare shoulder. "What?"

He stepped back and her stays fell to the rug.

She widened her eyes before chuckling. "You, Lord Blackmore, are a trickster."

"No, not a trickster. It is merely that I have great skill."

She put her hands on her hips and narrowed her gaze. "And how, pray tell, did you achieve such skill?"

"That is not a question any gentleman will answer. However, since it is you who asks it, I will tell you that what I learned, I learned before I met you."

"But you were barely two score and two?"

He gave her a cocky smile. "And well experienced at that."

She turned her back on him in a huff. Not truly upset, but more amazed that he would know so much of what was in Joanna's book at such a young age when she had been ignorant until now.

His arms wrapped around her waist and his lips found the side of her neck. "Do not be cross with me." He kissed upward toward her ear. "My practice was all for you."

She loved the feel of his lips on her and let her head fall back against him, her eyes closing. "I suppose I must forgive you then?"

His kisses moved to the top of her shoulder. "If it is your wish." He spoke against her skin. "I throw myself upon your tender mercy."

She shivered with delight when suddenly her left breast was lifted. She stiffened, her eyes opening.

"Shh, I promise this will be pleasant."

Despite his words and Joanna's book, she remained still, afraid that what he thought would please her would feel no different from her late husband.

"The devil take him." The harsh curse whispered across her skin.

She lifted her head and pulled away, turning to face him, now worried. "It's not good luck to curse the dead."

Shaking his head, he didn't reply, but his hands had fisted at his sides.

What was she doing? She crossed her arms over her shift. She didn't even like procreating. What had made her think it would be different with Marcus? Maybe she was deformed and what was supposed to be pleasant, wasn't.

"Mariel, I am only angry with your husband. As you put it, he did not procreate correctly and that hurt you, so now you fear touch. I understand."

"How can you understand so much?"

His hand moved to his thigh where he seemed to rub, his knuckles pushing into his muscle. "I have seen atrocities, the worst that humans can do to others, and have had to overcome them. Some I have not. I am no longer the person I was before I left for the battle on the continent. I will never be the same."

While she didn't want to know what he'd witnessed, she did understand being different from when they first fell in love. "But who you've become makes me love you more. While I'm now less of a woman."

"No." He stepped forward and cupped her face in his hands,

so gently, it belied his sudden movement. "You are more. You have grown into a woman who is witty, adventurous, and passionate."

She wanted to believe him as she stared into his penetrating silver-gray eyes and recognized the truth of his words. She needed to trust him. He'd never hurt her.

"If you wish to continue, I suggest telling me when you feel uncomfortable. Or we can stop now and I can bring you home."

The thought of going back to Craymore Hall knowing no more than when she'd left, when it had been her plan to seduce him at the first opportunity was too unbearable. "I want you to show me ecstasy." She wasn't sure she pronounced it right, but when his nostrils flared, her body heated in response.

"It would be my honor to show you a pleasure like no other." Gently, he moved his hands to her arms and tugged until she let go. Then he placed her hands on his shoulders. "Touch me."

"I am."

His mouth quirked up. "Yes, but caress me, wherever you wish to." He raised his brows. "Unless you don't want to."

Ah, she understood what he was about. She could touch him and then he could touch her. Having never touched a man's bare chest, she was happy to explore. She trailed her fingers over the upper section of the mounds that were his chest. They were so very large.

His chest vibrated beneath her finger tips as he chuckled. "I will not break."

Laying her hands flat, she ran them over the muscles just as he had moved his hands up her legs. She was not unaware that he had nipples like hers, and smoothed her hands over them. They seemed harder, so she moved her hands back. There was nothing in the book that showed a woman touching a man's nipple, but it had shown what a man could do with a woman. Deciding to experiment, she took them between her thumbs and forefingers and rolled them.

Marcus' chest rose and he sucked in air.

She snapped her head up. "Did that hurt?"

"No." The word barely came out. He cleared his throat. "No, it felt so good that it made me want you even more."

From the pleased look on his face that meant it was good. She went back to her study of him and ran her hands over the ripples between his upper muscles and the top of his pantaloons. As her fingers hit his waist, she noticed a large bulge beneath the fall. About to investigate, she found her hands suddenly grasped within his.

"Now may I do the same?"

It seemed only fair, and he certainly hadn't been hurt by what she'd done. She just needed to focus on him and not what her husband had done. She nodded. "Yes."

He bent and lifted her into his arms once again only to drop her onto the bed.

She laughed, fond memories of flouncing on her bed to day-dream filling her. Many of those daydreams included Marcus and what it would be like to be kissed by him. Now she knew and she so enjoyed his kisses.

Marcus joined her, laying on his side, his head resting on one elbow.

She smirked as she thought of how he could have been a model for Joanna's book. The only difference was that he still wore his pantaloons. For the first time, she wondered if complete-ly unclothed would he look like the man in the sketch.

"Elle, I'm going to touch you now, if you are willing?"

She nodded, forcing herself to think about their kissing.

He didn't grab her breast. Instead, he found the bow at the top of her shift and pulled, loosening the neck line. Then he gently moved it down over one shoulder and helped her remove her arm from the short sleeve, effectively baring her right breast for him to see.

She heated under his appreciative gaze. How did she look compared to the woman in the book? She'd never purposefully looked at herself in her looking glass.

Still, he didn't touch her, but pulled down the other side of her shift until she was bared to him from the waist up, like the sketch of a woman from another country that Joanna had shocked them all with while still too young to understand.

But she understood now, and having Marcus resume his position with his head on his elbow while she lay there half nude caused her heart to beat faster.

"You are beautiful. I could lay here all evening just looking at you."

Embarrassed, yet oddly pleased, she lowered her gaze. The book hadn't said anything about simply staring at each other. Though she felt a bit overheated and her breathing was far from normal, she viewed his naked torso from beneath her lashes. Her fingers itched to touch him again. Is that how he felt looking at her?

He lifted his hand. "Watch what I do."

Surprised, she widened her eyes. "Watch you touch me?"

"Yes." His answer came out far lower in octave than his last statement and sent a fire of anticipation sweeping through her.

Doing as she was told, she followed his hand as it hovered over her right breast. He left it there just a hairsbreadth away and her nipple hardened. Her body wanted him to touch her! Shocked at the realization, she licked her suddenly dry lips. "Please, touch me."

At her words, his fingers gently stroked her, sending tendrils of excitement through her chest and down between her thighs. When his fingers took her nipple between them and rolled like she did to him, she sucked in her breath and crossed her legs as a tightness developed in her abdomen, the pleasure seeming to make it stronger.

He ran his fingers across to her other breast and even before they reached it, her nipple turned hard. Amazed at the transformation, she stared, expecting him to do the same thing, wanting him to repeat his actions, but he didn't. Instead, he laid his hand flat against her, cupping her breast.

"So soft and perfect." His words were spoken as if he were mesmerized, his gaze completely focused on her body. It was as if she were being worshiped.

She was about to tell him she deserved no such accolades, when his palm lifted and brushed across her hardened peak. Slowly, he moved his hand in lazy circles, causing ripples of pleasure to pool in her abdomen and starting a wetness she remembered from reading the book.

A need to moan crawled up her throat, and she quickly bit down on her lips.

His hand stopped all movement. "Are you hurt?"

She shook her head.

"What is wrong? Do you wish me to stop?"

Again she shook her head, swallowing to make her voice work, though it still came out scratchy. "I didn't want to make any noises. That wouldn't be proper."

He blinked at her before his brows raised. "By Jove's beard, why would you think that? No, don't tell me. I don't want to know. Making noises while making love lets your lover know that they are succeeding in making you feel good." His soft smile turned purely seductive. "If I don't know if it feels good, I'll have to keep trying."

At his look, something tightened between her legs. He promised sinful pleasure with his eyes. She couldn't quite get her voice to work. "I like it." The whispered words sounded enticing, though she hadn't meant them to.

His eyes darkened as he sat up. "Then let's see what else you like. Uncross your legs and lift your hips for me."

In an instant her blood cooled, but she did as instructed. They must have reached the end of pleasure and now it was time to procreate. She stared up at the ceiling above the bed, wondering if it would take Marcus longer than her husband took.

As she felt the shift slide down over her hips instead of up, she frowned, but her instinct told her Marcus knew what he was about. When the bed dipped and his hands rested on her knees, she gritted her teeth. The book said that being moist made penetration pleasurable. Though she doubted that, after all the author was a man and how would he know, she did believe it would make it easier for Marcus.

"Mariel, what are you doing?"

She didn't look at him. "I'm not doing anything."

"You're looking at the ceiling. Look at me."

"As you wish." She tilted her head down to find him kneeling between her legs in his pantaloons. "I believe you will have to remove your clothes to finish this."

He stared at her for a moment before he shook his head. "I know you do not want me to speak ill of the dead, but your late husband was a bloody bastard."

Because he said the words in such a factual manner, she found her lips quirking up. "No, I do believe his ancestry was quite well established."

His brows raised. "What I mean to say is that he did not treat you as you deserved to be treated."

She wanted to argue the point because George had been a very solicitous husband, though if she were to be honest with herself, it was most likely that he wanted to be sure she was in good health to have his heir. But at that moment, Marcus' hands moved up her legs and to the top of her thighs, causing her breath to hitch. Her gaze flew to his face, where he was focused on her most private place. The urge to cross her legs was strong, but he knelt between them.

His hands moved to the inside of her thighs and nudged her to spread her legs wider.

"Marcus?" She wasn't sure exactly what she wanted to ask him. The feelings inside her were so jumbled, she didn't even know what she wanted.

"Open for me. You are so lovely."

Heat filled her cheeks at the realization he was looking at her very womanhood. But despite how improper it was, a strange feeling of excitement filled her.

And then his fingers were there, at her opening. They started to stroke her before moving up to what the book called her pleasure point. She hadn't understood the name until Marcus' fingers found the spot. A jolt of pleasure whipped through her. "Oh!" She slapped her hand over her mouth.

"No need to be quiet. We are alone." His voice held laughter.

If he thought it humorous that she tried to stay quiet, she definitely would not. Just as her pique began, it disappeared as another spike of feeling flew through her. It was strange to feel so alive and yet so weak at the same time. Letting her head fall back on the pillow, she watched Marcus as she could.

But soon the streaks of excitement had her panting, her breathing too loud to ignore and yet he continued his sweet torture. She wasn't sure how much more she could enjoy without fainting when something slipped inside her.

She opened her eyes wide, thinking it was him, but he still knelt between her legs. It was his finger. She'd seen that in the book, but hadn't realized, hadn't known it was—

He pulled his finger out and pushed it back in, but now there was more pressure inside her. The pleasurable waves flooded her and she whimpered with amazement. Closing her eyes, she felt them build one upon the other, spiraling higher, floating her up to some unreachable height.

Then her nipple was sucked, and she screamed as her body ignited into a thousand fireworks, exploding into a bright light before raining down, back to the bed to become one once more.

Marcus' lips feathered her mouth before his tongue darted inside. The urgency of his kiss nudged her from her dazed state and she grasped his head in her hands and kissed him back, thanking him for showing her what she hadn't known.

When he broke the kiss, his breath was ragged and he must have slipped his hands from her body because he leaned over her on his elbows. But as she viewed his closed eyes, it was clear something was wrong.

"Marcus, are you in pain?"

CHAPTER SIXTEEN

H E HEARD HER question, but the blood pounding in his ears made it hard to respond. Making love to Mariel with his hands and mouth was like experiencing a flower awakening to the sun. Beautiful, poignant, and far more stimulating than he'd ever imagined.

Yes, he was in pain in many forms. His erection was painful because he needed to be inside her. The pain of knowing that if he tried to, it would never work. And worse, the pain of knowing that now he must let another man have her.

He dropped his forehead to hers. "It is not that kind of pain."

"Your injuries?"

"No. It is that I feel as you did before you reached fulfillment, but I can't." He lifted his head and looked into her concerned green eyes and wanted her more than air.

"You did not feel what I felt because you were clothed."

At her naïve conclusion, his dark thoughts dropped away. "Yes. I would need to be naked."

"Then you must undress immediately."

He barely kept his smile from appearing. "Must I, now?"

"Absolutely. I want to see you like you have seen me."

At her words all humor vanished and his body reminded him that it wanted release. If he did as she demanded and attempted intercourse, he would fail miserably. The thought of her seeing him unable to please her had his ardor cooling considerably.

But that might be what needed to happen for her to let him go.

Straightening, he carefully removed himself from the bed, wishing there was a bottle of whisky in the room. This would be the hardest thing he'd ever done in his life, except possibly living after being shot.

He turned to face her to find she'd grabbed up her shift and used it as a blanket. Her innocence made it a bit easier to do what must be done. Looking down, he unbuttoned the front of his pantaloons, but didn't let the material fall. He was no longer as hard as before, but he also wasn't small.

"Now don't play shy, Marcus. I know what men look like."

He doubted that very much. "Men, as in more than one?"

She cocked her head and raised her brows. "As a matter of fact, I've seen sketches and even a half-naked male model."

He had no doubt which half that would be, but would still insist on knowing how that had come about, though his guess would be it had something to do with her sister, the artist. "Very well. If you insist." He kept his gaze on her face as he let go of the material.

Her eyes rounded in appreciation before her brows knit. "I'm not sure we will fit."

His heart lurched at the thought of actually sinking into her and his body responded. Quickly, he pushed down the tight pantaloons, and stepped from them, purposefully turning his back on her as he bent to the floor to lift them. At her intake of breath, he grinned. At least she liked that side of him.

Finally, he faced her completely naked and allowed her to view his scarred body. The courtesans he'd attempted to bed in France had been well practiced in hiding their true reaction to him, but Mariel would be honest.

Her gaze turned from delighted to concerned in seconds. "Do your scars hurt now?"

He rubbed the one on his thigh out of habit. "My leg can

sometimes pain me in the winter, but it is nothing. If anything, it reminds me that I survived a great war."

She rose onto her knees still holding her shift before her, her hair now free of its loose tie. She was a mixture of seductress and innocent. "May I touch you?"

Her request humbled him, so he moved toward the bed.

"Tell me if I hurt you."

He bit down his smile as she almost echoed his own words to her. What a pair they made.

With one hand, she held her shift while she used the other to lightly touch his scar. He hadn't expected that. Then she leaned forward and kissed it. As she did so, her loose hair fell against his erection and he hardened.

When she pulled back, she hesitated, obviously noticing the change. But she didn't stop. Instead, she ran her fingers down his shaft before enfolding it in her hand. Bloody hell, where had she learned that?

He swelled within her grasp and it was all he could do not to moan. He didn't wish to scare her, but he didn't wish to spill his seed in her hand. He covered her hand with his own.

Her gaze flew to his. "Does it hurt?"

How could he explain the kind of pain he was in to a woman who'd only reached fulfillment for the first time mere minutes earlier? He let go of her hand, and she pulled it to her, grasping her shift tightly. "It is only the pain of wanting you."

Her gaze lowered. "I really don't think we will fit."

At the slight shake of her voice, he gritted his teeth. He imagined her elderly husband had been smaller than himself and probably made no effort to please her. He'd seen it before at a couple of gentlemen-only events in the country. Somehow, he had to allay her fears, but he was at a loss. No matter how much he promised to be careful, she wouldn't understand. "I know I seem large, but you are very soft and will adjust to me, I promise." Even to his own ears he sounded unconvincing.

Suddenly, her eyes lit. "Could we perhaps not take the missionary position, but the rider position? I'm quite good at riding." She even gave him a sly smile.

Shocked at her knowledge, he didn't say anything, but as her suggestion registered his body reacted even before he recognized the sense of it. She could control her movements, which would ease her fears.

And he would lose his erection the moment he breached her entrance. Then the questions would start and he would explain, and she would finally understand why they couldn't wed.

Though he acted in an honorable fashion, now having her here with him, on a bed, made it so much harder to give her up.

"Marcus? Did you hear me?"

Her hand on his chest pulled him from his reverie. He placed his hand over hers. "I did. I am willing, but I must insist on two promises."

"What may they be?" She smiled softly, obviously pleased that she would have her way.

"First, you must promise to tell me how you learned of the rider position."

She wiggled her brows. "I suppose I could share that with you, if you promise to never tell anyone."

"Agreed." He laid his hand on her bare shoulder. "And the second promise I must have is that you allow me the pleasure of taking your shift and not returning it until I deem it appropriate."

Her eyes rounded and her hand left his chest to secure the shift against her. "Is that truly necessary?"

He nodded as he held his hand out.

"I suppose that is only fitting since you are without clothes." Still, she held the material. Her tongue came out to lick her lips, causing a tightening deep in his sac. Finally, she looked down at the material and with both hands threw it at him.

He wasn't sure if she'd meant to cover his face, but when he pulled the shift from his head, he saw the roundness of her buttocks before she dove beneath the quilt.

Grinning, he set the shift on top of the bureau before returning to the bed. Her strategy might have worked if she had wanted the missionary position, but in the rider position, he would have her in full view.

She lay beneath the quilt, smiling innocently, her hands above the covering folded across her torso as if she could stay beneath it.

He so enjoyed the various facets of her person, but in a battle of cleverness, she would never win. He stepped next to the bed and casually lay his hand upon the quilt. "Are you quite ready to assume the position you asked for?"

She cocked her head and raised her brows. "You must lie down first."

If he'd thought her ignorant of the position she requested, her answer negated that. His erection jumped.

She gasped, her gaze flying to his shaft and in that moment, he grabbed the quilt and whipped it from the bed.

"Oh, you do not play fair." Though she complained, there was humor in her voice as she flipped over, showing her pretty arse.

He threw himself onto the bed, to land beside her on his back. "I am ready."

She pulled herself onto her elbows, her brow knitting.

He laughed, unable to help himself. She obviously had just realized she would be in full view. "Your ride awaits, my lady."

Though her eyes widened, a seductive smile formed upon her lips. "So it does." As if she had not a care that she was naked, she rose to her knees next to him and stared.

Bloody hell, she learned fast. He felt harder than a mounting block and barely kept from dragging her across him. But his instinct kept him in control.

When her hand reached across to stroke him, he thought he would release in her hand, but the moment his control started to slip, she stopped.

"Let me know if I'm doing this right." She lifted herself to straddle his legs just below his erection.

Dread filled him. Despite knowing it would happen, he kept

her need in mind. Lifting both hands, he cupped her breasts. "Do you know how much I enjoy the taste of you?"

Her breathing sped at his touch. "No, but I know how much I enjoy your kisses." She leaned forward, surprising him.

Not one to question a boon, he quickly took one taught peak into his mouth to gently suck, even as he twirled the hard nub in his hand. She arched her back, pushing her body toward him, not just accepting but asking for more.

Running his hand down her stomach, he reached the warmth between her legs and coated his finger with her readiness before circling her most sensitive spot.

"Yes." Her word came out on a hiss, causing a spike of need to run from his sac, straight up his spine.

In response, he sucked harder on the nipple in his mouth.

Her moan of pleasure urged him on and he tugged at the hard peak, even as he kept his touch light below. He needed to stay focused on her.

"Marcus, I need you." Her words came out in a whisper.

He understood, and pushing back the darkness hovering just beyond his consciousness, he moved his hands to grasp her hips and bring her above him.

The screams started in his ears, but he kept his gaze on Mariel. Her eyes closed, her face flushed, and her body warm beneath his hands. Still, the images flashed. Cobby's grin. Limp bodies.

"Marcus, I need you closer, inside me. I've never felt like this. Please, love me."

Her confused, anxious words pulled him from the images, and he squeezed her hips. "Lower yourself onto me."

She moved down his shaft an inch, her strong muscles against him, proving her own ability. Then she moved a bit lower. He closed his eyes, the screams still surrounding him, but the images were fading.

Her warm, tight, softness called out to him, enticing him inside, but he held his hips still, allowing her the control she wanted. When she continued down, slowly sinking onto him, the images in his head vanished.

Too stimulated to help himself, he pressed his hips up, sinking to his hilt inside the woman he loved with his entire self.

The screaming stopped.

"Oh, yes." Mariel pressed her hands upon his chest and began to ride him in earnest. She needed no further coaching as her body pulled at him to release his seed deep inside her.

He held back, determined to allow her to finally understand what it meant to find ecstasy.

Just as his control slipped, she arched against him, her hips grinding into his as she screamed her release. He found his at the same time, filling her, loving her, grasping her to him as they rode the wave of fulfillment together.

Their hearts beat out a staccato rhythm against each other while their breathing finally began to slow. Mariel lifted her head. "Is that how it's supposed to be?"

He brushed her long hair back behind her ear. "Yes. When two people love each other, that is how it's supposed to be."

"Thank you for showing me. I wasn't sure you could."

He moved his hand to her back. "What do you mean?"

"I mean, you told me you couldn't have children, so I wasn't sure if it was an injury from the war that made you sterile or if you could no longer function in that male capacity." She smiled. "I'm so pleased you can still function, even if you can't have an heir."

At her words, he froze. He did it!

He'd made love to her, something he hadn't been able to accomplish in years. The ramifications were life changing and happiness of a whole new kind, exploded within him. Rolling them over, still inside her he looked upon her in awe. "You saved me. I should have known. It makes sense. I've been an idiot."

She scrunched her nose. "Marcus, you aren't making any sense, except maybe the idiot part."

Her grin had him laughing. "No, I don't suppose I am making sense. I must explain myself, but first I must thank you properly."

He leaned down and gave her a thorough kiss before raising his head and finally slipping from her.

Rolling to her side, he lay back and pulled her against him, cradling her head on his shoulder. "I will spare you the details, but while in the war I witnessed an atrocity against humankind that affected my performance as a man, as you put it. Because of that, I thought I would never be able to have children."

Her arm came over his chest, even as her leg found its way between his. "But you just performed, so why did you think you couldn't?"

This might anger her, but he had to be honest. "After I healed from my injuries, I made my way to Paris where I learned of your marriage. My heart broke. I drank heavily, not caring if I stumbled into the road to be run over by horse and carriage."

She squeezed him hard, but didn't say a word – typical Mariel.

"I'm ashamed to say I tried to drown my sorrows in women." Though he felt her stiffen against him, she didn't speak, so he continued. "That's when I discovered I could no longer perform. Whenever I tried, the images and sounds of what I witnessed would overwhelm me and I couldn't continue. To be honest, I never expected to have you in my life again, so I thought by not being able to procreate, the only person I would be disappointing was my mother."

She finally lifted her head to look at him. "Did this event you witnessed involve a woman?"

She was far too intuitive, but he wouldn't lie to her. "Yes. When you arrived at Ravenridge, I didn't know what to think. I thought keeping you away was the best thing. But now I realize that you are the balm for my tortured mind. I should have known. Can you forgive me for keeping you away?"

She moved her hand from his chest to his face. "I can. I will." Her gaze turned shy. "Does that mean you can marry me now?"

At her question, the final burden lifted from his shoulders and a euphoria he hadn't felt since they were young filled him. "Yes!"

He pulled her on top of him. "If you'll still have me."

"Oh, yes. Most definitely." She kissed him, then lifted her head to gaze at him.

"Then we will post the banns this Sunday." He briefly thought of attempting a special license, but he doubted he'd be successful. "No one need ever know that we were not betrothed in truth. I can now sign the marriage settlement your sister and father created."

She leveraged herself up, sitting across his stomach. "So it really was just the fact that you couldn't give me children that held you back?"

He grasped her waist, loving the view of her nakedness. "It was, though I was sorely tempted to marry you anyway."

"Well then. I guess my seduction worked." She wiggled in her delight, causing his already hardening staff to take notice of her rounded arse.

Quickly, he rolled her onto her back and further, so she lay facing away from him. Locking his arm around her waist, he threw one leg over hers, and braced his head with his other hand. "Yes, about that seduction." Not that she'd truly seduced him so much as asked him to make love to her. "You promised to tell me about how you learned of the riding position."

Her cheeks turned rosy in an instance. "I did promise, didn't I." Her hand intertwined with his at her waist. "My sister gave me a book called *The Illustrated Pleasures of Seduction*. I learned about many positions, but it was meant for a man to read, so it focused on what women liked." She glanced up at him. "I had no idea there was so much to procreation."

Even at the thought of her reading such a book, his erection pressed against her arse cheeks. "Your sister the artist?" If there were sketches, maybe she used them for intimate paintings, though he couldn't see the talented Lady Sommerset doing so.

"Oh, no. Not Amelia. Joanna. She has a book on every subject there is."

"The duchess?" Now he was truly shocked.

Mariel looked askance at him. "Yes, that would be Joanna. She is a teacher after all. She thought I knew most of what was in the book. I could never admit how ignorant I was as a widow."

He definitely needed to see this book. "These illustrations must have been very detailed. You rode me like an expert."

She looked down, her face reddening once again. "It is very detailed. It showed and explained every part of a man's and woman's bodies. I admit, there were things I didn't know about mine."

At her admission, he wanted to teach her even more. "And is this where you learned about a man's ability to *perform* as you stated?"

"Oh, no. That was another book. After you told me you couldn't have children, I went to our library at Craymore and looked in one of the medical books there. I thought not being able to have children was the woman's problem. I didn't dare ask Joanna, whom I sure would have known."

"And that is where you found the answer."

"I did. I actually found two answers, so I wondered which was your case. Both were possible since you had been injured in the war."

Some of his contentment vanished at her statement. "What were the two possibilities for a man who could not father a child?"

"The first was that a man had been surgically made a eunuch or had some injury that made it impossible."

His leg muscles tightened and an imaginary pain swept through his sac.

"The second was that a man could not complete the act in some fashion. There were three reasons given for that. They—"

"I think I'd prefer to be ignorant of what they were. I much prefer proving to you again that I can make you feel pleasure." He moved his hand from her waist up to cup her breast, his thumb naturally brushing the hardening peak.

She sighed. "I like how you make me feel." She pulled one leg out from under his, opening herself up.

Now *that* was an invitation he didn't plan to ignore, even if she didn't realize she made it.

A knock sounded on the door "Lady Beaumont?"

Anthony! He looked toward the door, and noticed for the first time the darkening of the room.

Mariel grabbed the sheets and crumbled them up against her.

He whispered in her ear. "Tell him one moment."

She nodded before swallowing. "Yes. One moment." Her voice was not loud, but it would be enough.

Jumping from the bed, he picked up the quilt and covered her before grabbing up his pantaloons and pulling them on. Then he bent over the bed to press a kiss on her cheek. "You'd best dress. I'll be back in to help you finish."

Striding toward the door, he found her sitting up in bed with the quilt pulled up to her neck, her eyes round with nervousness.

He opened the door only as far as needed and slipped out. "You're back."

Anthony took one look at him and grinned. "Indeed I am, but I fear not in time to save a lady's virtue." He lost his smile. "Or was it the same?"

It was his turn to grin. "It was different in every way."

Anthony clapped him on the shoulder. "This is good news. You'll marry her then?"

"I'm having the banns posted next week."

"Congratulations." Anthony looked pointedly at the door and lowered his voice. "You looked like you'd been to hell and back this morning. Another night of dreams?"

He grimaced. "Dreams from hell." He glanced toward the closed door. "I have a feeling I'll sleep well tonight though. I believe marriage will agree with me."

"Before the wedding, you may want to search out Cobby. He's here."

Cool anger rushed through him. "At Blackmore House?"

"No, but he's in Town. He's taken lodging at the Broken Oar, near the Thames. I have a man watching him. If you wish, we can go tonight."

Grabbing Anthony's arm, he moved them further down the corridor. "We go tonight. The sooner I dispatch the bloody miscreant, the safer all women will be."

"I agree. Do you want to take your sword or your flintlock?"

"Both." And he'd bring his dagger as well. "The man is sly. I'll use whatever is required.

Anthony started to leave. "Wait. Tell Gibson to have the coach brought around. Lady Beaumont's swollen ankle is doing better and I will escort her home."

His friend grinned at the fabrication and nodded before hurrying off.

He turned back toward the room where Mariel was no doubt dressing. If he didn't already have enough reason to rid the world of Cobby, he had more now. He could not allow the man to live while he had someone so precious in his life.

Opening the door to find her completely dressed including her hair tied back once again, he forced a smile. "Turn around and I'll finish your ties."

She did as he requested. Once he had her clothing secure, he reached into his fob pocket, where he always kept it, and pulled out the garnet necklace. Laying it around her neck, he locked the clasp. "You always did and always will have my heart."

Her intake of breath told him she understood. Her hand came up and held the stone as she turned around to face him. "And you always did and always will have mine."

CHAPTER SEVENTEEN

MARIEL PULLED ON her gloves and brushed down the skirts of her dark green riding habit, pleased to be seeing Marcus so soon. She rarely was able to ride while in London, so the fact that he was taking her to Blackmore House where she could work with Hector made her even more anxious to leave.

Stepping before her looking glass, she scanned herself with a critical eye. Despite the fact the banns had been read last Sunday, there were still two more weeks to go and she wished to impress upon Marcus that he'd made the right decision.

Part of her knew she didn't need to impress him, but after having a lovely dinner with her parents and his mother at Blackmore House, she did feel she should try to be as proper as—

A knock at her door had her looking away and the door opened. "Joanna. I didn't know you were calling."

Her younger sister, dressed in a purple day dress, strode in. When Joanna walked like that, it always meant she had something on her mind. "I'm not calling. I'm here to talk to you specifically."

Before she could offer her sister a seat, she sat in the wing-back chair near the window.

Obviously, Marcus would have to wait. Pulling the chair from her dressing table, she sat. "What would you like to discuss?"

"I have a number of questions for you pertaining to your marriage."

She could always expect Joanna to come to the point. Maybe Marcus wouldn't have to wait after all. "I'm happy to answer what I can."

Joanna rose and walked to the fireplace. "It has come to my attention recently that Lord Blackmore has returned from the continent changed."

"Yes, that's true." She thought only she had noticed, but Joanna must have been watching them very closely.

Joanna paced back toward the chair, her skirts swishing with her quick steps. "Do you find the change acceptable?"

She wanted to grin, but could tell that Joanna was truly concerned for her. "I do."

"You do." Joanna faced her. "Is there anything about the lord that concerns you?"

Confused, she frowned. "No. He's been very attentive."

Joanna paced back to the fireplace. "And have your feelings for him waned, grown, or changed?"

Again, she bit back a smile. "Actually, they have grown much stronger. We are both older and much wiser."

Again, Joanna faced her. "So you do still love him?"

"I do. And before you ask, he loves me. He's not only shown his love but told me multiple times." She was quite proud that her betrothed willingly told her how he felt about her.

Joanna paced back to the chair and slumped into it.

She smiled, unable to hold it back any longer. "Joanna, what is it? Can you not believe that after all these years we are still in love?"

Her sister seemed stymied as if she didn't know how to tell her something.

"Come, tell me what's on your mind so I may put it to rest."

"He hasn't signed the Marriage Settlement and the banns have already been read." Joanna leaned forward, her elbows on her knees, her chin in her hands. "I'm worried he will beg off."

At first it gave her pause. Why would Marcus have not signed the settlement? "Did he agree to the revisions Father told me about?"

"He didn't not agree." She looked uncomfortable. No doubt because of how she and Father had presented it.

Not above punishing her sister a bit for how she'd handled the settlement, she smiled brightly as if still ignorant of what occurred in the library between them. "I will be happy to mention the subject when I see him today. It may be that it slipped his mind. He's been quite busy. He has some business he wishes to complete before we wed."

Her sister nodded absently, obviously still not satisfied. "I just don't want to see you hurt again. If he postpones the wedding again, I will be on his doorstep in a thrice."

"Again?" At her sister's assumption, she finally put the pieces together. "Why do you say *again?*"

Her sister sat up. "Because he didn't marry you before he left for the war. And now…."

"Joanna, Marcus did not postpone the wedding before he fulfilled his commission, I did."

"You?" Her sister's shock was almost humorous.

"Yes. I know you think I always do whatever a woman is supposed to, and for the most part I do, but when Marcus said he wanted to marry me before he left for the continent, I convinced him to wait until he returned."

Joanna's mouth opened then closed, then opened again and closed. Finally, she seemed to gather her thoughts. "Why would you do that?"

Only Marcus knew the truth, but it seemed unimportant now to hide the truth. "I didn't wish to live alone with servants in a new home. At the time, he was simply Mr. Stratton. He would have to purchase a house in the country and rent a town home in the city. While I didn't mind the tasks necessary to make that happen, I didn't wish to be in a new home without him. I preferred to stay with my family until he came home."

"And you never expected that he wouldn't."

She shook her head. Marcus was always so full of life and an abundance of energy, much like a young stallion. It had been what drew her to him. But now she preferred the more mature version of the man she loved. Maybe she'd be even more in love as they grew older together.

"Curse it, I owe the man an apology."

"You do?" She couldn't imagine why.

Joanna rose and stopped in front of her. "I need to write a letter immediately. I judged your betrothed without the facts and found him lacking. I'm sorry." Joanna took her hand. "I want you and the viscount to be as happy as James and I."

She squeezed her sister's hand. "I promise you. We will."

"I believe that now." Joanna released her hand and walked to the door. Opening it, she paused. "Amelia says you make a good aesthetic couple. That's high praise from her. I should have taken that as a sign. I'm sorry." With that, she closed the door.

Mariel contemplated her past decision. If she had married Marcus and he died, she would have been back at Craymore Hall anyway. Looking back, the only piece of her life that would have changed was she would have been alone that year he'd been dead. But once he had returned to England, he would have come to her. They missed two years of being together because of her decision. But her family would not have been financially comfortable either.

Shaking her head, she rose. As Belinda always said, the past made the present possible, but it wasn't worth dwelling on too long because it can never change, but the present could. For a younger sister, she'd been wise well beyond her years.

Now it was time to start her new future and if she didn't hurry, Marcus would be cooling his heels for well over half an hour. She didn't want to miss one moment together. Descending the stairs, she grinned as Channing opened the door and Marcus entered.

Pleased she hadn't kept him waiting, she quickly descended.

"I believe I'm ready."

He looked up and his face broke into a smile. "Indeed you are, and especially lovely in blue."

She blushed, which was silly. She was far beyond having her head turned by a compliment, but still it pleased her. "And you are looking dashing, as usual."

Marcus wore a dark gray tailcoat, lighter gray waistcoat and black boots and hat. His broad shoulders appeared broader in the coat and with his hat, he seemed very tall. She would never tire of seeing him dressed so fittingly.

"Shall we? I brought the coach to allow my coachman to fight the crush so we can enjoy chatting."

As Channing held the door open, she walked past and Marcus followed, then descended the three steps ahead to help her inside. Once she settled in and the coach moved forward, Marcus switched his seat to sit next to her.

She liked that he did so. It made her feel that he wanted to be with her. "Did you have anything in particular you wished to discuss?"

"Yes, I do." He grinned like a boy who had just absconded with freshly made flummery and the cook was unaware. "I want to talk about your lips."

She frowned, touching her lips. "Whyever for?"

He leaned closer. "Because they taste so sweet, I find I'm dreaming about them."

A tingle ran from her chest to her toes as his gaze focused on her mouth. "Oh."

His hand moved to her neck and he pulled her closer. "May I?"

She licked her lips even as she nodded. As his mouth met hers, she closed her eyes, grasping his arm with her free hand.

The next half hour was over far too soon. As they moved up the short drive to Blackmore House, she made Marcus return to his seat and brushed out her skirts. Despite how much she'd enjoyed kissing him, she was inordinately pleased that he had not been able to loosen her riding habit. At least she had one piece of clothing she could wear and remain in it.

The coach rolled past the front door and stopped at the small stables. Blackmore House was situated on the outskirts of London and provided roads and lanes where she could ride far more appropriately than in London proper.

As Marcus led her into the stable, she felt a familiar excitement at learning a new horse. What unique trait would Hector have? Hector was a courageous name, like the hero of Ancient Troy who defended his family and people.

She stopped before the stall, her horse standing as far back as possible, watching. Unfortunately, her Hector had been treated poorly and she needed to gain his trust.

Marcus opened the stall gate, and she stepped inside. She looked behind her to find him closing it and staying outside. She smiled her appreciation. Approaching Hector as she had upon her last visit, she held out her hand and allowed him to recognize her scent. "Good afternoon, Hector. Would you like to go outside? The sun is shining and there's a slight breeze that I know you will enjoy."

She moved her hand to his neck and gently stroked. "I promise you will always be treated kindly."

When he didn't pull away, she ran her hands over his back. He had excellent stature and with a bit more weight would be a healthy horse. "We are going to make sure you have plenty to eat and fresh bedding and lots of exercise. Would you like that?"

She continued her inspection running her hands over his side and hind quarters where scars marked his abuse. It brought tears to her eyes, but she didn't let her sadness change her voice. "I would very much like to take you for a ride and see what you like to do. Would you enjoy that?"

Marcus' soft chuckle had her looking at him. "Why do you laugh?"

He pointed to Hector's head. "Every time you ask him a question, his ear flicks."

"Truly?"

Marcus dropped his hand. "He just did it again."

She turned her attention back to the horse and watched his head as she patted his back. "We're going to have you saddled, but I'll be right here with you. Then we'll go for a short ride. Are you ready for a gallop?"

Sure enough, his left ear flicked. "Oh, you are such a smart horse. I will have to teach you to answer my many questions. I have a feeling you could learn to. Are you that intelligent?"

At the flick of his ear, she grinned. "I think it's time to bring a groom in."

She continued to speak soothingly to Hector until Marcus came back, but instead of a groom, he'd left his tailcoat and waistcoat behind and carried the saddle.

"I think it best if we take this slow until he feels safe with us."

Her heart filled that he used the word "us." They would soon be man and wife and they could share their love of horses and riding. They could work together with the horses. It had been a young woman's dream and now it would be her life.

She remained with Hector, continually talking, as Marcus fitted the sidesaddle. Once it was cinched, she walked the horse outside.

He brought out a mare. "Hector, this is Ebba and she's the kindest horse you will ever meet."

The two horses sniffed at each other. She waited, to allow Hector time to know Ebba. When the mare rubbed against Hector, he quivered. Had he been ostracized by other animals too? With her heart breaking, she stepped between the two horses. "I think we should go for a short ride."

"I agree." Marcus pulled Ebba away. "There is not much property here, but it's a short ride to the parish church." He walked Ebba outside.

After Marcus helped her into the saddle, he mounted.

"Hector, let's go for a walk." The horse started to move, keeping pace with Ebba as they started down the drive at a sedate pace. Once on the road, she flicked the reins to see what Hector would do, but he didn't do anything except continue as he was. Puzzled, she tried again, but still nothing. She looked at Marcus. "Why don't you and Ebba ride ahead. Maybe he'll want to catch up."

With a quick nod, he urged Ebba into a trot.

She flicked the reins again, but still Hector didn't show any interest in moving faster. Why had he started walking when they left the stable? "Hector, would you like to follow Ebba?" His ear quirked back but he didn't move any faster. Not sure what to do, she patted his neck and flicked the reins, but nothing happened.

Maybe she needed to state her wishes. "My dear Hector. Follow Ebba, please." She flicked the reins and he started into a trot. She tamped down the surge of success. She may have simply been lucky.

Ebba and Marcus were still far ahead. "Hector, catch up to Ebba." As soon as she flicked the reins and leaned forward, he shot forward into a pleasant gallop. She laughed, thrilled that she'd discovered Hector's preferred direction.

As they shot past Marcus, he grinned, before giving chase. Soon they were racing down the road. He pulled ahead on Ebba and turned them down a left fork in the road where she noticed a church not far off. "Hector, slow down." She pulled back on the reins and he slowed.

She turned him into the churchyard and brought him to a halt. "Good boy. She patted his neck and stroked him, encouraging his good behavior.

Marcus turned to face them. "His stride is smooth. I see no reason why anyone would have problems with him."

She grinned. "I do. I don't know who trained him, but he only obeys commands when I say his name, and it can't be in a question."

He raised his brows, obviously not convinced. "Show me."

She appreciated that he didn't dismiss her knowledge out of turn like he had at the horse jobbers when she'd told him of her horses' defensive talents. "Of course. First, I will flick the reins and lean forward."

She did as she stated and Hector stood there. Smiling triumphantly, she nodded to Marcus. "Hector, walk back to Blackmore House." She flicked the reins and the horse started walking back the way they'd come.

Marcus and Ebba joined them. "I wonder if he could be trained to go to specific places."

She stroked the horse, feeling proud of both herself and him. "I think he's very smart. I wonder if a woman trained him."

"We'll never know. At least he has a safe home and a compassionate rider now."

Warmth filled her. Since he called Blackmore House Hector's home, that also meant it was her home. And for the first time since Marcus had been revealed as alive, she could think of Ravenridge as her home as well. No longer would she stay at Craymore Hall during the season or return to Thornwood Park for the winter. These would be her new homes.

She glanced over at Marcus, whose profile had changed in the last four years. Though she'd been in love with him before he left, her heart told her she loved him more now and understood him better.

He caught her looking at him and smiled. "What are you contemplating?"

"Just thinking about how in a few weeks, I will be living in a new home." She gazed into his gray eyes appearing even lighter in the sun, the trickle of excitement in her chest catching her by surprise. "I'm also contemplating whether Hector could beat Ebba in a race."

She leaned forward in her seat. "Hector, run like the wind!" She flicked the reins, tapped her foot against his side and he shot forward causing her bonnet to come off, held on only by the ribbon around her neck. She laughed loudly before the pounding of hooves behind her had her lowering her torso close to Hector's neck.

Just as she reached the short drive, Ebba pulled alongside.

Quickly, she sat straight again. "Hector, slow." She pulled the reins back a little, allowing the horse to slow at his own pace.

Marcus did the same. "He's fast off the start. I wonder how long he could run full out."

"I'm sure we will discover his endurance and many other things about him in the days to come. But mostly, I want him to be happy." She patted the horse. "Hector you deserve to be happy here. Don't you think?"

Hector's left ear flicked, and he slowed to a stop before the stable.

Marcus jumped down from his horse and walked to her, holding his arms up. "I believe we all deserve to be happy."

Now that, she could agree with. Slipping into his arms, she found she wished to stay there, but a groom came from the stable to meet them, so she reluctantly stepped back and turned to Hector. "You did very well. I'm so proud of you." She gently stroked his nose then turned toward Marcus.

As he instructed the groom to fetch another to walk the horses, her bonnet was tugged from behind. Turning to look, Hector set his head on her shoulder. She stood frozen for a moment, shocked by the affection. Tears sprang to her eyes, and she patted the side of his face, leaning her own against him. She closed her eyes, too overwhelmed by the love she felt for her new animal.

"It appears we found you that horse you've been wanting. I would not have guessed he'd behave in such away after all he has gone through. I believe he is grateful."

She opened her eyes to find Marcus gazing at her, his own love shining in his eyes. His support of her love for horses meant more, now that she could see what life would be like with him. "And I'm grateful to you for giving him to me."

The grooms strode out and she let go of Hector's head, but turned to give him reassurance. "We'll go for another ride soon."

As the grooms took the horses for a walk to cool and be rubbed down, a tear slipped down her cheek.

"Mariel, what is it?" Marcus was at her side in an instant.

She waved her hand in front of her face. "I'm just so happy."

He pulled her into his embrace. "And I pledge to keep you happy at all times."

She laughed at him. "Really, you cannot make such a pledge. That is impossible."

"But I can try."

Before she could respond, his lips descended upon hers and desire flamed to life. She wrapped her arms around his neck and kissed him back, loving how his kisses made her feel so weak. A need started to build inside and she pressed herself closer, wishing their clothes were off.

He broke the kiss. "I want to taste you."

She let her head fall back as he kissed her neck. "I think you are."

"No, not here." He pulled away, leaving her a little lightheaded, but then grasped her hand firmly. "Inside."

"Inside?"

He pointed to the stable.

Her heartbeat raced at what he was suggesting. Then he pulled her with him into the darkened interior. Letting go of her hand, he closed the doors.

As her eyes adjusted, she looked about, vaguely wondering if there was a cot nearby, then scolded herself for thinking such a depraved thought.

Marcus grabbed her hand again and strode to the back of the stables, past the stalls to where the phaeton was stored. "I'm going to help you up so you can sit on the floor of the phaeton."

Seeing as there was no cot, her curiosity had her complying. She grinned at him as he stood before her. From her vantage point, she could see over his head into the other stalls. "I do believe this may make kissing a little difficult. Was there something you wanted to show me?"

His hands on her ankles immediately brought her mind back to kissing.

"Yes. I want to show you what I mean by tasting you." Letting go of her ankles, he lifted the skirts of her dress over his head.

Her heart skidded to a halt as his hands ran up her legs and nudged her thighs apart. It was only then that she remembered the sketch in *The Illustrated Pleasures of Seduction*. A lightning bolt of excitement flew through her abdomen before she felt his first lick. "Oh." She had no chance to say anything else as he demonstrated exactly what he'd meant.

CHAPTER EIGHTEEN

MARCUS STARED OUT the window of his study, his view on the stables as if they could somehow help him. The last three weeks courting and loving Mariel had been both exciting and concerning. He and Anthony had found Cobby multiple times, but they still hadn't caught him. The man was more slippery than an eel and just as hideous.

He and Anthony had arrived at Cobby's room only to discover it empty and the window open. It was obvious he heard them in the tavern below and had climbed down to the ground via the trash piled against the building. They didn't expect that to be a problem as Anthony's man had followed.

For weeks now, they arrived moments too late to confront Cobby, and Marcus was losing patience.

A single knock on the door heralded the entrance of Anthony. "We've got him. He's at the Devil's Own pub playing cards. I suggest we wait until the middle of the night and then corner him."

He would have agreed, but that was what they'd been doing for weeks. They needed to change their tactics. "No."

"No?" Anthony strode forward to sit on the arm of a nearby arm chair. "But we have your quarry in sight."

"Yes, but in sight is not in hand. I feel like a street dog chasing a rat that slips beneath the building just as its cornered. We must trap the rat."

Anthony's brows raised. "Ah, that is true. I should have thought of that. But to trap a rat, we need bait."

He rubbed his thigh as he anticipated Anthony's reaction to his next suggestion. "There is only one thing Cobby wants, and that's me."

His friend jumped to his feet. "Absolutely not. The man will kill you on sight."

"Maybe, but I don't think so."

"What do you mean?"

He strode over to his desk and pulled out the papers he'd been using to write down every detail he knew about Cobby. Anthony had suggested it after their last foiled attempt to capture the man. He spread the three sheets out next to each other.

Anthony strode across the room to join him. "What is this?"

"These are the notes I compiled about Cobby."

His friend grinned. "So you did write everything down. May I?"

He moved to the side to make room for Anthony to read through what he'd written.

"Don't forget we found his dagger in that room next to the Three Tups and a Jug. That could mean he no longer has one."

"Or that he's stolen another." He unplugged the ink and dipped his quill into it and added the information to a sheet. That reminded him of something else he'd forgotten. "His gloves. He left his riding gloves behind as well at that place. We must have surprised him."

"Do you think he stabled his horse nearby?"

He shrugged. It was hard to know what a man like Cobby would do. "If he has his horse nearby, it won't be pleasant riding without gloves."

"Unless he steals those too."

There was little doubt that Cobby would do whatever necessary to fulfill his own needs.

Anthony propped his hip on the desk. "So how do you suggest we trap him?"

He turned over one of the papers. "I sketched out a rough map of where he's been. I'm not surprised he's staying near the Thames. Fewer questions asked and no witnesses. I thought to go to one of the pubs near the one he stays in."

Anthony just shook his head.

"You have a better plan?"

"I do. I'll dress as you and go to one of these pubs. when he jumps me, you shoot him."

"I cannot allow that. You already saved my life once. I will not allow you to take my place. The danger is mine to face. I'm the one who saw what Cobby did. I'm the one who planned to turn him in. I must be the one to take the risk." Even at the mention of what Cobby had done, the images began to flash through his head.

"That may be true." Anthony clapped him on the shoulder. "But you have something to live for now."

Mariel. Even as he thought of her and the time they spent together in his very bedroom two days ago, all images vanished. She was the balm to his soul. He couldn't die on her…again. Yet, it was still his responsibility to rid the world of Cobby. "That may be, but that only means I need to be more careful. I will not allow you to bait the trap."

Anthony rubbed the back of his neck, clearly not happy with his decision. "Then I have another suggestion."

"I'm willing to listen to all ideas." He smirked. "Even if I reject them." He used to tell his men that, and Anthony had heard it a few too many times.

"I know. I know." He waved off the comment and walked around the desk to face him, setting both hands flat on the papers. "I suggest that we don't go after Cobby and we lure him out, but we do it in town in the less dangerous areas. But instead of staying to the streets, you take the alleyways when you walk. It will lull him into thinking you gave up, plus set the trap in a better area." He grinned. "It also allows me to disguise myself and be your shadow."

The idea had merit. He was about to agree when Anthony straightened.

"No, it still puts you in danger. Cobby could get off a shot and run off and you'd be dead." He grimaced. "I don't relish the idea of telling Lady Beaumont that you're dead."

"You won't have to. Cobby won't kill me."

"Bollocks."

He held up his hand at Anthony's swear. "Follow the clues." He pointed to a spot on the paper. "Cobby first came to our attention when he spooked my horse in the village of Northampton." He moved his finger to another spot. "But before that, don't forget there was the broken wheel on the carriage." He moved his finger yet again. "At Ravenridge, he came the closest. Yet again, he shot near me, not at me."

Anthony shrugged. "So he's a poor shot."

"No, he isn't. He was one of the top three best shooters I had."

"What about that carriage mishap? You could have been killed."

He sat in his desk chair as the new information fell into place. "No, I couldn't have. That road is known for its rough terrain and no one with a logical mind would race down it. Our pace was forced to be slow. If we lost the wheel and the carriage had tipped, then I may have been hurt, but not killed."

Anthony turned away, walking past the wingback chair before the desk. Finally, he stopped and turned back, one hand on the chair. "If you're right, then what does he want with you? I doubt very much that he wishes to confess."

He scowled. "That's a confession I never want to hear. No. I believe he wants to make me suffer for causing him so much distress."

"What? You causing him…? Oh, I see it now." Anthony sunk down onto the arm of the chair. "A man like that thinks only of himself. I fear you may be right. I don't even want to contemplate what he might think is a fitting punishment for you."

He rubbed his thigh, his mind running in that direction. Already the images of the woman on the table in the farmhouse had him rising. "I think your plan is a good one. We will try to flush him out before Thursday. The final banns are being read tomorrow and I will need to be rid of him by wedding day."

"I'm confident we can—"

A knock at the study door had Anthony standing.

He remained in his chair. "You may enter."

Gibson opened the door. "My lord, a Madame Fontaine is here. Would you like me to—"

"Gibson, is it? Move aside." The woman pushed Gibson as she brushed by him. "Me and the fine capitaine are well acquainted, are we not, mon ami." She walked briskly toward him, her pale blue dress rustling.

At the sight of Madame Fontaine, Marcus jumped to his feet, quickly striding around the desk. "Madame, I did not expect you."

She waved off his comment before accepting a buss on each cheek before sinking down into the chair before his desk. She crooked her finger toward Anthony. "Come here and greet me proper, filou."

As Anthony, or trickster, as Madame referred to him, did as bidden, Marcus studied the older woman who had saved his life. From her dress and better English, he'd say the allowance he'd given her had greatly aided her.

After batting Anthony's arm, she shooed him away. "Now you go. I have très important matters to discuss with the capitaine."

He held back a grin at Anthony's surprised look.

"I am hurt that you could not take me into your confidence, Madame."

She rolled her eyes. "No you're not. Now go."

"Anything for you, ma belle dame." With his hands crossed over his heart, he gave the woman a bow then left the room.

Madame Fontaine waited for the door to close behind her

before she looked up. Her face broke into a wide smile. "You look hail and hardy my guerrier brisé."

No one called him broken warrior anymore. "I am." He held his arms out wide, before leaning his arse against the desk and grasping the edge with his hands. "And you, my angel, are doing well."

She shrugged, the gray curls about her face swaying with her movement. "We do well, thanks to your generosity."

He was pleased he could do something for her. Before the war, she and her husband had owned a great farm that was prosperous and then not only was it stripped of its harvest, but also burned, leaving nothing but the house standing. Napoleon's army took both her husband and son into service and they were killed in the wars, leaving only her young granddaughter who she'd hidden beneath the floorboards whenever soldiers were about.

"Still the nightmares?" Her brow knit with concern.

The question caught him off guard. "They are rare, now that I have Mariel."

Her smile was back. "So you are married. I wish to meet this woman that kept your heart beating, even when it should not."

"I promise, you will. We marry in a few days. I would like very much if you could be there."

She shook her head in disbelief. "You English are so slow. It is difficult to believe you won the war." She winked. "But I'm glad you did."

He agreed. At first, he hadn't understood the significance of it, but after knowing Madame Fontaine, he understood how important it was to win.

"I've come to ask for your help yet again. I do not know if it is considered proper in your country, but I treat you like my son and so I ask you like a son."

He tried to imagine his mother and Madame Fontaine conversing about him. That would never occur as his mother would immediately know that the older woman was not of the French

Aristocracy, though she was most likely on a level as their gentry. "You know you have only to ask. I can never truly recompense you for saving my life."

She sat a bit straighter in the chair. "Très vrai. I am thankful my mother taught me what I needed to know to save you. For you are an important ally, non?"

"Yes. Tell me what I can do."

"It is Lissette. I wish her to marry an appropriate English gentleman."

He widened his eyes in surprise. "Little Lissette? Marry?" He tried to remember how old she was. She'd dressed as a boy for safety and had the curiosity of an innocent child.

The woman raised one eyebrow much higher than the other. "That petite fille is grown now. Overnight, she became woman in body but not yet in mind." Madame Fontaine snorted. "She thinks she is a woman, but she is not. Much trouble she causes me." The woman sighed. "She is much like me when I had dix-neuf ans."

Nineteen. Little Lisette was nineteen? And ready for marriage? That wasn't exactly his specialty, but he would figure out what needed to be done. "Of course, I will help you."

"I knew the moment I heard you speak that you were un homme bon. I do not allow her to marry yet. She must know more of English ways. I let you guide me on it all."

She rose quickly, and he offered her his arm. "I promise, I will put a plan in place so that little, I mean, Lissette will have the best opportunities for a good man." He knew exactly who was good at planning and could help immensely with this task.

She patted his arm as they walked toward the door. "Bon. I will tell her."

When he opened the door for her, she let go and faced him, her smile wide. "I will be here for the wedding. Oui?"

"Yes. I will have an invitation sent today."

She gave a single nod then waved on Gibson to show her the way out.

He watched her as she reached to open the door and Gibson quickly yanked it open first. His new butler must think him a lord with strange happenings. But he wouldn't have it any other way.

Walking back into his study, he gathered the papers on Cobby and returned them to the drawer. He couldn't put Mariel in harm's way. The threat from his past needed to be put to rest. He must find Cobby and soon. In four days, he was to start a new life with the woman he loved. He planned for it to be a safe life.

CHAPTER NINETEEN

Wedding Day

MARIEL SAT IN the coach before the parish church not far from Blackmore House. It was half past ten, but no one had come to tell her to alight. Surely, they realized they couldn't start the ceremony without the bride. Tired of waiting, she opened the door and the footman helped her down. She lifted the hem of her new green dress, the color of spring leaves that Marcus had suggested for the wedding when she'd told him she'd had it made, but had yet to wear it. He said it must match her eyes beautifully.

A warmth filled her chest at the memory as she walked to the back of the coach to check on Zephyrus. Her stallion would be going directly to Blackmore House after the ceremony, so she could ride him in the morning. Just the thought of waking up in Marcus' London home as the new Viscountess of Blackmore had her stomach jumping. She couldn't believe she was finally marrying him.

After giving her horse a pat on the neck and some reassurance that he would not be there forever, she walked around the coach to find her family standing outside the church. She hurried forward. They should be inside by now. "Joanna. Amelia. You and your husbands need to go in. We're late."

Her sisters looked at her worriedly.

Frowning, she turned to her parents. "Mother, why are you out here? The plan was to be inside by now. Is the vicar not here?" He was an older man, but he didn't seem to move particularly slow.

Her mother took her hand. "Mare, my darling Mare. We are just waiting for the groom."

"Marcus? He's not here yet?" She didn't want to have an argument on the first day of their marriage, but if he didn't arrive posthaste, she wasn't sure they could avoid it. "I do hope whatever it is, is very important. Has his mother arrived?"

Joanna answered. "She arrived before we did. She's very excited."

"And did anyone ask her what delayed Marcus?"

"We did." Amelia nodded toward her husband. "She said when she left, he'd called for Merlin to be saddled."

She nodded. "Yes, we planned for him to ride Merlin and Mr. Taylour would bring the phaeton, so we could ride back together after the breakfast. Is Mr. Taylour here?"

Joanna's husband, the duke, shook his head. "Neither Mr. Taylour nor the conveyance is here."

"Then it appears they've been delayed. There's no hope for it, but to wait."

The church door opened and the vicar joined them. "Oh, I'm so pleased we have a bride." He smiled kindly at her. "Do we have a groom?"

She returned his smile. "Not yet. It appears he's been delayed."

The vicar scanned her family. "But we have all the family?"

"Yes." She did have all her family. Or rather almost all. Teddy was still about on the continent and Belinda was gone. She glanced skyward, or perhaps Belinda was watching from above. She liked that thought. "Please tell the guests we will begin shortly."

There were only a score of people including the six who were her family. She fervently hoped Marcus hadn't acted impulsively and become hung up in a bind. Marcus being late for his own wedding was not acceptable.

The vicar gave her a slow nod, scanned her family, then returned his attention to her. "I will do as you request, but you should know I have another event to oversee in a short while."

"Of course. Thank you for waiting." Even as the vicar disappeared inside the small church, a foreboding crawled up her spine, but she staunchly ignored it.

She strolled over to a stone bench in the front walled-in yard of the church and sat. The day was warm and pleasant. Perfect for the wedding she'd waited years for. Why would Marcus make her wait longer? She'd seen him just three days past, and he'd seemed ready to whisk her away to Gretna Green. So why was he late now?

Unless he'd decided to disappear again. She shook her head. He'd been a bit distracted as they strolled through the arcade, and it was strange that he'd left her to ride home in his coach alone as he went to take care of some business he wanted completed. But he'd been as excited as she, even suggesting that they forgo the obligatory tour of his estates to simply enjoy each other's presence for an entire fortnight. She blushed at the thought of what he'd meant by that. No doubt *The Illustrated Pleasures of Seduction* would be used to the utmost.

Then again, he'd been just as eager before he left for the continent, and yet when he came back, he had not sought her out. She worried the trim on her neckline, too anxious to sit still. Her thoughts buzzed as her heart thudded loudly in her chest.

Had she only seen what she wished to see with him? Had she said something wrong?

The church door opened again and the vicar strode toward her parents, not seeing her sitting on the bench. She should rise, but her knees felt too weak to hold her.

Her parents directed the vicar to her, coming with him.

"Lady Beaumont, as much as I hesitate to say so, I cannot

wait any longer. I must be off as I have half a day's ride. If whatever has kept the groom is rectified, I would be pleased to marry you tomorrow." Though he was kind, she could see the pity in his eyes. Then he proceeded inside, no doubt to tell their guests that there would be no wedding.

She looked at her mother, who had tears in her own eyes, her father clasping her hand.

This could not be. Her heart beat loudly in her chest as she curled her fingers into her hands. Stubbornly, she refused to accept that he'd leave her at the church. Marcus would not abandon her to face such a public shaming. He loved her. He said he loved her. He even made love to her. The tightness started in her chest just as it had the day her sisters told her he was alive. Betrayed again. Her breath seemed caught in her throat and she forced herself to breathe. She would not faint.

The church door opened again and the guests started to file out. She couldn't stand and face the pity. Their fake betrothal had been to spare her such pity and yet here she was. She wanted to laugh but she couldn't, the pain too harsh. And soon, all of London would know of how she was left standing at the altar. She focused on breathing, finding it more difficult by the moment.

Lady Blackmore stopped, looked at her with puzzlement, then continued to her coach.

Did Marcus' mother think she'd done something? Did she, or was she simply bad luck? Her eyes stung with the need to cry, but she held her tears back, refusing to accept that Marcus didn't love her.

As people filed out, her family gathered around her like a protective wall. Her mother now dabbed at her tears with a handkerchief, her father's arm around her waist. Amelia stood arm and arm with Lord Somerset, both of them with sympathy in their eyes. Even the Duke appeared affected and looked saddened by the event. But as she moved her gaze to Joanna, she encountered something different.

Fury.

At the sight of her sister's anger, she remembered the words she'd written in the letter she'd left with the book. *And if Lord Blackmore dares to break your heart again, I promise retribution.*

Something inside her shifted. She pressed her hand to her chest and touched the garnet stone around her neck. Her doubt dissipated like the morning mists. Marcus loved her.

Joanna started to pace. "How dare he! How dare he put you through such public humiliation."

"I'm so sorry, Mariel." Amelia sat down next to her. "You did nothing to be treated so poorly. He obviously doesn't respect you."

That didn't fit Marcus, the man who would endure a fake betrothal just to save her from being pitied. He wouldn't do this, not a-purpose. It was something else. He could be hurt. No, he was an expert horseman. He could handle any eventuality, unless… Memories of him scanning the area every time they were in public flashed through her mind.

"Mademoiselle Mariel?"

At the sound of her name, she turned her head toward the open church door. An old woman looked at her around her parents.

She'd never seen the lady before. "Yes?"

The lady bustled forward, forcing her parents to move to the side. "I am Madame Fontaine."

At her blank look, the woman shook her head. Then she lowered her brows at Amelia, who rose at the unspoken command and allowed Madame Fontaine to sit. The older woman took her hand and held it tight. "Something is wrong, oui? Marcus, he take three bullets and still he lived only because of you. Yet, he is not here now."

"Lady Fontaine." Joanna approached. "Please explain who you are."

Madame Fontaine didn't look at Joanna, which was surprising in itself. "I am the woman who found him. I drag him back to my home. I nurse him, thinking he will die. But it was you he lived for. He had to come home to *you*. You comprendre?"

She did understand. In other words, nothing would keep Marcus from coming to their wedding. The fear that had started in her stomach, skittered up her spine. She squeezed the woman's hand and gave her a slight nod before pulling her hand from the woman's grasp.

"I'm leaving." She stood and pushed through the protective wall that was her family, striding toward the Mabry coach.

"Mariel, what are you doing?" Her mother's concerned voice stopped her.

She turned around. "I'm going to find Marcus." She bit down to keep from saying more. Now that the chance he was hurt had taken hold, it wouldn't let go. She might be wrong, but she'd rather be wrong than do nothing.

Joanna's eyes lit with delight. "I'm coming, too. I have a few words to say to that man."

"Oh, I'm not going to miss this." Amelia started forward with Joanna.

Though her sisters didn't understand, she appreciated their support. She glanced toward the sky. *I hope you're with me too, Belinda.* Continuing her way to the back of the coach, she untied Zephyrus. "I need you now, boy." Motioning the footman over, she gained her seat and glanced once more at her family, then turned toward the road that would lead to Blackmore House and kicked him into a gallop.

If she was wrong, she was about to be humiliated again, but it was worth the risk. She'd always told her sisters that love was more important than anything. She would follow her own convictions to the end, whatever that may be.

She gave Zephyrus his head, hoping that everything was fine and Ebba had simply come up lame. But even then, she could imagine Marcus walking the rest of the way to the church. As she came around the bend in the road, she could see Blackmore House, the entrance to the drive, and Lady Blackmore's coach pulling up at the front. Because of that distraction, she almost missed the black hat sitting not far off the road.

Pulling on the reins, Zephyrus reared. Since it was one of his favorite actions, she held on, well used to it. Once he landed, she walked him toward the black blot in the small field before the house.

Her heart hitched. It had to be Marcus' hat. She scanned the short grass, seeing no one. Peering closer, she could see horse-shoe marks, more than just one, but how many she couldn't tell. Highwayman? They usually preyed on coaches, and doing so in view of Blackmore House would be most unusual. Then again, it had been a harsh year and people were desperate.

About to follow, she heard a coach on the road and looked back to see her family coach slowing. Not willing to wait, she walked Zephyrus along the faint trail until it reached the wood not far from the road, which did make an excellent place to hide. As the coach rumbled to a stop behind her, she turned to find Blackmore House was no longer in sight.

Joanna hopped out first, no footmen in attendance. Then helped Amelia down, before striding toward her. "Why are you here?"

"I found Marcus' hat where I turned off the road and followed the trail to here."

Joanna looked up at her. "I saw that hat. Do you think he may have been taken by a highwayman?"

"I don't know."

Amelia joined them. "Should we not gather our husbands and launch a search?"

Though she knew that was what she should do, she didn't dare delay. She'd lost Marcus before and she refused to lose him now. At the remembered look of Madame Fontaine's near-panicked eyes, she firmed her resolve. "You may gather them if you think it best, but I'm following this trail no matter where it leads right now."

"Then we're going with you." Joanna stepped closer. "I have

medical knowledge in case anyone is injured."

Amelia joined her. "I can always act like a maiden in distress." She looked at Joanna. "I certainly have had plenty of practice."

Joanna rolled her eyes at the reference to all the plays she'd had them perform for their parents at Christmastide.

"I hope we need neither." Mariel looked at her sisters, who hadn't thought twice at staying with her, even though they'd thought Marcus had purposefully abandoned her.

"So do I, but the coachman will wait here in case we need to go for help." Joanna sighed. "I'm sure our husbands will follow soon."

She glanced above the coach. It wouldn't be seen from the road, so they'd have no idea where they were, but it didn't matter. She had to continue because the man that was to be *her* husband was in trouble.

"No. Tell the coachman to go to the duke and the earl and have them follow us. Then follow the trail if I lose you." With those directions, she urged Zephyrus into the wood.

At first, the trail was easy to follow, but as she rode deeper, the ground was full of last year's leaves. If it hadn't been for a broken twig here and there, she would have wandered off in the wrong direction. As she wound her way through a particularly dense area, she suddenly found herself in a small clearing. Unfortunately, she wasn't alone, and from the pistol the wide-chested man with the bleeding bruise on his cheek pointed at her, she wasn't welcome either.

CHAPTER TWENTY

"WELL, IF IT isn't the pretty bride."

Marcus forced his eyes to open, though they'd already started swelling. *Mariel!* His heart seemed to stop in his chest. What was she doing? She should be at the church or home with her family. Far from Cobby. Dread gave him renewed strength.

Desperate, he tried to wriggle his hands from the rope cutting into his wrists, holding him to the tree, but they were half numb as it was. The juxtaposition between Mariel's beauty and Cobby's ugliness was like a reflection of opposite souls.

Cobby motioned with his pistol. "Do come and join us."

He wanted to tell her to gallop away, but even Zephyrus wasn't faster than a bullet. And he knew from the wound in his shoulder that Cobby was anxious to shoot.

Mariel did as she was bid, her horse taking just a few steps further into the clearing, opposite from where he was tied. Cobby approached her, limping from their fight, still holding the gun on her. "Throw me those reins."

Again she did as told, keeping her focus on the man.

"Well, captain. What a pleasurable turn of events this is. I do enjoy an audience, don't I Stiff?"

The man with a cut lip, who had tied his hands after Cobby shot him, grinned. "Yeah, you do. Seen how you made that pretty sing last night, I did." The man had the audacity to wink at Mariel. "An' you sure is a pretty one."

Unfortunately, that brought Mariel's attention to Stiff, who stood next to him, making sure he didn't lose consciousness. Her eyes widened in shock before all emotion seemed to leave her face. She lifted her chin. "I just came to discover where my future husband had gone off to. You do realize that you interrupted the most important day of my life. I am not pleased. No, not pleased at all."

Cobby blinked, obviously not sure what to make of her.

If she could just keep the man talking, he might be able to get his flesh to give way and use the blood from the oozing cuts to slip one hand out. He just needed one hand. His heart pounded. How long did he have before Cobby grabbed for Mariel?

Mariel set her own hand on her hip. "Now he's going to need weeks of recovery. That is not at all helpful. Untie him at once and go on your way. I'm sure you have already emptied his pockets."

Despite the pain in his right hand as he tried to work through the rope, he was tempted to smirk. Mariel's suggestion gained them time.

Cobby looked at Stiff. "Did you check if he has anything in his pockets?"

Stiff shrugged. "You didn't say to look."

"Well do it, you rattlepate."

Stiff made the mistake of stepping in front of him, and he kicked the man hard, letting his frustration add force to his movement.

"Argh!" Stiff fell back on his arse, clutching his thigh. "The nabob kicked me." The man glared at him before rising again.

"Bugger it." Cobby pointed at Mariel. "You stay there." Letting go of the reins, Cobby strode toward Stiff.

Marcus kept his eye on Mariel, who lifted her finger to her lips before dropping her hand as Cobby turned his head to make sure she wasn't moving. His former soldier yanked Stiff up before approaching him, the man's foul breath fanning his face. "Now, you're going to behave when Stiff reaches into your pocket, or I'm going to shoot your woman." He turned his head and raised his flintlock at Mariel's head.

A chill filled him as the image of the last woman he'd seen with Cobby whispered through his mind. With no choice, he let Stiff reach into his waistcoat and fob pocket on his breeches. All the man got for his efforts was a pocket watch.

Stiff grinned, holding the watch up by the chain. "Can I have it, Cobby?"

Cobby swiped the watch from the man's hand. "No, you can't. After I sell it, I'll give you a shilling."

Stiff's eyes rounded with excitement. "I can have me own lady then." He eyed Cobby hopefully. "Unless you will share."

Cobby shook his head. "No. This one is too pretty to share." He turned back to stare at Mariel. "Bet you'd be mouthy and want to fight, but I know how to take care of that."

Marcus' blood ran cold. If Cobby thought he'd touch Mariel, he was bound for disappointment. Having stopped moving his hand when Cobby approached, he started sawing the rope against his skin, the pain nothing compared to his fury. He'd saw off his hand if he had to.

Cobby limped back toward Mariel. "And what do you have of value, captain's lady?"

Mariel kept her poise. "Nothing. I was expecting to be married, not going to a ball."

"That will fetch a living for the year." He pointed at her throat with the gun. "Throw it here."

Mariel's façade broke as her hand flew to the necklace he'd given her. It was his heart and she'd promised to always keep it safe. But if she kept it, he'd lose her. Her gaze flitted to him and he gave a quick nod, hoping Stiff hadn't noticed.

She flipped the stone. "This? It's hardly worth much. More sentimental than valuable, but if you wish it, you can have it. You are obviously in great need." She reached her hands behind her neck and unclipped it. Then she tossed it past where Cobby stood.

"Fool woman. You think I'm going to go after your bauble and let you get away? You females always underestimate me. Now, what else do you have?"

Marcus felt a piece of bark chip from beneath his wrist. Glancing at Stiff who stood to his left, he checked to see if the man noticed, but he was focused on Cobby. As long as Mariel stayed on top of Zephyrus, she could still escape.

Mariel held both her gloved hands palms up in front of her. "I told you. I don't have anything." Her voice took on an imperious tone. "I was supposed to be getting married."

"What about the horse, Cobby? I bet that would buy a whole cottage. If you wanted one, that is."

Marcus wanted to kick Stiff again, but he had to focus on getting his hand to work.

Cobby, who turned toward Stiff, grinned. "It's a better mount than I have."

Zephyrus stepped sideways as if appalled at the idea, but Marcus had no doubt Mariel directed him to.

"That would hardly be smart." Mariel frowned at Stiff. "Even this man, Cobby, knows that a mount like this one would cause questions. Not only is he well known in horse circles, but he's also quite ornery."

As if Zephyrus had heard himself called that before, he pulled at the reins in Cobby's hand.

Cobby sneered. "I never said I'd sell him, and I'm very good at making a horse come round to my way of thinking." To emphasize his point, he tugged the reins.

Zephyrus' eyes grew round.

"Shh, calm down." Mariel patted the horse then glared at Cobby. "No one's taking you away from me."

Marcus stifled a groan. The only thing Cobby liked better than a fearful woman was a challenging one. He tugged hard and his thumb slipped beneath the rope. Success gave him hope. Just one hand. It was all he needed to be free. His breath came fast as he struggled, his eyes on Cobby, who moved closer to Mariel.

"Don't lie to the stupid animal. Now get off—"

A noise on the opposite side of the clearing had Cobby going silent. Everyone froze in place. Could it be that Anthony had survived? Or had Mariel enlisted her sisters' husbands in aiding her? If so, he'd have a word with them about allowing her to come into such a dangerous situation.

The sound of someone walking through bushes continued. That wouldn't be Anthony, unless he was so badly wounded, he didn't know what he was about. If it was the duke or earl, he hoped they brought a gun as that was the only weapon that could stop Cobby.

Cobby took three more steps toward Mariel, then trained his gun on the noise.

Marcus stiffened. Mariel only had a chance if Cobby released the reins. Whomever was about in the wood obviously didn't know anything about soldiering, which had his hope dwindling. He worked harder at getting his hand out while everyone was focused on the intruder. His only hope was getting his hand free or that the person about to arrive in the thicket was a hunter with a fully loaded rifle.

Finally, a bush rustled at the edge of the clearing and Lady Sommerset stepped out.

"Oh, good day." She smiled sweetly as if she had no idea of what was happening.

His hope plummeted. He'd seen the earl with his wife and there was no way he'd allow her into such a dangerous position. Is this why Mariel had motioned to be silent, because she'd brought her younger sister with her?

Even as fear for both women filled him, the rope on his hand gave way. He stilled as it was placed in his hands to let go as he chose. He didn't dare turn to see who was behind him as he now understood Lady Sommerset had been a distraction. Though he'd like nothing better than to wrap the rope around Stiff's neck,

Cobby was the greater threat.

"Stiff! Stop ogling the woman and grab her."

At Cobby's order, Stiff walked toward a very docile Lady Sommerset.

She shrugged one shoulder. "I was just out for my usual walk when I heard your voices. Are you having a picnic? I haven't been on a picnic before."

The quiet snort that came from behind him gave him pause before he heard the slightest rustling as whoever it was left. Though he wished that person would attack Cobby, his knowledge of his adversary meant he had to be the one to do so. He just needed Cobby to step away again.

"Wait! What are you doing?" Lady Sommerset sounded truly disgusted. "Take your hands from my person, you filthy man."

"Sorry, miss. Cobby said I need to hold you. You smell real nice."

As if Stiff's words had been too much, the lady suddenly fainted, almost toppling the man to the ground.

Releasing the rope from his left hand, Marcus watched Cobby keenly. *Let go of the reins.*

"Stiff, drop her." Cobby's attention on Stiff had the pistol waving, but a shot still could hit Mariel.

In the next instant, another person tackled Stiff.

Marcus didn't wait to find out who it was. He dropped the rope and ran toward Cobby.

The man turned at his movement, finally letting go of the reins, and aimed the gun at him.

"Mariel go!" He kept his eyes on Cobby's hand as the man drew back the hammer.

A shrill whistle split the air.

Suddenly, Cobby's head snapped to the side as his body flew through the air, Zephyrus' front hooves coming down where he'd been standing. The shot rang out, going wild as the pistol fell to the ground.

Knowing Cobby always carried two pistols, he grabbed the

second from the man's trousers before he could get his wits about him and held it over him. "You're done hurting women, Cobby."

The man held his middle, trying to breathe through what was no doubt broken ribs. "You can't...tell me...what I can...do. Not...my captain."

That Cobby had no regret proved how thoroughly depraved the man was. "I don't have to be your captain. I'm simply a subject of the crown who has discovered a criminal."

"Ouch! Cobby, she's hurting me." At Stiff's complaint, he glanced back to see the duchess tying the man's feet. The duchess?

"A knife! Marcus!"

At Mariel's warning, he turned, caught the gleam of the sun on the knife in Cobby's hand and without hesitation, shot. The weapon about to be thrown at him fell to the ground from Cobby's lifeless grip.

"Marcus?"

He turned in time to catch Mariel to him as she threw herself into his arms. She smelled of orange blossoms and all that was good, and he grasped her tightly, relief flooding him. When she lifted her head, he didn't wait for an invitation but kissed her with all the love he had inside him.

"Mariel, are you bleeding?"

At the worried sound of Lady Sommerset's voice, he broke the kiss.

Mariel stepped back. "No, but Marcus is. We need to dress the wound. Joanna?"

He looked past Mariel to find the duchess, finishing a knot on the rope tied around Stiff's ankles.

"I'm almost finished here." Lady Northwick motioned with her head. "Amelia, find a place for him to sit down."

Within moments, he found himself seated on a downed tree at the edge of the clearing with all three sisters gathered round.

Lady Northwick knelt before him. "I need clean linen. We'll pack the bullet wound and wrap his wrists."

Mariel sat next to him and lifted up her dress. She held her hand out to Lady Sommerset who stood in front of them. "Let me have your knife."

The lady pulled a knife from her boot and handed it to Mariel, who proceeded to rip her shift.

With so many unanswered questions, he asked the first that came to mind. "You carry a knife in your boot?"

Lady Sommerset grinned. "I do. I never know when I'll need to sharpen a pencil. And before you ask, yes, I always have a pencil with me." She bent to her other boot and lifted out said pencil.

Mariel handed back the knife and lowered her wedding dress, which was stained in his blood.

This wasn't the wedding day she'd planned on, and he knew how she hated when her plans went awry. "I'll buy you a new dress."

She took his hand. "I don't need a new dress. All I need is you."

Her green gaze was so filled with love that he started to lean in for a kiss, when a sharp pain hit his other shoulder as his tailcoat was pulled off. "Och."

"I'm sorry, but this can't be helped." Lady Northwick didn't actually sound very apologetic. "The bullet went straight through, but I need to pack the wound, or you'll lose too much blood by the time we get back to your home."

He gritted his teeth as his shirt was ripped open and Lady Northwick expertly wound his shoulder up.

"Mariel, let go of his hand."

Reluctantly, he let her go as both his wrists were wrapped.

Lady Sommerset, who'd wandered off, returned. "Mare, I think you'll want this." She opened her hand to reveal the garnet necklace. "I know how much it means to you." Then she looked at him. "She never took it off the entire time you were away."

The slight rebuke in her tone was noted. "So I have come to understand."

Lady Sommerset then gave him one of her secret smiles before dropping the treasure into Mariel's hand.

With no hesitation, Mariel looped it around her neck and closed the clasp. He could sense her relief at having it back, filling him with awe that he could mean so much to her. To have such a brave, observant, shrewd woman, who had actually taught her horse to attack was far more than he deserved.

Lady Northwick sat back on her haunches, her dress covered in dirt. Lady Sommerset stood next to her, with a dress in no better condition. He turned to Mariel taking her hand again. "You saved my life." He looked to the other two sisters. "You all did. Thank you."

Lady Sommerset's eyes twinkled. "Well you are, or will be, family. And we are an unusual one."

Lady Northwick nodded. "Damn, if we are at that." She winked, a smile lighting her face.

He looked to his love. "I will never doubt you again."

She squeezed his hand even as she cocked her head and raised her brows. "Or Zephyrus?"

"Or Zephyrus." The horse lifted its head from the tender grass he enjoyed then went back to it. "I promise to be as odd as I can to rub along better with everyone."

Mariel leaned in and kissed him lightly. "We are happy to have you as you are."

Shouts rang out in the wood and the two ladies before him looked at each other. Lady Northwick swore. "Bloody timing. I'd hoped we'd have everyone at Blackmore House before our husbands arrived."

Lady Sommerset lifted one shoulder. "I'd rather have the help." She turned toward the trees. "Andrew! Is that you?"

Swearing could be heard, and he rose. He'd need to recount to the duke and earl what had occurred. Even as he remembered being shot from his horse, his fear rose, causing him to stumble.

"Marcus!" Mariel grabbed his arm.

"We have to find Anthony. Last I saw him he'd been shot

while driving the phaeton and it spooked Legend and Lore. I can only hope he's still alive. While Cobby wanted me alive to exact his revenge, he didn't have such compunction about Anthony." His gut tensed with worry for his friend.

"I promise we will find him, and Joanna can tend to him."

"Joanna!" The duke's deep voice swept through the woods like a cannon ball, his worry obvious to them all.

"I'm here, James! We could use your assistance!"

The sound of branches being pushed aside could be heard just before the duke and earl emerged upon the clearing, one in black and one in brown. They stopped for less than a moment before they both rushed to their wives.

Marcus took that moment to slip his arm from Mariel's grasp and clasp her around the waist. It was clear from the way her sisters' husbands held their wives that they too knew well what it was to marry a Mabry. Now if he could just save Anthony and get Mariel to the altar, he could truly be part of the family.

Clearing his throat, he drew their attention. "My friend, Anthony, was also shot. We must find him." He glanced to where Stiff was trying to roll himself into the woods. "There is also that man over there to contend with and a body to bury."

At his words, the earl let go of his wife and strode over to Stiff. "I'll take on the live one. Newgate seems a fitting place for him. Who tied him up so well?"

The duchess preened. "I did, after I dropped him."

Her husband scowled at her. "What do you mean, you dropped him?"

She grinned. "The girls were not the only ladies attending the physical defense classes this past winter."

At the widening of his eyes, it was clear the duke had no indication his wife had been involved in such lessons. His gaze narrowed. "Do tell me you didn't kill the other one."

Before the duchess could answer, Mariel answered. "No, Zephyrus injured him, but when he tried to kill Marcus, he had no choice but to shoot him."

"Your horse injured him?"

Marcus could tell there would be a lot to be retold, but they needed to find Anthony. "I know you all have questions, but Anthony could very well be dying."

Mariel pulled from his grasp. "Yes, we need to search for Mr. Taylour posthaste. Lord Sommerset, you can take care of Stiff. We can send the footman for the body later. James, I'm assuming you brought a coach."

The duke nodded, a bit taken aback that she took charge. Marcus quite liked that.

She took his good arm. "Then let us return to the coach so that our search can be underway." She gave a soft whistle and Zephyrus walked over. "Good boy." Taking his reins she started through the wood.

Thankful that she'd set them all into motion, he shared his concerns. "I was on the ground when Anthony was shot. He stood when he saw me fall and was an easy target. I saw him fly back, but I don't know if he flew out of the phaeton or is still in it."

"We did not see the phaeton on the road, nor did we see him, so I would conclude he is still in it."

That gave him a bit of relief. "Legend and Lore wouldn't go far. Hopefully, we can find him quickly. He saved my life. I very much wish to do the same for him."

When they broke through the trees, they found two coaches. Without waiting for the others, she tied Zephyrus to the Mabry coach, then he and Mariel climbed in and headed for the road.

Mariel, sitting beside him, patted his good arm. "I think we should check at Blackmore House first in case anyone saw the phaeton and already brought him back."

Though he was ready to scour the roads all the way back to the center of London if he needed to, he recognized the logic of her council. "I agree. We are not far."

After giving instructions to the coachman, they both watched out the window for any sign of the phaeton or Anthony, but they saw none, none that is until they pulled into the short drive of Blackmore House.

He was out the door in an instant, causing a wave of dizziness to take him, but he kept moving. The Sommerset coach was there along with the phaeton. "Anthony!" He strode toward the conveyance where two footmen were lifting his friend's prone body.

He stopped them and with a lump in his throat, he set his fingers to Anthony's neck, hoping the blood all over his torso did not mean what he feared. At the movement of the slight pulse, he dropped his hand in relief.

Mariel stepped to his side. "Take him upstairs immediately and be careful." She turned to the Mabry coachman. "Intercept the Northwick coach and tell them to come here immediately." She turned to her parents, who remained by the Sommerset coach. "Come inside. Thank you for finding him."

Despite his fears for Anthony and his own pain, he wasn't unaware of what a service her parents had done. "Lord and Lady Wakefield. Thank you. Whatever chance he has is because of you."

Lady Wakefield put her hand to her mouth, but her husband replied, "I packed the wound to stem the flow of blood, but I don't know how long he was there on the side of the road. Joanna is far better read on the subject of bullet wounds than I. Are you injured?"

"Yes, he is." Mariel grasped his arm once again. "And we can all discuss it once we are inside and have a cup of tea in our hands."

He grimaced. "Or a bit of whisky."

She looked askance at him, but didn't say anything as she ushered them all up the three steps. The door opened and Gibson stood there, mouth agape.

"Gibson, show my parents to the parlor and have tea brought. Then have water set to boiling and have it and some cloths sent upstairs to Mr. Taylour's room. Lord Blackmore will need a hot bath filled immediately. Is Lady Blackmore about?"

The man closed his mouth long enough to shake his head. "She has taken to her bed, my lady."

"Then don't disturb her. When my sisters arrive, send the duke and duchess to Mr. Taylour's room and Lord and Lady Sommerset to the parlor."

Mariel turned to him and kissed him on the cheek. "Now go bathe and retire. You need to rest to heal."

As she turned toward the parlor, he pulled her around with his good arm and clasped her to him, amazed at how calmly and astutely she arranged them all. "But I want to marry you."

A smile tugged at the corner of her lips. "You will. Tomorrow." Then, in front of Gibson, she raised on her toes and gave him a kiss that promised an exciting consummation.

After shooing him with her hand, she strode into the parlor.

"She will be a welcome member of the Blackmore family, my lord."

He turned to find his butler smiling. "Yes, she will, Gibson. Yes, she will."

CHAPTER TWENTY-ONE

MARIEL SIPPED HER tea as Amelia explained to her husband and their parents what had occurred in the woods. Even as she listened, her palms grew hot and her heart pounded. She'd almost lost him again. What if the vicar hadn't needed to be somewhere? Would she have waited too long before searching for Marcus? Would she have been too late? And what if she'd gone alone?

She took a deep breath. Wondering what might have happened was hardly productive. Marcus was safe. They were all safe, and she dearly hoped Marcus' friend would be well again. It was important to be thankful, something Belinda had never forgotten, even being grateful for the months she'd lived beyond the Scarlet Fever, despite being so weak. That's what she needed to remember, to be grateful. Now they would focus on Mr. Taylour.

Joanna had come down to tell them he'd lost much blood and dared any of them to suggest they send of a physician. None of them dared, nor wished to, which required an explanation to Lord Sommerset about Joanna's foray into medicine when Belinda had been ill.

A part of her envied her sisters for being able to have their husbands near, but as much as she wished Marcus was at her side as they waited, it was better that he rest. Even as the memory of the man, Cobby pulling back the hammer on his flintlock filled her head, her hands began to shake and she found it harder to breathe.

She clasped her index finger with her other hand. She'd just needed Cobby to turn his back. It was all she required, but it had been so close. She closed her eyes, trying to push the image away, but all she saw was Marcus tied to the tree, bleeding, barely able to see, then suddenly free and rushing toward the gun. She'd thought she would lose him. Her heart raced and she couldn't seem to swallow.

"Lord Blackmore."

At Amelia's surprised greeting, she snapped her eyes open to find Marcus dressed, his left arm in a sling and the skin around his eyes already turning blue from his beating. Relief made her eyes itch with tears. Blinking them back, she rose. "I thought I told you to rest."

He shook his head. "How can I rest when my friend fights for his life? I bathed as you requested, but I was with Anthony until your sister told me I was in her way. If I can't be by his side, then I wish to be with you. You are more comfort than a lonely room."

She felt the heat rise in her cheeks. "Then please sit."

He gave her a soft smile and took the other side of the settee. It was hardly proper, but right now she didn't care, and she sank down beside him.

"Has my mother come down?"

"No." She gestured upward with her head. "I did send a message up to her maid, so when she woke, she'd know you were safe."

"She must think the worst of me for leaving you at the church."

She'd removed her gloves earlier and had them discarded since they were covered in blood. Still, she laid her hand on his. "When I saw her, she gave me a strange look as if I were cursed."

"No, she believes our family is cursed after all that has happened."

Her heart squeezed. She could understand why. "Then she will be very happy that you are well, and we will marry on the morrow." She moved her hand back toward her lap, but he captured it.

She glanced at her sister and mother. Her mother smiled kindly and her sister smirked. Relieved they wouldn't say anything, she gave his hand a squeeze.

He turned a worried gaze toward her family. "Do you think I should send for a physician?"

"No."

"No."

"No."

His brows raised, though his eyes did not widen, the swelling quite considerable, as she, her mother, and Amelia negated his suggestion one after the other.

Taking pity on him, her mother explained. "Joanna will care for your friend better than any physician."

Amelia chimed in. "Yes. She knows more about medicine than they do. Mr. Taylour is being well cared for."

"Then I must invite you all to spend the night. It is the least I can do for all that you have done." He looked to Amelia and then herself. "And I believe I need to replace three gowns."

Lord Sommerset shook his head. "My wife has plenty. No need, but we will accept your invitation."

Her mother poured another cup of tea. "As will we."

For the first time, her father who had been quiet, but avidly listening spoke up. "Lord Blackmore. Who was that man and why did he wish you harm? Was he the man you mentioned to myself and Joanna?"

Marcus looked at her and then addressed them all. "He was. He committed crimes under the guise of war, and I planned to have charges brought against him. But our regiment was attacked before I could meet with my commanding officer. I was shot, and he and four other men left me for dead as you know. Three of them died in the war, and one died shortly after coming home to

England. The man that attacked me is the last one."

Her father finally sat back. "Then I can assume my daughter will no longer be in danger?"

Marcus let go of her hand and pressed his fist to his chest. "You have my oath that I will never allow anyone to harm her."

Her eyes misted at both her father's concern and Marcus' pledge.

Footsteps on the stairs beyond the room drew everyone's attention. Joanna and the duke strode into the parlor. Joanna looked victorious but the duke looked concerned.

"He's going to live." Joanna smiled, obviously pleased.

"She thinks. We can't be absolutely sure."

Joanna turned on her husband. "I'm sure. Do you doubt me now?"

"What I doubt is that you will stay awake all the way to Haven House."

Mariel rose. "No need to go home. Marcus has invited you all to stay." She started past the couple to give instructions to Gibson for a light supper and to have rooms readied.

As she passed Joanna, her sister pulled her arm to stop her. "Put our room next to Mr. Taylour. I will check on him during the night."

"No, you won't." The duke leaned in, his voice almost a growl.

Joanna waved him off. "You can come too. Just don't growl at me when I wake you from a sound sleep."

Mariel bit down on a smile and gave a quick nod before stepping into the corridor. As she expected, Gibson met her.

"Is there something you need, my lady?"

"There is. I'll need three bedrooms readied for my family. One should be next to Mr. Taylour. Also, have Cook prepare a light repast in about two hours from now. I'm sure my sisters will need a bath filled as well."

"Is that all, my lady?" He looked at her as if she'd forgotten an important detail.

Since she could think of nothing, she gave a confident nod.

"Would you also like a room and a bath?"

At Gibson's question, she gave a self-effacing grin. "I think that would be lovely. Thank you for thinking of me, Gibson."

"It will always be my honor to assist, my lady." Though the butler didn't actually smile, his mouth was quite a bit less stern.

Pleased with not only the arrangements but also the rapport she built with Gibson, she returned to the parlor. "All is arranged."

The gentleman rose at her entrance and Marcus held out his hand. "If only we could arrange for Anthony to be at our wedding. He has been by my side since the war."

"I think I can help with that."

They looked to the duke.

"If you have ink and paper, I can send off a note and have a special license for you to marry here."

Feeling Marcus' body relax, then stiffen, she had no doubt he was about to politely refuse.

She quickly stepped in. "Thank you, James. That would make our wedding complete."

Though Marcus squeezed her hand, he did not naysay her.

"Now, I suggest we all repair to our rooms for some rest after our day. Dinner will be ready in a couple of hours."

Her sisters with their husbands filed out, but her mother stopped. "Mariel, I don't think I've ever told you how proud we are of you and the woman you've become. It wasn't until this moment that I truly realized what your sister Belinda told me long ago."

At the mention of Belinda, she swallowed hard, always willing to hear something of her. "What did she say?"

Her mother laid her hand on her cheek. "She told me that you were the strongest of them all and loved like no other."

Her mother dropped her hand and moved out of the room with her father.

She felt her eyes misting with tears. She'd never sought

recognition, but receiving it almost undid her.

"Come." Marcus took her arm with his good one. "You deserve to rest too."

Unable to speak, she nodded and Marcus brought her to her room. After giving her a light kiss, he left. Tiredness seemed to suddenly weigh her down, and she pulled her dress from her body. At the sight of all the blood, she dropped it to the floor and collapsed upon the bed, sobs wracking her as she cried out all the fear she'd held at bay.

⇥⇥⇤⇤

MARIEL AWOKE TO lamp light. The curtains had been drawn and from what she could see, food had been left on a table near the window. She sat up quickly. Had she slept through dinner?

"You're awake. I had hoped you'd sleep through the night."

At the sound of Marcus' voice, she turned her head to find him sitting in an armchair near the fireplace, a half-filled glass near at hand, wearing a dressing gown, his sling of linen a stark white against the russet fabric. "Did I miss dinner?"

"You did, but as it was, only your parents joined me and my mother. They didn't want any of you disturbed."

"Your mother?" Her voice rose to a squeak and embarrassment filled her. "She must think me horribly rude."

"Not at all. In fact, she plans to apologize to you at her first opportunity. She was quite put out that she slept through the events." He paused, obviously puzzled. "She even blames herself for Anthony's condition. She said if she had been awake, she could have sent the grooms out to look for him."

"That isn't logical." She didn't understand how his mother could assume that. "Even were she awake, she wouldn't have known to look for him."

"Very true. I'm afraid that the recounting of events by your father may have been slightly embellished and the timeline somewhat obscured."

"That does sound like my father."

"My mother is sorry that you had to take on the hostess duties after being through such a harrowing experience." He gave her a soft smile. "But like myself, she is happy everyone is in good health."

She grasped the quilt. "Not everyone." She gestured with her head to his left shoulder and his swollen eyes. "You were shot, beaten, and Anthony is barely alive."

His brow furrowed. "I did visit Anthony after the meal. He is eating a little, so no harm was done to his stomach, so he tells me. But he lost so much blood. Your sister stitched him up nicely and said he could eat and drink as much as he wished." His face relaxed. "He will live because of you and your talented family. I will enjoy being a part of it."

Relieved that Anthony was doing well, she smiled. "I do believe you will need to make some changes to rub along well."

He rose from his seat, carrying his glass and setting it down on the end table by the side of the bed closest to him. "For you, I can make any change. What did you have in mind?"

She pretended to think, setting her chin upon her hand. "Well, you need to be odd, too. Do you have any strange habit or hobby that is out of the ordinary?"

He sat on the bed, prying her fingers from the cover to entwine his with hers. "Only loving you."

"I do have to admit, since you are the only one who does so, that would qualify."

He lifted her hand to his lips and kissed her bare knuckles. "I will be eternally grateful that every other man to meet you has been blind."

Her cheeks heated at his statement. "And I am eternally grateful that you lived through the war and came home."

"I'm sorry I remained hidden from you. I nursed a broken heart and a broken body never realizing that you were all I needed to heal."

At the regret in his gaze, she let go of the quilt and cupped his cheek. "I'm just happy you are here with me now, and we can have the future we used to dream of."

"Only we are a little older and wiser now."

She smiled, her heart filling with joy. "Yes, and thankful for what we have."

His gaze lowered to the open neckline of her shift.

Heat started in her belly as her state of undress registered. "Should you be here, my lord?"

"There's nowhere else I belong, my lady. From here ever after, I pledge to be by your side. And tomorrow I will make that pledge before witnesses. But tonight, I want the wedding night we were denied."

She couldn't help scanning his chest where his dressing gown opened. His own state of undress becoming more obvious. "Did you truly walk the hall in your bare feet and dressing gown?"

A sly grin turned his lips upward. "Not at all. I simply used the connecting door to your dressing room." He pointed behind him.

She forced her gaze from the larger view of his chest to look where he pointed to find a doorway she hadn't noticed. Then again, she hadn't noticed anything when she walked in. The significance of where she'd slept was not lost on her. "And your chambers are on the other side."

"They are, but I don't plan to use them tonight."

At his mere words, an ache deep inside her started. Revealing the viscount and all the pain that he'd hidden, though difficult, how well been worth it. "I do not think it wise to participate in any extraneous activity. You need to heal. The wisest course of action would be to wait until our wedding night."

His brow rose quickly, before he chuckled. "Already acting the lady of the house I see. As the lord, I see no reason why you cannot ride tonight. I can simply lie here on my back." Sliding from the bed, he pulled the sling from over his shoulder.

He tugged on his sash and shrugged the dressing gown off his right shoulder before carefully extracting his left arm from the sleeve. Then he lifted the glass by the bed and toasted. "To our long life, health and happiness." He threw back the drink before whipping the quilt from her.

She squealed, then covered her mouth over her own laughter.

Marcus lay down upon the bed next to her, unabashed by his nudity. "Do you need help with your shift?"

Though she had been naked with him before, she felt a certain shyness at his request. "I think I would need a sip of whatever you had in your glass to give me the courage."

"That won't give you courage. That was merely lemon water."

"Lemon water? You were drinking water?"

He reached up and took the opportunity to untie the top of her shift. "Yes, dear Mariel, water with a bit of lemon squeezed in. Cook brought it from Ravenridge. I haven't sipped liquor since I left the continent, and I have no plans to do so in the future."

At his statement, she crinkled her nose. "Oh, you are just as odd as the rest of us."

"So I am." His chuckle warmed her right down to her toes. "Now, what do you say to removing your shift? I allow no clothed riders."

Meeting his gaze she could see his love for her, but beyond that was a hunger only she could fulfill. The ache inside her turned to need, and she lifted her shift over her head, letting it fall to the floor. Then leaning forward, she kissed him.

As his hand came up to cup her breast, she leaned into his touch. "I have always loved you."

His hand moved upward and he touched the garnet lying against her bare skin. "I know. And I've always loved you." He dropped his hand to the bed. "Now make love to me, Elle."

Her heart filled, knowing everything was as it should be. She moved over him and lowered her head to kiss one of her new favorite parts of her viscount.

His gasp made her smile before she took them on a ride to love fulfilled.

EPILOGUE

Blackmore House
One month later

MARCUS HANDED THE duke his scotch then returned to the sideboard in his study to pour himself lemon water. Mariel's first dinner party with her sisters and their husbands was going well. Now he simply needed to host her brothers-in-law for a drink or two and return them to their wives.

Sommerset, dressed in a brown tailcoat, stood at the cold fireplace admiring the new painting his wife had painted, his drink on the mantel.

After filling his own glass, Marcus approached. "You must thank Lady Sommerset again for me. She captured not simply Mariel's image but who she is inside as well." He shook his head. "I have no idea how she did it."

The younger man smirked. "She caught your likeness exactly, too. Did you know you usually stand more on your right leg?"

He sat in the chair next to the duke before the fireplace and studied the painting. "I hadn't thought about it, but it makes sense. When I recovered after the war, I couldn't put weight on my left leg for what seemed like months."

The duke, having taken a sip of scotch, motioned toward the painting with his glass. "Was it necessary to have all those horses in the background?"

He smiled at the memory of trying, and failing, to keep Hector away while Merlin and Zephyrus stared each other down. "Yes, it was." Mariel just didn't have the heart to lock Hector in his stall. He turned from the painting and faced the duke. "You have your books and we have our horses."

The man gave an accepting abbreviated nod then set his glass on the small table between them. "Has Lord Wakefield requested time with you to explain your experiences during the war?"

"He has." He grimaced, not looking forward to it. "I've been able to put him off until next month. Duties of a newly married man and all that." That and he was nervous how discussing it would affect his new found peace.

"You need not worry. Our father-in-law will not wish to know personal details. He is far too curious about the mechanism of war from the actual weapons, to combat, to formations, to the tents the foot soldiers used."

That did relieve his mind somewhat. "Is your wife as interested in such knowledge?"

The duke grinned. "My wife is interested in *all* knowledge."

"And I'm grateful for that. If not for Lady Northwick, Anthony would not be alive today." He raised his own glass of lemon water in a silent toast.

"And you do not mind that he is looking into something for me?"

At the duke's question, he stifled his protective instincts over his friend. Anthony was a grown man to do as he wished. He knew best whether he had healed enough to aid the duke. "I do not mind. He is a good friend, but he is his own man."

Sommerset chuckled, quickly taking another sip of his drink.

"What do you find so humorous, Sommerset?" The duke sounded as if he regularly asked that question of the man.

"At Blackmore's remark about his friend, I couldn't help thinking the same could be said for our wives."

He found himself nodding his head, yet the duke grinned.

"They are definitely our wives, but their own women. It's a wonder we were able to bring them around."

At that, he almost choked on his water. "Bring them around? You jest."

He and Sommerset stared at the duke as if he'd turned into a statue before their very eyes.

"Very well. I withdraw my statement." The duke's blue eyes grew shrewd. "Do you have a better one?"

Sommerset nodded. "I would say it's a wonder they allowed us into their lives."

"No." He shook his head. "It's a wonder they found something in us to love."

"Here. Here." The duke raised his glass.

As the other two men finished their drinks, he glanced at the clock. Though he enjoyed a drink with his wife's brothers-in-law, he'd much rather be with Mariel. They had barely been married a month and he still wished to spend every moment making up for the years they lost. He idly wondered if it would always be that way.

"Northwick, I think we best join the ladies in the parlor or our newly married host is going to fall over watching that clock." Sommerset threw back the rest of his drink and set it on the fireplace to emphasize his statement.

He laughed, not at all embarrassed that his motives were so easily ascertained. "And you both would rather be here talking about our wives than in there with them?"

At the sheepish looks on both men's faces, he laughed again.

The duke rose and spoke to Sommerset, but pointed at him. "And that, my friend, is the result of marrying a Mabry."

Sommerset nodded enthusiastically. "Damned, if it isn't true. Why are we still standing here?"

Marcus opened his arm toward the door and they filed out. As they walked toward the parlor, laughter could be heard in there as well. How long had it been since Blackmore House had had such happiness? He was sure it was too long.

"There you are, Andrew. You must hear about this lad Tiernan." Lady Sommerset held her hand out to her husband. "Mariel says he's excellent with training horses. Didn't you just say the other evening that we needed a new stableman now that your last one has gone to live with his daughter?"

Tiernan as a stable master? He moved to where Mariel sat on the settee and joined her. "I don't know if he'll want to leave his father's business."

She wore her second wedding gown made of the same bright green material as her first. It made her eyes seem more expressive, and she looked radiant. "A young man who is currently beneath his father's and uncle's thumb might well be excited by the prospect of being in charge of his own stables. He does have Mr. Clancy's blood in him after all."

He hadn't thought of it that way, but she was right. She had a skill for understanding people very well, specifically, himself. "Then we should ask him, if Sommerset is interested." He turned to look at the man, who was nodding his head as he took the chair next to his wife.

The duchess addressed her younger sister. "I received the oddest letter from Teddy this week."

"You did?" Lady Sommerset looked to him. "I don't know if you remember, but we have a cousin."

Before he could answer, the duke frowned. "How could anyone fail to remember Lord Mabry."

The duchess ignored her husband. "As I was about to explain, I received a letter from Teddy and in it he apologized to me for his cruel words before he left."

Lady Sommerset's eyes widened. "That is quite unexpected. Are you sure he was serious?"

The woman nodded, but Mariel smiled softly. "Perhaps our Teddy has found someone who has made him see the error of his ways." Sommerset shook his head. "I doubt that." The man nodded to him to confirm the assumption that the continent was not a place where one fell in love. He silently agreed with that sentiment, but didn't respond. His experience there had been nothing short of hell.

Mariel clasped his hand, bringing him back from his dark thoughts as if she sensed his emotions, a trait he thoroughly appreciated. "Did you ask James about Lissette?"

Before he could explain that he had not, the duchess spoke. "Who's Lissette?"

Mariel answered for him. "Her name is Lissette Fontaine. You met her grandmother in the churchyard on our first attempt to be married."

He squeezed her hand, silently communicating how happy he was that their second attempt in the upstairs solar with Anthony in a wheeled chair and been successful.

The duchess' eyes rounded. "She's the woman that saved Lord Blackmore's life, correct? She has a granddaughter?"

"Yes, she does." He knew it was a large favor, but only by asking could he know what his options were. "Madame Fontaine has found that her granddaughter is too interested in social events, but too young to understand the ways of English society." He looked to his wife, who gave a nod of encouragement. She knew her sister far better than he. "She feels that Mademoiselle Lisette needs further education to distract her from her primary focus."

The duke's eyebrows rose. "And that is?"

Mariel answered. "Men. Madame is afraid that Lissette would be too easily swayed without having a better education."

"And you think Belinda's School for Curious Ladies would be the place for her?" The duchess crossed her arms, which was not an indication of her sympathy.

"Yes, I do." Mariel released his hand. "First, the young woman needs a distraction." She tapped the palm of one hand with her other index finger. "Second, she needs to be among young ladies who are curious about other subjects." She tapped two fingers into her palm. "Third, she has already had the typical education of women of status in France, so she needs more than a finishing school." Mariel tapped three fingers into her palm and closed her hand around them. "She needs Belinda's school."

The room was silent as both the duchess and the duke appeared to contemplate the matter. Lady Sommerset looked at her husband and they both grinned.

His wife was truly amazing. First, she had opened their home to Madame and Lissette whenever they wished to visit, and now she'd argued on their behalf. He couldn't believe he once thought he could live without her.

Finally, the duchess nodded. "You make a good argument. I can find no clear objection."

"I can." At the duke's words, everyone froze, but his wife.

"You can?" The duchess' eyebrows rose in disbelief. "Pray tell, what could it be beyond proof of her lineage."

His satisfied smile that he'd thought of something his wife hadn't was not appreciated. "Payment."

Lady Sommerset rolled her eyes. "Truly, James?" She waved at Mariel and himself. "Do you not think they have already made arrangements?"

The duke shrugged. "It is still a consideration."

Having seen a similar exchange a few days ago, Marcus knew it was no more than a simple intellectual challenge between the couple. That they enjoyed it was obvious, but he preferred his and Mariel's mode of communication.

The duchess' smug look turned serious. "As long as the young lady follows the school's rules."

"Have you had any problems with your students?" Mariel's concern for the school was clear in her tone. "I don't remember you mentioning anything after the season started."

The duchess glanced at her husband, who was also no longer smiling. "We haven't. But we have been asked to call upon one student's mother tomorrow. It appears one of our curious ladies is not curious enough, and the mother wishes to discuss it with us."

Sommerset frowned. "Did she say what the problem was?"

"No. But we will do whatever we can to help."

Lady Sommerset genuinely smiled at her sister. "With two of the most learned people in London helping, I'm sure everything will be fine."

The sisters' affection for each other was strong, and as he'd seen, they would do anything for each other. He looked to his wife, thinking he had married the best Mabry sister by far but found her holding her stomach. It wasn't the first time, and his smug happiness turned to worry in an instant. He lowered his voice, knowing his wife would not want to be embarrassed. "Elle, what's wrong."

She waved him off with her other hand. "Nothing important. I imagine my stomach didn't care for the mutton I ate at dinner."

That was not the first time she'd said something she ate made her uncomfortable. In fact, he'd lost count of the number of times she'd said that lately. He turned to the duchess, whose gaze had already fastened onto her sister.

Before he could say anything, the woman spoke. "Mariel, you are unwell." She rose from her seat and strode over, kneeling before his wife.

This time Mariel didn't try to smile. "It's something I ate."

He'd risen when the duchess stood, so he moved, allowing her to take his place on the settee. "That's what she's been saying for at least a fortnight now."

The duchess' gaze snapped to him before returning to Mariel.

That look froze him to the spot.

"Do you need me to ask for anything?" Lady Sommerset, who also stood, took the few steps to aid her sister.

"I do not think so." The duchess took his wife's hand. "Mariel, I want you to think back on the last few weeks. Have you felt uncomfortable mainly in the evening or mornings?"

"Mornings, but occasionally after our evening repast like now." She glanced at him, clearly worried now that her sister was concerned.

"And has it always been after you have eaten?" The duchess

set her hand against Mariel's forehead.

Mariel looked to him before shaking her head.

His heart started to thunder in his chest and the need to protect her rose like a wild bear inside him. He fisted his hands to remain where he stood.

The duchess then leaned in and whispered something in Mariel's ear.

Again his wife shook her head, but her cheeks turned rosy and she clasped the garnet about her neck.

Rising, the duchess patted Mariel's hand, a wide smile on her face. "You are going to be just fine in about three months."

"Three months?" The exclamation escaped before he could think about it. "Why must she suffer for so long?"

His sister-in-law smirked at him. "Because of you."

"Me?" Whatever it was, he'd never do it again.

She nodded, then looked at her Mariel. "You're with child. What you have is pregnancy vomiting, which usually, though not always, occurs in the morning. It should go away in about three months' time."

Child? He looked at his wife then dropped to one knee at her feet.

Her eyes rounded filling with unshed tears. "A baby." She gazed unbelievingly at him. "We're going to have a child."

He could feel himself grinning, but he had no control over it. Grasping both her hands in his, he looked into her beautiful eyes. "All that you wished for." His heart filled with happiness to know that he'd fulfilled her dream, even though he'd thought he couldn't.

Before he could fully comprehend it all, Lady Sommerset dropped onto the settee and hugged Mariel.

He rose from his knee and the duke clapped him on the shoulder. "Well done, Blackmore."

Sommerset strode for the parlor door. "I'll alert Gibson. We need to celebrate."

Among the hugs of her sisters, Mariel looked at him with

such love in her eyes that it almost buckled his knees.

He rubbed his thigh before the duke's hand pressed on his shoulder. "Sit, before you fall."

He did as instructed, the wonder of becoming a father now filling him. Would it be a boy or girl? Did it matter? In his heart, he found the truth. Not at all. Either way, he'd teach her or him all about horses.

The next hour went by in a haze, his only anchor, his wife, who he eventually was seated next to. There were toasts and questions about names and education and who would tell the parents, but all he could think about was that he wanted to have his wife to himself.

Finally, everyone left, and he found himself alone with her. Taking her hand as Gibson closed the door, he silently led her back into the parlor, closing the doors behind them. Guiding her back to the settee, he sat with her, taking both her hands. "You are happy?" For some strange reason, he needed her reassurance, which made no sense.

She squeezed his hands in hers and sighed. "I am very happy. I'm also surprised."

This is what he liked best, or almost the best. Talking with her, learning what she thought and how she felt, never knowing what new insight she might have. "Why are you surprised?"

She cocked her head and raised her brows, what he'd learned her sisters called *the face*. "Because I didn't know…I mean I didn't feel…."

Knowing he shouldn't, he couldn't help the laugh that escaped.

She pulled her hands from his. "It's not a laughing matter."

He grasped her closest hand, not willing to let her go. "I apologize."

She frowned, still not happy with him.

Maybe if he explained, she'd see the humor. "After all the time we've spent *procreating*, as you call it, it was bound to happen, don't you agree?"

She scrunched up her face. "Well, that's true. We have been doing it according to the book."

The book. The wonderful book the duchess had given her. They weren't halfway through it, and even he'd learned a few new tidbits of information. Though learning what his wife's favorite positions and caresses were had him completely enchanted. He cupped her face with his free hand. "My beautiful, sweet, kind, and proper Elle."

"Perhaps not always so proper."

At the twinkle in her eye, he chuckled. "And glad I am of that. I hope our daughter or son will have all your characteristics."

She rested her hand against his on her cheek. "And I hope he or she has all your energy and excitement in life."

He shook his head. "I'm not sure you'll want that. Best talk to my mother about what it was to raise me."

She pulled away. "Oh, we must tell your mother as soon as possible. She will be so pleased."

That was his wife, always thinking of others. "Yes, but let us have tonight to enjoy our wonderful news."

"I agree. We had best decide on names so we can politely turn down all suggestions." She smirked. "You really don't want to know what my father wished to name me."

"Having spent more time with him of late, I'm going to guess it was Hippocrates."

She laughed. "You are closer than you think. He wished to call me Medusa."

He froze like one of the men who gazed upon the hideous Greek legend with snakes for hair. He tried to determine a reason why a father would want to name a child after a monster, but couldn't fathom it.

"Father said he liked saying the word, but of course my mother was having none of such foolishness. Obviously, if it's a girl, a name like Andromeda would be more fitting."

"Andromeda? Why not something like Morgana?"

She widened her eyes. "Oh, my. You realize we are suggesting names like those we use for our horses."

This time, he laughed. "I guess we aren't very good at this."

"No, but we will be. Let us tell everyone that we have decided on names, and we are keeping it a secret until the baby is born. People will try to guess the names and that will give us so many wonderful ideas, but it will still be our decision."

"Lady Blackmore, you truly are the most intelligent woman I know." He held up his hand as she opened her mouth to no doubt say her sister was. "The duchess may be the most knowledgeable, but you are the most intelligent. You are also my wife and the mother of my child and the keeper of my heart. You will always be the most everything to me."

"Oh, Marcus." Leaning forward, she kissed him.

Wrapping his arms around her, he returned the favor before pulling away a hairsbreadth. "I will forever be grateful for you."

"And well you should be." Though the words were said sternly, Mariel couldn't keep her lips from twitching.

The little minx. Without warning, he leaned back and pulled her on top of him.

She squeaked before raising herself up as best she could, her body stiff. "Marcus."

"Allow me to show you how truly grateful I am." He gave her a wink.

She looked toward the doors. "In the parlor?"

Oh, he would enjoy making love to her in every room in the house and then at Ravenridge, too. "Yes."

Her eyes rounded before a sly smile filled her face. "I read that the danger of discovery could be exciting."

Desire raced through his abdomen at her words. "Then you'd best be quiet so no one hears while I try my best to make you ecstatically happy."

Her smile softened. "You breathing is enough to make me happy."

His heart filled and his love seemed uncontainable. Now he understood why he didn't die on that battlefield in France. It was

Mariel, always and forever her. "I promise to make you happy for the rest of our lives." Not waiting for a response, he pulled her head down for a kiss to seal his promise that their love, lives, and happiness would be entwined forever.

The End

About the Author

Lexi Post is a New York Times and USA Today best-selling author of romance inspired by the classics. She spent years in higher education taking and teaching courses about the classical literature she loved. From Edgar Allan Poe's short story "The Masque of the Red Death" to Tolstoy's *War and Peace*, she's read, studied, and taught wonderful classics.

But Lexi's first love is romance novels so she married her two first loves, romance and the classics. Whether it's dashing dukes, hot immortals, sizzling cowboys, or hunks from out of this world, Lexi provides a sensuous experience with a "whole lotta story."

Lexi is living her own happily ever after with her husband and her two cats in Florida. She makes her own ice cream every weekend, loves bright colors, and you'll never see her without a hat.

Website: lexipostbooks.com
Lexi Post Updates: app.mailerlite.com/webforms/landing/c1w1g3
Facebook: facebook.com/lexipostbooks
Twitter: @LexiPost
Instagram: instagram.com/lexipostbooks
Amazon Author Page: http://amzn.to/1IEL2cc
BookBub: bookbub.com/authors/lexi-post
D2D: books2read.com/author/lexi-post/subscribe/1/16171
Goodreads: goodreads.com/goodreadscomLexiPost
Instagram: instagram.com/lexipostbooks
Blog: happilyeverafterthoughts.com
Pinterest: pinterest.com/lexipost77
Email: lexi@lexipostbooks.com